I0597470

By SARIA BRYANT


ELEMENTAL THRONES
Shadow's Wound

UNDERWORLD MAGES
Mage's Marines


Published by DREAMSPINNER PRESS
www.dreamspinnerpress.com

# SHADOW'S WOUND

❖ SARIA BRYANT ❖

Published by

## Dreamspinner Press

8219 Woodville Hwy #1245
Woodville, FL 32362 USA
www.dreamspinnerpress.com

This is a work of fiction. Names, characters, places, and incidents either are the product of author imagination or are used fictitiously, and any resemblance to actual persons, living or dead, business establishments, events, or locales is entirely coincidental.

Shadow's Wound
© 2025 Saria Bryant

Cover Art
© 2025 Andrei Bat
https://99designs.com/profiles/bandrei
Cover content is for illustrative purposes only and any person depicted on the cover is a model.

All rights reserved. This book is licensed to the original purchaser only. Duplication or distribution via any means is illegal and a violation of international copyright law, subject to criminal prosecution and upon conviction, fines, and/or imprisonment. Any eBook format cannot be legally loaned or given to others. No part of this book may be reproduced or transmitted in any form or by any means, electronic or mechanical, including photocopying, recording, or by any information storage and retrieval system, without the written permission of the Publisher, except where permitted by law. To request permission and all other inquiries, contact Dreamspinner Press, 8219 Woodville Hwy #1245, Woodville FL 32362 USA, or www.dreamspinnerpress.com.

Any unauthorized use of this publication to train generative artificial intelligence (AI) is expressly prohibited.

Trade Paperback ISBN: 978-1-64108-802-2
Digital ISBN: 978-1-64108-801-5
Trade Paperback published January 2025
v. 1.0

*To my family for always believing in me and The Persistent Quill writers for keeping me encouraged and motivated.*

# Chapter 1

*"YOU'LL BE stabbed and left for dead."*

Cal stared out the window of the carriage as Julius' words echoed in his mind. Unfortunately, unraveling a Seer's vision to find who could possibly want him dead wasn't even the most pressing issue he needed to deal with.

His father's death had brought the court and general government processes to a grinding halt. Part of that was his own fault, as he refused to be crowned, but a month seemed like far too little time to pass before he accepted the throne.

He might have brushed Julius' vision aside as a nightmare, but his Sight was never wrong. Still, his experience with visions was that they were confusing at best, and Fate's way of fucking with everyone involved at worst.

The carriage jolted as the cobblestone road gave way to the dirt and gravel of the seedier part of the city. He'd been working on plans to restore the worst areas within the next few years, but even that would have to wait now.

"We're here," Julius said as the carriage rolled to a stop in front of the prison.

Dread and excitement burned hot in his gut as Cal stared at the large iron building. He glanced briefly at his left hand, at the shimmer of a red Fate string coiled around his little finger. It'd been there for as long as he could remember, stretching into the distance, so faint he'd been convinced it was just his imagination. Until several weeks ago, when it started growing brighter and he couldn't deny its existence anymore.

Whoever his fate was tied to, they'd finally arrived in his kingdom. And now the string was brighter and thicker than ever, pulled taut and leading directly into the prison.

He sighed and climbed out when Julius opened the door. He straightened his tunic and smoothed his hands over the fabric before striding inside. The threshold sparked along his senses, but the original function of the prison was so long forgotten, the lingering magic laid into its boundary was little more than an echo.

One of the guards took a single, imperious step towards them before shock settled on his face. He quickly bowed and fell into step behind Cal. "Your Highness."

Cal left the guard to Julius as he glanced at his hand, following the string deeper inside, past the iron-and-silver-wrought walls that still stood as testament to darker times, when they were needed to protect against the creatures and beasts that ruled the night. Creatures that hadn't been seen in Ages.

He ignored the oppressive weight of metal towering over him, his heart thrumming in his ears as the string brightened and seemed to pull tight enough to snap. He stopped in front of a solid iron door and found it locked. He flicked a glance to the guard. "Open it."

The guard hesitated. "Your Highn—" he started, but Julius didn't let him finish.

Julius stepped forward, grabbed the handle, and with a burst of condensed magic, wrenched the door open so hard the metal gave a sickening screech as it bent and twisted. He preceded Cal inside, but stopped two steps in.

Cal's heartbeat skipped at that hesitation, before the scent of blood, piss, and worse hit his nose. He grimaced and stepped inside, scanning the room. There were instruments strewn on iron tables and hung on the walls that wouldn't have been out of place in a torture chamber. Which, he realized, was exactly what this was. Most had signs of old blood, and all of them were iron or silver or sharp-edged metal.

His gaze landed on the table in the center of the room and the man bent over it, his back a bloody mess, his thin pants torn and soaked through. Two others stood near him. Not guards, they were dressed like human nobles. One held a whip, the other a single long strip of leather with jagged metal pieces woven through it, glinting with malicious spells.

His Fate string stretched out across the room, connecting him to the one strapped to the table.

"Release him," Cal snarled, taking another step into the room.

The man with the whip turned with a sneer that melted into horror. The other man ignored him completely and lifted his weapon for another strike.

Julius surged forward, but Cal was faster, lifting his hand as he gave his magic and rage an outlet. Coils of light wrapped around the man's wrists and throat, and he screamed as the magic burned him enough that he dropped his weapon, the stench of singed hair and skin mixing with the filth.

The other man hastily dropped his whip and scrambled back, hands lifted in surrender.

Cal stalked to the table, intending to release the man tied down, but Julius planted a hand against his chest.

"Don't you dare," Julius hissed, pushing him back a step and giving him a warning glare before going to the table himself.

Cal twitched at being denied, but he'd waited thirty-five years. He could wait a few more moments to get a look at the man Fate had decided belonged to him.

He ordered the new guards, arriving due to the commotion, to arrest the two men, as well as the first guard. Only then, as he turned back to Julius, did he notice his finger. The string was still there, glowing pure and bright and leading to the man now collapsed on the floor beside the table. Except it was thinner than before, because there was now another string, just as pure and bright and stretching to the other side of the room.

His breath stuttered as he moved to follow, faltering to a halt in front of what looked like an upright, rounded iron casket. He reached for the lock, but even when he strained with all his strength, it wouldn't budge.

"Juls," he said, his voice rough as his stomach twisted with a fresh wave of unease.

Julius appeared a moment later, pressing Cal back before studying the casket. He found the seam, gripped it, and heaved. Metal scraped against the floor with an ear-piercing screech. As soon as it was open, a slim form slumped forward.

Cal reached out instinctively, in time to keep the young man from being impaled on the spikes sprouting from the lid.

"Don't—" Julius started, but it was too late.

The magic inherent in the Fate bonds shimmered through him, and a heavy pulling sensation he'd never even realized was there eased away. It was almost enough to distract him from the very soft, furry ears brushing his chin.

"Don't fucking touch him." The words were slurred and rough with pain, but laden with a promise of violence.

Cal turned in time to see the other man he was bound to struggle to his feet, leaning heavily against the table to stay upright.

The man took an unsteady step forward and nearly collapsed again. "Give him back."

Cal ignored Julius' protests and slowly closed the distance to his other bonded. The man in his arms was barely coherent, but he was aware enough to keep his feet and seemed possessed of the same frantic need to be reunited with his partner. Once they were close enough, Cal released his hold and watched as the two clung to each other, like they'd never expected to survive this room.

He had a feeling they hadn't been meant to.

He turned to Julius. "Get a healer. And you," he said, pointing at one of the new guards. "Bring me whoever is in charge here."

# Chapter 2

Murder.

That was the crime his bondeds were accused of.

He had to set aside the fact that he had *two* bonds for the time being. One was rare enough. He'd never heard of two.

Nearly three hours after arriving at the prison, he'd finally finished getting what little information the warden could tell him about the men. It was clear no investigation had been done. They had allegedly murdered a low-ranking human noble in cold blood, but the only witness turned out to be the man Cal had burned with his magic, and he had been stubbornly silent when questioned.

He'd sent for a Truth Seeker, but there were only two in the kingdom, and neither was currently in the city.

Cal dismissed the warden with clear instructions to ensure no other prisoners were tortured, or he'd be a prisoner himself by morning.

Once he was alone, he took a moment to breathe. He'd known there were problems that needed to be addressed in every level of the government, but it wasn't until his father died that he started to see just how dire things were. He refused to believe his father was so incompetent, but the alternative was unthinkable. His father had ruled for nearly a thousand years and should have ruled for thousands more, but now that the responsibility for the kingdom came to Cal, he had to do things differently.

The realm had changed. Beyond the edges of the kingdom was little more than barren wasteland. The Wound, left behind by the war three hundred years ago. Ylrendorei was the last of the inhabitable land on the southern coast, an elven kingdom harboring the remnants of the magical creatures who'd fought in the war, and the descendants of the humans who'd tried to destroy them. After the humans were stripped of their magical abilities, they'd been much more agreeable to peace. For the most part. Cal had sensed growing tensions between humans and the magical community over the past few years.

He pinched the bridge of his nose and carefully set aside every outrage and desire to tear this entire prison down. Balance would be restored, he would see to that, but first he needed to ensure the two men he was bound to were recovering.

When he stepped out of the warden's office, he found Faelan waiting for him. He should have been surprised, but even half an hour would have been long enough for Julius to get word to the palace.

"Faelan," he greeted, motioning for the other elf to follow as he navigated the halls. They'd taken over one of the solitary infirmary rooms before Cal had started his search for answers. The healer had taken care of the worst of his bondeds' injuries when she arrived, but the damage to the back of the one who'd been tied down was severe enough to require a clean room and more time.

The door was closed when he found his way back to it, and he paused outside it as he turned to Faelan. "Enough food to feed ten, please," he said. "And nothing procured from the prison."

Faelan showed no surprise at either request, simply bowed and turned for the nearest exit.

Cal waited until he was out of sight, then let himself inside, finding Julius standing watch two steps in. "Well?" he asked quietly, glancing at the bed on the far side of the room. The man who'd been tied down was stretched out on his stomach, the healer in a chair next to him. A soft golden glow pulsed around her hands as she worked.

Julius shrugged. "About half done, I'd guess. I already sent word to the palace for a fresh healer. Should be here soon."

Cal nodded and surveyed the room, then lifted his hand when he didn't see his other bonded. Both strings glowed bright and stretched towards the bed. When he glanced at Julius, all he got was a rueful nod towards the far corner.

He moved along the wall to the other side of the room and stepped around the end of the bed. Tucked into the scant space between it and the wall was the young man who'd been locked in the casket. His legs were drawn up, one arm wrapped around his knees, the other lifted beside him as he clasped hands with the man on the bed.

Cal drew in a sharp breath as he finally got a good look at him. He hadn't been imagining the furry ears. Black fox ears twitched towards him before green eyes met his. For a moment, all he could do was stare. Beastkin weren't rare, a couple even served in his princeguard, but there weren't many in the city. As far as he knew, their kind still thrived in what remained of the forests on the other side of the Wound.

For a new one to arrive here and be bound to him? As relieved as he was to finally find who his Fate strings tied him to, he couldn't ignore the wariness curling in his gut.

"Hello," he said, crouching at the end of the bed. One black ear swiveled towards him, and he couldn't help the smile that tugged at his lips. "My name is Callith Ratearynn."

Bright green eyes blinked at him as the man's lips moved, as if shaping Cal's name. A few moments later, he spoke. "You're him, then? The Sun King?"

Cal couldn't stop the flinch, but he breathed through the fresh wave of grief until he could speak again. "No," he answered. "My father—" He stopped and forced out a slow breath. "I haven't been crowned yet."

The man visibly paled. "Why not?"

Cal considered that for a moment, feeling the sharp need to soothe away the fear singing along the newly established bond. Even knowing where that sensation came from didn't prepare him for the intensity of it. "My father died a month ago," he said. "Taking over so soon doesn't feel right to me."

"You have to be crowned. There has to be a king."

Cal tilted his head, glancing at Julius where he still lingered beside the door. Those were the same words he'd heard countless times the last few weeks. "There will be," he said, turning back to the fox. "In due time."

"No! The crown must be worn!"

The man on the bed made a sound that was nothing more than a slurred whisper, but the young man jumped as if it'd been a yell. He twisted onto his knees to face the bed, leaning in close.

"Haru," the fox said, tangling his free hand in silvery hair matted with dried blood.

Cal straightened from his crouch, the movement catching the prone man's attention. Dark amber eyes focused on him with far more clarity than they had a few hours earlier. There was no hostility in the gaze, but there was no welcome either.

It didn't last long. A few heartbeats later and unconsciousness claimed him again. Cal watched the two of them in silence, torn between leaving them to their healing or getting answers, but there was no time to spare. The prison had operated unchecked for long enough, and the longer this took, the more resistance he might encounter.

He cleared his throat and waited for green eyes to focus on him again. "Are you hungry?" he asked, motioning to the small table on the other side of the room. "Food should be arriving shortly, and there are some things I'd like to ask you."

The man glanced back to his partner, his expression twisting with reluctance before he untwined their fingers. He carefully pressed his partner's arm into a more comfortable position on the bed before standing. His black fox ears twitched back towards the bed as he stepped away, but he moved forward until he stood in front of Cal.

With a smile, Cal motioned to the table again, following the shorter man and letting him choose his chair, not surprised when he chose one where he could see both the bed and the door. "Will you tell me your names?" he asked, sitting with his back to the bed.

"Rashi," the fox replied, his gaze drifting towards the bed before focusing on Cal. "That's Haru. Masaharu, but he prefers Haru."

Cal nodded and crossed his legs, folding his hands on top. "Can you tell me what happened?" He asked as gently as he could, sure it was an unpleasant memory, but he still flinched from the sudden spike of terror that wasn't his own. By the Wound. He gripped the edge of the table as he controlled his breathing, sparing a quick look at Julius when he moved. He hoped it was reassuring, but he doubted it. The way Rashi had paled and frozen in his seat was telling, and his chest ached in sympathy even as black rage threatened to eat him alive.

"Rashi," he said, forcing calm into his voice despite the fresh desire to raze this entire prison to the ground. He lifted his left hand, palm up, and slowly extended it between them.

Rashi's ears flicked back, not quite pressed against his head, but close enough.

"You are safe here," Cal said firmly, wiggling his fingers a bit. It was enough to catch Rashi's attention, and he didn't miss the way those green eyes focused on the Fate string, slowly following it to where it attached to his own finger. He blinked as if noticing it for the first time, looking up with wide eyes. "That's—" he started, biting his lip and glancing at the bed. "Him too?"

Cal nodded, relieved when Rashi's shoulders slumped and the pressure of fear receded. "I've spoken to the warden," he said. "You were both arrested for murder, but I suspect there's far more to the story than that."

"Yes," Rashi bit out, indignant anger thrumming along their bond.

He wasn't sure what to make of that, feeling Rashi's emotions so clearly and strongly. That was unheard of for newly forged bonds, but it was yet another issue to be dealt with later.

"We arrived in the city at night and were trying to find an inn. Two humans approached us, said they could help." His ears pressed flat and his fingers tightened their grip on his shirt. "They led us into an alley and shoved me against the wall. Said they'd never seen a fox feral bred before." He sneered briefly before looking across the room, focusing on Haru. "Haru grabbed the one holding me and threw him against the wall. They started screaming, more humans came. They had sticks that sparked with lightning. I blacked out when it hit me," he said, his ears drooping as he dropped his gaze to his hands. "When I woke up, we were in a cell here."

Cal breathed out, forcing his hands to unclench from fists. "And no one asked you what happened before bringing you here?" he asked, already knowing the answer before Rashi shook his head. He flexed his fingers, grateful for the knock at the door. When Julius opened it, Faelan and Laena, another one of the palace healers, stepped inside. "Ah, good," he said, motioning Faelan to put the large bag of food on the table.

He stood and helped unpack the contents, setting out flatbread still warm from the ovens and an assortment of diced vegetables, chicken, and sauces. He passed two pieces of bread to Rashi and motioned for him to fill them with whatever he liked. Then he stepped aside, guiding the exhausted healer to his vacated seat. He made sure she took food for herself while Laena settled beside the bed, then stood beside Julius.

"Chances of this being a rare situation?" Cal asked, almost smiling when Julius gave him a pitying look. "I don't know where to start with this," he said, and immediately regretted it, because he already knew what Julius' response was going to be.

"By taking the crown."

He sighed and rubbed the ache forming between his eyes. "I mean after. Every worker, every guard, every criminal in here will have to be questioned and reprocessed."

"Justice isn't going to like that."

Cal bit back a sneer through sheer force of habit. Justice was the highest-ranking human official in his kingdom and oversaw the upholding and enforcement of the laws. He was also the most unpleasant human Cal had ever had the displeasure of meeting.

"Good," he said, glancing across the room to where Haru still lay motionless on the bed. "I think perhaps it's time to reshape this kingdom."

Julius straightened with a fierce, "Fucking *finally*."

# CHAPTER 3

IT TOOK the healers well into the night to heal Haru enough he could be moved. Most of that was due to the small, jagged pieces of spelled iron someone had embedded along his skull and under his toenails. At some point in the afternoon, the healers realized he wasn't recovering nearly as quickly as he should have been and did a more thorough examination. Between that and the long list of injuries, from broken ribs and bruised lungs to a fractured ankle, Cal was ready to murder the warden and every worker under him all over again.

His princeguard arrived with a fresh healer sometime after moonrise. He set half of the guards to the task of searching every room and cell to ensure no other atrocities were being committed.

Before the moon began to set, they got Haru and Rashi loaded into a carriage with Faelan, who Rashi had taken an instant liking to, and made the journey back to the palace. He would have liked to see Rashi's reaction to approaching the ylren tree the palace was built inside, but the city was still cloaked in the dark of night, with only the small sunstones along the streets for light.

Cal slumped in the seat of his own carriage instead, exhausted and angry and barely coherent. He closed his eyes, but he knew sleep wouldn't come to him for several hours yet. As soon as they returned, they had to announce he'd be accepting the crown at dawn. It was sure to cause a panic on a dozen different levels, but he couldn't care less. Not now, when his refusal to ascend the throne meant he didn't have the power he needed to keep his bondeds safe. It would be even more necessary now, when word of his long trip to the prison would have spread to those who cared. He needed to make the first move.

Julius had gotten word that one of the Truth Seekers received his summons and would return within the day. As soon as Cal was crowned, his first order of business would be locking all the advisors and officials in the audience chamber and questioning every single one, starting with Justice. Or perhaps saving him for last. Cal was well aware that if he had to execute Justice, he would be facing a civil war, but he refused to suffer corruption and the oppression of nonhumans.

"This is going to get messy," Julius murmured.

Cal cracked an eye open with a flutter of guilt, there and gone again, when he saw Julius looked as exhausted as Cal felt. "Regrets?"

Julius' smile was more a grimace and all teeth. "Only that it took you too long to get here."

Cal sighed and closed his eyes again.

After a long minute of silence, Julius asked, "Do you have a plan?"

"Isn't that your job?"

"You don't like my plans."

"I'll make an exception this time."

Julius hummed in disbelief. "Don't kill Justice."

"You're right, I don't like your plans."

"You'll need him. At least for now. Even if he is responsible for this mess, he holds more sway than he did a few years ago. Especially among the laborers."

"I thought Clarence was the favored of the labor class." Clarence was one of three financial advisors and oversaw the labor duties of the Waterside district.

"He was, until he and your father both voted in favor of building the new refinery in Waterside."

Cal frowned, keeping his eyes closed as he dredged up memories of an issue from four years ago. New mythril and crimson ysazicite veins had been found deep underground, just outside the Wound to the east. The first to be found since before the war. Dwarves didn't like working with ysazicite—it was far too brittle and easily crumbled into fine dust— but it stored magic almost as well as sunstones. Humans had devised a way to mix it with sand and heat it to form beautiful red glass, durable enough for jewelry and adornments.

The debate on where to build the refinery for the ysazicite had lasted a week. In the end, the risk of dust getting into their water supplies won out against the inconvenience of a full day's ride from the city.

"We built it near the mines," he said.

"That was Justice's idea."

"Fuck." He didn't need to be told that Justice was behind other similar votes in the past few years. Especially ones that seemingly benefited humans. Waterside was a predominantly human district. As the non-magical creatures they'd become since the war, humans made up the largest portion of the city's manual labor, from the farms to the city guards and sanitary workers to support for nearly every business in the city.

But humans were so very greedy in every aspect of their beings, as though, even generations later, their loss of magic was a void inside them that they were driven to fill with anything and everything. No matter the cost.

The more important question now was, was Justice's goal simply to protect humans, or to gain enough favor for a coup?

IT WAS still late enough that getting Haru and Rashi into the palace without undue attention was easy. Even the more nocturnal nobles and courtiers were fast asleep. The hardest part was getting Julius' agreement to put them in one of the spare bedrooms of Cal's apartments. Considering the entire purpose of one of the rooms was to serve whoever was attached to his Fate string, it was a short argument. He needed the peace of mind of having them secure, especially after the state he'd found them in.

One of the palace servants slipped inside ahead of their group with fresh linens and towels. Cal recognized him, though it took him a moment to recall the human's name. Aster was young, but he'd been promoted to the royal floors about two years ago. The servant made quick work of changing the sheets and stepped out of the bedroom as the healers and guards were carrying Haru inside.

"Thank you, Aster," Cal said.

The human looked at him with startled, wide eyes before bowing and backing out of the apartments.

Cal managed a quick word with Rashi, assuring him they were no longer prisoners and that he'd be crowned within a few hours, before he was dragged away to clean up and prepare for the ceremony. He used the time to meditate while aides combed his golden hair and wove it into an intricate braid along the right side of his head, applied red kohl to his eyes, and rubbed oils into his skin.

He felt like a Second-Age maiden being made ready for her wedding night and wished the ritual wasn't necessary, but the oils had absorbed scents and spells worked into the herbs that soaked in them. By the time the sheer crimson and gold robe was tied in place and he made it to the throne room, he had precious few minutes before sunrise.

He wasn't ready. He was a few hundred years too young to be king, and more than one voice had whispered such from the palace alcoves over the past weeks. His father should still be on the throne, ruling for hundreds more years. Grief threatened to choke him anew, and he closed his eyes, forcing air into his lungs until it released its grip. And then he was out of time.

He stepped into the center of the balcony behind the throne and bent his head, accepting the gold crown of delicate, intertwined leaves with a sun at the center. Carved from a single sunstone, it glowed faintly with Ages of stored magic. Then he turned to the east, where the light of sunrise was breaking over the horizon, glittering on the waves of the sea to the south. He took a deep breath and spread his arms, calling his magic to the surface. Warmth suffused his limbs as sunlight filled him, matching the warmth of the sun as bright light spilled over the city.

The spells in the oil sparked to life, making his skin glow, and he whispered the words of ascension, claiming the city, the kingdom, every life under his rule, be it elf, human, or any other creature. When the sun finally lifted above the horizon, the heat intensified until it felt like high sun on a summer day, but he held still, submitting to the Sun's judgment.

A small eternity passed as the sun hung motionless in the sky, the bottom edge touching the horizon far longer than should have been possible. As it had when his father died, it paused in its journey across the sky.

His eyes stung, but he couldn't blink or turn away, held in place, unmoving, by magic and will. His arms grew tired and shaky with fatigue as he waited and waited, until finally he felt new magic crack into place inside him.

He sucked in a startled breath as his awareness grew, touching against every elf he'd been granted rule over. Those in charge of the farmland, ensuring the crops remained pest-free and hydrated, the livestock healthy. The dock workers who spelled ships for swiftness and nets to catch just enough fish to sustain both land and sea. The city workers who kept the streets clean and buildings in good repair. His princeguard—kingsguard now, most still restoring some semblance of structure to the prison, while the rest secured the palace for what was to come.

His advisors, most awake and taking in first light, already realized what was happening as the sun lingered at the horizon. The healers and chefs preparing their concoctions for the day. Laena and her partner, sharing pleasure after their long night. One of his cousins, beyond the border of the city and swiftly moving closer, his other cousin farther away, near the smaller villages spread along the coast. Faelan, sound asleep as he snatched what few hours of rest he could.

Julius, ever loyal and steadfast, watching Cal's back even now.

The sun flared bright and resumed its ascent.

The magic released him and he gasped, grasping the rail of the balcony and slumping against it to catch his breath, his subjects' presences settling at the back of his mind.

Truth be told, this was another reason he'd hesitated to take the crown. Ruling the kingdom was one thing, but to be linked to every elf, to feel the weight of their lives for the rest of his own....

He pulled in another deep breath and straightened, glancing at the sun once more before turning. He stepped inside and moved to the thrones. Both were ornate, each carved from their own single sunstone and equal in size, though the one on the left was set a pace back. Where his mother had sat before she died, and where he'd sat for the last decade in her place. Now his younger sister would sit there, as he took his father's place.

The moment he sat, bright sunlight radiated from the throne and the crown, filling the entire room with a low thrum of ambient magic. For several long moments, it was too bright to see even shadows in the corners.

When the light finally returned to normal, Julius stepped forward and sank to one knee, bowing his head and pressing his right fist across his chest. "My King," he said.

Cal swallowed his protests. He could no longer hide behind the title of Prince. He lightly touched his fingertips to Julius' head.

"My guide," he said. "Rise. We have work to do."

# CHAPTER 4

AN EAGLE arrived with a missive, stating the Truth Seeker had forgone the waiting carriage and would arrive by horseback by high sun. He was grateful for the expediency, but it also set him ill at ease, sure there would be still another, more pressing concern to deal with when they arrived.

He left the detaining and gathering of the advisors to the guards, relieved to see the captain overseeing the task herself. Duaia was Julius' sister, a rare sorceress born from a noble elven family. She was three decades older than them, but she'd been as much a steadfast presence in his life as her brother. He could trust her to deal with anyone who might dare protest the first orders of the new king, though the few he'd spoken to in passing seemed eager to finally get back to their work. His father's death had brought the entire kingdom to a standstill, and there was plenty of work to be done.

He slipped away to the kitchens while he had the chance. He wouldn't start the interrogations until everyone was accounted for, in case any rumors made it to Justice or his potential accomplices.

It took no time at all for the head cooks to press a tray with several plates of food into his hands, and then he was making the trip back to his own apartments. He knocked lightly at the guest room door, smiling when Rashi's soft voice called for him to come in.

The fox was tucked into the sofa with a book, empty plates already stacked on the table in front of him.

"You've already eaten?" he said, pleased someone had seen to their needs, even if he was disappointed it hadn't been him.

Rashi snorted softly and motioned to the bed across the room with his chin. "Haru ate most of it before he passed out again," he said, somehow sounding both amused and annoyed.

Cal glanced at the bed, where Haru was stretched out on his stomach, fast asleep. His back was still mottled with a few fading bruises, but his injuries were far better than they had been even a few hours ago. He couldn't even see any scars where the whip had cut into flesh, which was odd, since Haru's back had been a mostly solid bruise with deep-but-fading lash marks when Cal left them here earlier.

"He needs the food and rest," Cal said, setting the tray on the edge of the table. When he looked up, he found Rashi staring at him. Or rather, at his head.

"You're king," Rashi said, slumping into the couch with a brilliant smile. "Good."

Cal raised an eyebrow, sitting next to him before offering a plate. "You said something before about needing to be crowned."

Rashi took the plate, staring at it as he bit his lower lip. "The Thrones must be held," he said, watching Cal from the corner of his eye. "The lines cannot be broken."

Cal picked up his own plate. "The lines?" he asked, not missing the quick twitch of dismay before Rashi smoothed his expression.

"The Thrones," he said again, as if that explained everything. When Cal remained silent, Rashi's brow furrowed. "The five Thrones. Light, Frost, Sea, Nature, Air. All set at the junctures of the strongest ley lines."

"I know of the Thrones," Cal said slowly. The elves had sat on Ylrendorei's Throne of Light for thousands of years, stretching back into the First Age, though now it was more commonly referred to as the Sun Throne. He could trace his lineage to the very first queen blessed with the Sun's power.

The sirens ruled the Sea, largely untouched by the war that had ravaged the land. The Frost Throne had been ruled by dragons when they existed, but the others had always been in flux with what species sat upon the thrones. As far as he knew, the Frost Throne had never been reclaimed. And of course, the Shadow Throne no longer existed, destroyed in the war three hundred years ago.

"Then you know they each need a ruler to maintain balance."

Cal nodded, though he couldn't remember ever hearing such a thing, but too much of their magical knowledge and history had been lost along with most of their elders in the war. It made sense, as the thrones were set in place to reflect the higher elements, the ley lines filling them with raw magical power.

Rashi let out a groan and rolled his eyes towards the ceiling. "You have no idea, do you?"

"Not a clue," Cal admitted. "But I'm crowned and have accepted the Sun's gifts, so your worries are unfounded." Which was good, because he truly could not handle another crisis on his list yet. He motioned for Rashi to eat and picked up his own pastry, filled with cream and fresh berries. He'd given Rashi the plate with eggs and cured ham, since he'd gone for meat every time food was offered.

They ate in silence for several long moments before Rashi glanced up at him. "I never thanked you," he said softly.

Cal nearly broke the handle off his cup when his grip tightened. "You don't need to," he said, letting out a slow breath. "That situation should never have happened. I'm sorry that was your first impression of our city."

He set his cup aside and shifted to face Rashi. "As soon as I get things sorted here, everyone involved will be held accountable." He might even hold a public execution for the man who'd dared taken a whip to Haru, and the warden for allowing it to happen. The last execution had been when he was fourteen, and he'd sworn to get rid of the practice when he became king, but he could see the necessity of such punishments now.

Rashi's smile was small and sweet, disappearing behind a huge yawn.

"I'll let you rest," Cal said, taking Rashi's empty plate and stacking it with the rest.

Before he could get to his feet, Rashi made a sound of protest and lightly grasped the sleeve of his robe. "Stay?"

Cal hesitated. There was little he could do before the Truth Seeker arrived, and perhaps it would be better to let the palace stew in confusion and impatience until then, rather than risk giving away his intentions.

"All right," he said, sitting back in his seat. "Would you tell me where you're from?" he asked, and was rewarded with a brilliant, tired smile before Rashi eagerly told him about the lands far to the northeast, on the other side of the Wound. Lands where rain fell in great torrents for entire months, where humans and beastkin grew rice and orchards of apples and tiny sweet oranges. Lands that were green as far as the eye could see, with trees so old and big it took fifty men with arms outstretched, touching fingertip to fingertip, to encircle one. That was a fraction of the size of the ylren tree the palace was built in, but it still must have been a magnificent sight, to see so many at once.

Rashi told of how when he'd been ten, he'd followed the bright red string on his finger into a pretty stranger's arms. "When I said the string meant we were going to be mated, all he said was yes," he said with a soft laugh. At some point he'd moved closer, until he was tucked against Cal, a warm, solid line along his side.

As Rashi's words slowed and his head grew heavier against Cal's shoulder, he couldn't resist running his fingers through the unruly black hair. Rashi sighed and went completely lax, his ears going limp with the rest of him. Cal pressed a smile against the top of his head, breathing in his unique scent, like the green of the forest he spoke so fondly of and the lemongrass soaps Cal kept in his apartments. It was such a comforting scent that he closed his eyes to enjoy it, just for a moment.

CAL WOKE with a jolt and the foreboding sense he was late to be somewhere. He squinted blearily at the room, finding everything placed wrong, and frowned in confusion, until a soft snore drew his attention. He glanced down to find Rashi's head in his lap, his limbs hanging off the edge of the couch. It looked entirely uncomfortable, and he winced in sympathy. Then he noticed the angle of the light coming through the window and swore. If it wasn't high sun, it would be shortly.

He scrubbed at the grit in his eyes and took a breath to center himself before getting up as carefully as possible. He held Rashi's head up and replaced his lap with a pillow, then lifted the fox's sprawled limbs onto the cushions. There was a light blanket over the back of the couch that he spread out over Rashi, taking a moment to appreciate having his bonded here before turning to the door. Halfway there, he became aware of a heavy gaze on him and glanced towards the bed to find glittering slits of amber watching him.

He froze, torn between going to Haru or leaving as quickly as possible. He couldn't explain the lance of unease bordering on fear in his chest, but he knew Haru was eyeing him as a predator would its prey. Despite still healing from grievous wounds, he had no doubt Haru could be on him in moments if he chose to attack. He might look human, but Cal sensed the magic in him, even if it was unfamiliar.

Neither of them moved, locked in each other's gaze.

The soft knock on the door was a surprise and a relief.

"Your Majesty, the Seeker has passed the city gates," Aster called.

"I'll be there shortly," Cal replied without breaking eye contact.

He gave Aster a moment to leave before nodding to Haru. "Rest. I'll have more food sent up for lunch," he said, before continuing for the door.

He disliked having his back to Haru, but he wouldn't treat his own bonded as a threat or an enemy until he proved to be one. He made it out the door without being attacked and closed it softly behind him.

He stood there for a moment, breathing out and calming his nerves, then turned his attention to where it needed to be. Where it should have been weeks ago, before this mess first had a chance to develop.

He shed the robe on his way to his own bedroom, tossed it over his bed, and changed into something more sensible. A loose silk shirt, with one of his formal blue tunics over it, and trousers to combat the discomfort of the long day ahead. He pulled on his usual boots and headed to his office, retrieving the ivory tablet with a thin sheet of pure gold centered on top. It was a magical aid used only in the most formal or extreme situations, but as he'd just become king, he doubted it would raise any questions.

As he passed through the assembly chamber, he stopped in the center, taking a moment to turn and observe the advisors and higher-level workers gathered, filling nearly every seat of the long, curved desks positioned in a widening spiral around the room.

"Thank you for gathering today," he said, raising his voice to be heard over the quiet conversations. "I'd like to speak with each of you privately. If you have pressing concerns that need addressed, please have them ready. We'll begin shortly."

He moved to the smaller room to the side, where the spells in the threshold ensured complete privacy against any who might try to eavesdrop.

Julius was already propped against the wall outside with a vaguely annoyed expression. "Where did you disappear to?"

Cal huffed softly and moved into the room, waiting until the door closed behind Julius before responding. "You mean did I complete the bond with Haru? Of course not." Even if Haru weren't still healing from torture, he did know better. Fate bonds might be a gift, but they could also be dangerous, especially for those in power. Rashi had been an accident, and he certainly didn't regret it, but he did need to know why they were here, and why now. And why he was bound to two of them.

When Julius sighed in relief, Cal glared at him in offense. "If you're done," he said pointedly.

Julius held up a hand in peace and retreated to take his place beside the door.

Cal moved to the desk and set the tablet down, closing his eyes as he focused on the framework of the spells he needed. A revealing of loyalties and intentions, not just in regard to the throne, but the people of the city, human and nonhuman alike. A need to speak truth and to keep silent against repeating any of their conversation, with a high-level enforcement spell. Too low level, and the spell would only muddle the words if someone tried to speak of what they shouldn't. He needed one that would prevent them from speaking in the first place, or communicating in any way. It might have been too cautious, but he needed answers, and there was too much anxious energy coursing through him that hadn't been there before, as though time were running short.

He shaped the spells in his mind, encompassing the room as the border and extending its essence to the prison. Anything regarding crimes or punishment, or mistreatment of magical creatures, all of it would be locked by the spell, ensuring no one could speak of their conversation in this room before the investigation was done.

It felt good, working his magic outside of mock battle. Elegant symbols and script of old Elvish appeared in the gold as he released the spells. Once they settled in place, he nodded in satisfaction and set the tablet aside. A few minutes later, the side door opened and an attendant bowed before the Truth Seeker stepped inside, her long wheat-brown hair in a windswept mess, as usual.

His lips twitched as he held back a laugh. "Cousin," he greeted.

Aeliria glided forward, pulling off her riding gloves and tossing them to the table. He fully expected to be pulled into a bone-crushing hug, but she dropped to one knee in front of him, pressing her fist across her chest and bowing her head. "My King."

His expression froze into place, though he'd known this was how things would be. At least he'd thought he did. Seeing his best friend and confidant bow to him had been hard enough, but his own cousin was worse. Still, protocol existed for a reason. "My eyes and ears," he said, resting his fingers on top of her head.

The magic settled around them with a distinctly satisfied thrum, something he'd never felt before. He glanced at Julius, but neither he nor Liria seemed to notice. "Rise," he said, pushing away the strange moment. Figuring out the Sun's gifts and changes in his magic could wait.

Liria pushed to her feet and offered a quick, fierce smile, pulling him into a familiar embrace that left his lungs aching for air. Well, at least things hadn't changed too much.

"About time," she said, pulling back and glancing up at the crown. She nodded and stepped back, throwing a wink at Julius before glancing around the room.

When she saw the tablet and the spells ladid out, she turned serious. "So, what is it you need me for?"

"A bit more than what I originally needed, sadly."

When she raised an eyebrow, he explained the situation at the prison and his need for Liria's magic to ensure he found everyone who had any knowledge of what was happening there. Her expression darkened as he spoke, and she let out an explosive sigh when he'd finished. "Well. Let's get started, then."

Her skills weren't as necessary for the elves, as the crown allowed him to sense if they were lying to him or not, but she still set out her tools as Julius motioned the first advisor in.

The next several hours were tedious and full of inane information that he unfortunately couldn't ignore. The past month of little actual work being done meant that everyone had a stockpile of issues they needed his approval or direction on. His unease grew as each advisor and official passed through and he realized even the day-to-day tasks were completely out of sorts, and not just from the past weeks. The financial records from each district hadn't been balanced in months, and wages for the guards and city workers had been cut to nearly half of what they'd been a year ago.

How had his father not been aware of his own kingdom crumbling to pieces from its very foundation?

By the time Julius returned with two trays laden with food for dinner, and a glower that demanded at least a short break to eat, Cal had a migraine that wasn't going away. Ever prepared, Julius set a small vial of tonic next to his cup of tea.

"Drink that," Julius ordered.

Cal sighed, but he was too grateful to even offer a token protest. He tossed back the tonic before devouring the food without tasting it, the drain on his magic and nearly three days with little sleep making him ravenous.

"The only ones left are Justice and the humans he worked most closely with. Are you ready for him?" Julius asked as he stacked the empty plates.

"Oh, will I finally have a challenge?" Liria asked, voice dry.

Cal ignored her and nodded to Julius. The humans had stewed long enough. They were sure to be tired and irritable by now, and hopefully more apt to admit to their crimes.

Liria moved her sunstone to the center of the table, within easy reach and sight of anyone sitting there. It was one of the best Cal had seen, clear enough it was almost translucent. The cut was natural, a large chunk rather than shaped into a globe, but it'd been polished to a bright shine and glowed with ambient magic. Beside it, she set her small ceremonial needle. Blood magic skirted the edges of the laws, especially after the war, but Truth Seekers relied on a single drop to work their own sun magic.

Julius watched until she gave a small nod, then stepped out of the room. A few moments later, Justice came in, his usual glower firmly in place. He was an older human, his hair graying at his temples and the edges of his short beard. His mere presence in a room always brought the feeling that the air had been doused with kitchen grease.

Cal forced a bland smile and motioned to the chair across from him and Liria.

Unlike everyone who'd come in before him, Justice didn't go to a knee or bow from the waist, merely inclined his head. "Your Majesty," he said, slanting a hooded sneer at Liria before taking a seat. He eyed the tablet, then the sunstone and needle with an air of bored distaste. "Is all this truly necessary?"

"Yes," Cal answered. "Now that the crown has accepted me, I mean to ensure everyone is working towards the same goals."

"Which are?"

"The safety and prosperity of this kingdom, of course."

Justice gave him a thin smile. "Wonderful. As you no doubt know, that has been my only goal since I began working for your father."

"Of course," Cal replied with a nod, before motioning to the sunstone. "If you would." He kept his posture relaxed despite tension seeping into him when Justice stared at him without moving. They both knew Cal couldn't force him. Liria's magic would work whether Justice freely gave his blood or not, but the moment such magic was used without consent, the humans would riot. Even without magic on their side, a civil war would tear the kingdom apart.

Minutes passed in utter silence before Justice gave a soft snort. "I will not be enslaved by you."

Liria flinched as if slapped. "How dare you," she hissed. "I have never used my magic in such vile ways."

"And yet you insist on needing my blood," Justice said, disdain dripping from his words. He flicked his fingers to the tablet with a sneer of distaste. "And your spells are written in your ancient script. How can I possibly agree to such blatantly underhanded schemes?"

Liria drew in a sharp breath, undoubtedly to start an hour-long tirade none of them had the patience for. "You served my father for thirty years, yes?" Cal asked before she could speak a word.

"Twenty-nine."

"And you are responsible for ensuring the laws are upheld and communicated to the people, both old and new." When Justice nodded, Cal motioned to the tablet. "Then surely you are familiar enough with Elvish to recognize the core of these spells. Or is there an interpreter you would like to join us?"

"Don't bother," Justice said. "I knew the moment you took the crown that you would begin removing us from our positions. You seek to return to the previous Ages, when creatures slaughtered humans for their lands and wore parts of them as trophies."

Cal couldn't keep his expression from twisting with disgust at that gross fabrication. "Those are the lies you intend to spread?" he demanded. "To sow fear and start a new war?"

Justice's lips twisted into a slow, taunting smile. "Those are the truths that humans already know. That's why we're here, is it not? I heard you were at the prison. So many creatures have been causing trouble lately. Like rabid beasts."

Cal snarled, a burst of magic heating the air around him before he forcibly snuffed it out. He didn't need Julius' glare to remind him he couldn't kill Justice here. "You will suffer every injustice you caused against another," he swore.

"Perhaps," Justice replied, once again appearing bored. "You'll have to get me to the prison first."

Liria sneered. "Where you no doubt have an easy escape waiting for you," she said, as Julius moved to the side door. Two guards were already waiting outside, and they strode in with iron manacles to secure Justice's wrists and ankles.

"Take him to an inner chamber with only one door," Cal ordered. "No one sees him, and he doesn't move until I send for him personally." When they'd gone, Julius following behind them, he turned to Liria.

"That was too easy." She sat back and crossed her arms. "And I still haven't been of any use."

"Not true. Matthias was so focused on your chest, he admitted to his own incompetence," Cal said, snickering when she elbowed him. Needless to say, Matthias was on the list of officials he'd be releasing from duty.

"I find it hard to believe no one knew about the prison," he said, staring at his tablet. None of the elves had known; he'd sensed that for himself. But the other magical creatures and humans? Justice wasn't well-liked among the rest of the officials, that was clear, but there was a sense of grudging respect among them.

"He has an aide, doesn't he?" Liria asked. "Or a servant maybe."

Cal swore. He should have thought of that himself. Most of the officials had aides or personal pages, and they'd be more likely to hear and spread gossip. He stuck his head out the door, spotted Duaia, and motioned her over.

"My King," she said as she approached, pressing her fist over her heart. "Ready for the next one?"

"Not quite," he said. "Justice's aide, have you seen him?"

"I can find him. I'll send Juls back with him if I see him."

"Thank you." He turned back to his seat and sank into it with a sigh, rubbing his forehead.

"You're being too hard on yourself," Liria said, patting him on the back. "You can't handle everything on your own."

"My father did," Cal muttered, before wincing. The past hours had proven what a terrible example his father truly was, as painful as that was to admit.

Liria sighed. "Your father refused even your advice and help most of the time. But you have Juls and D, and me and Aelin. And two new bondeds," she added with a sly grin, proving they hadn't avoided as much notice as Cal had hoped. "Plus your sister is always eager to get her hands into things."

Cal snorted quietly, about to make some flippant comment about the kingdom being doomed, but the door opened before he could. That was probably for the best; he didn't need anyone spreading word that the king thought they were doomed.

Julius held the door open and motioned a young man inside. Cal had seen him before, following Justice or running errands for him. He'd always seemed withdrawn, but Cal assumed that was a result of working for Justice.

"Good evening," Cal said, motioning to the chair.

The man swallowed, his green eyes wide as he looked from Cal to Liria. He was pale and looked nervous enough to be sick. His dark blond hair was a shaggy mess, plastered to his forehead with sweat and curling over his ears. "Your M-majesty," he stammered, stumbling to the chair and sinking into it.

Cal wanted to assure him he wasn't in any trouble, but if he'd been working with Justice, that might turn out to be a lie. He waited for Liria to offer the needle, and the man willingly pricked his finger, letting a drop of blood fall on the sunstone. When the magic flared and brightened, he leaned forward. "What is your name?"

"Kithiel, Your Majesty," he replied softly, staring at the sunstone as if expecting it to call him a liar.

"That's an elven name," Cal prompted. It wasn't unusual for humans to adopt elven names, but considering Justice's bias, he would have expected even an elven name to be too much.

"I'm half blood," Kithiel replied, dropping his gaze to his hands, his fingers twisting in the loose, worn linen of his tunic.

Cal glanced at Liria, saw her nod, then studied the young man with a frown. He reached out with his own magic and found a connection to Kithiel. It was faint and muddled, and he couldn't get much of anything from it, but it was there, evidence of his bloodline. "Do you know what Justice has been doing? With the prison?"

Kithiel sucked in a deep breath, opening his mouth as if to answer, but no sound came out. He whimpered softly, twisting his fingers tighter until his knuckles turned white.

"Do you know of his plans and desires to harm anyone of magical descent? To sow dissent among the people?"

Kithiel's breathing became ragged, and he paled further as he made a choking sound.

Julius straightened and took a step forward as Cal's own unease grew. He reached along the bond again and felt a tremor of something dark, before Kithiel coughed and lurched to the side, vomiting blood.

Cal swore, his chair toppling behind him as he lunged to his feet, but Julius was faster, grabbing Kithiel and pushing him upright before ripping the top of his tunic open. A gold collar sat on his throat, gleaming with powerful spellwork.

A slave collar. They'd been outlawed even before Cal was born, but they still appeared from time to time.

"Liria!" he snapped, calling on his own magic as he stalked around the desk. The spells were powerful, but they were no match for the three of them. He wrapped two fingers around the collar as Julius did the same on his side, his fingers already glowing with red-gold magic. Liria swiped a line of blood on the collar on her side before grasping it as well.

Cal took a deep breath and let his magic wrap around the collar, around himself, around Julius and Liria, around Kithiel. Julius and Liria did the same, creating a trifold layer of defense, their magics melding together with a familiarity and ease borne of working magic together for years. When he breathed out, their magics tightened and pulled, snapping the collar and the spells woven through it.

There was a moment of complete, unnatural silence, and then the backlash hit, a ripple of force powerful enough it sent all three of them flying.

Cal grunted as he crashed through the powerful enchantments and solid wood of the desk before slamming into the wall. His footing slipped and he crumpled to the floor, his vision wavering as something warm and wet trickled down the back of his neck. Everything flickered black, and a blink later, the room was swarming with guards, Duaia stalking through all of them with a thunderous expression, her sword gleaming in one hand and crackling blue magic swirling around the other.

"What the *fuck*," she snarled, her eyes landing on each of them in turn, before she spotted a brightly glowing piece of the shattered collar. Her face twisted with disgust as she plucked it off the floor, then turned a familiar, utterly unimpressed look on Cal.

"You know I could have dispelled this without nearly losing another monarch."

And that… that was a very good point, but he could barely breathe through what he was sure was a broken rib, much less speak just yet. As she called for healers, Cal let himself slump with a quiet groan. Considering how exhausted he was, he accepted the valid excuse to let unconsciousness claim him for a bit.

# Chapter 5

Waking without pain should not have been the luxury it was.

Haru cracked his eyes open to soft golden mage light illuminating the room. His sense of time was completely broken, but the smell of food told him it was likely far into the evening. Soft breaths against his arm and the warm weight of a body pressed into his side let him know where Rashi was, and the sensation of drool on his skin told him the fox had been asleep for a while.

He closed his eyes again with a sigh, but his body was finally recovered thanks to Rashi's healing, and he'd slept enough to last him a week. He carefully shifted off the bed and to his feet, examining Rashi and reassuring himself that they were both still alive. Rashi's hair was a mess, and Haru ran a hand over it in vain; it refused to be tamed, as if perpetually caught in a lightning storm.

Rashi sighed in his sleep and burrowed deeper into his pillow.

Satisfied that Rashi was safe and whole, Haru turned his attention to the warm food. He devoured the baked fish, fresh bread, and strange soft green slices of some fruit or vegetable. His hunger sated, he stripped off the loose pants he'd been dressed in on his way to the bathroom. Once he was under the hot spray of water, he closed his eyes and tipped his head back, letting the sensation ground him back in his body.

The spelled iron they'd used to weaken his magic had deadened his senses, which had been a blessing in the prison. Now that he was healed, he could feel his magic again, and he sank into it, letting it course through his body. He flexed his fingers, a silver-white glow building around them. The water froze into ice in the space above his hands, falling to the marble around his feet with soft *tink, tink, tinks,* before melting into water again.

He blew out a deep breath of relief and let his magic fade as he set to work cleaning himself. His hair had been pulled into a loose braid, and he shook it free, letting it hang down his back. He washed it twice, grit and dirt and flecks of iron swirling down the drain. Then he moved on to scrubbing the sweat, dried blood, and lingering medicinal ointments from his skin.

When he finally turned off the water and stepped out in a billow of steam, his pale skin was pinked from the heat and rough treatment, but he felt clean and whole for the first time since entering the Wound.

He stood dripping on the plush carpet and surveyed the room, frowning when he saw no sign of his or Rashi's belongings. With a tsk, he rummaged through the wardrobe and pulled on some simple pants and a loose shirt. They left him feeling naked and vulnerable without the enchantments and magic woven into his own clothes, but there was nothing to be done about that now. He found a comb and worked the tangles out of his hair, then wove it back into a loose braid.

Since Rashi was still asleep, he moved to the window and pushed open the curtains. An elaborate garden stretched out far below and beyond the window. It was too dark to see any color, but he could sense the blooming flowers, the slow beat of plants thrumming beneath the magic of the city. Some were familiar thanks to Rashi's inherent need to share his love of plants—jasmine, hibiscus, and foxglove. Others less so—fruiting trees and bushes full of ripe berries. The palace itself had a slower beat, old beyond ancient, and so vast that he could barely comprehend that he stood inside a living tree.

Even the view when they first approached the city, with the ancient trees stretching nearly to the clouds, hadn't prepared him for the enormity of their existence.

The stables were past the garden, and then the palace walls, and then the city itself. Tiny points of golden light marked the streets and flickered in the windows of buildings.

The last refuge of the south, Ylrendorei was called. The kingdom reached from the east to the west for nearly the entire continent, but just beyond the city gates to the north, the Wound stretched as far as he could see, all the way north to what was left of the singing forests. Rashi's homeland diminished every year as the Wound ate away at healthy soil. If something wasn't done, eventually the entire continent would be reduced to a barren wasteland.

He'd thought the stories of Ylrendorei being a golden jewel of safety meant they could find the start of a solution here, but the moment the city had come into view, he'd sensed the core of rot festering inside. He would have turned back then, but their Fate strings led directly to the heart of the city, and Rashi was far too eager to find their third.

And then those humans found them.

He snarled softly before reining in his anger when the glass frosted over, obscuring the view of the city. He closed his eyes and breathed, the strength of Rashi's bond soothing the anger and fear of nearly losing him. That couldn't happen again.

He turned his attention to the room's threshold. The protective spells laid into the foundation were old and foreign, but the purpose of them was familiar enough. He slipped his magic into them to add his own, weaving spells to keep out any who intended harm, to protect against fire and hostile spells, to alert him to poisons or hidden weapons. His magic sang along his senses, and he took pleasure in embracing it again after days without it.

There was resistance in the ambient magic, as if something held the non-elemental aspects in a loose grip, but he blamed it on the rot that seemed to be coming from the ley lines themselves.

No sooner had he set the wards in place than he felt the rush of magic in the palace, a powerful backlash that rattled the dishes on the table as though the ground itself were shaking. Rashi thrashed on the bed with a sharp cry, curling in on himself as his breathing turned ragged.

Haru gritted his teeth against the echo of pain in his chest and the throb of a sudden headache, but when he reached along their bond, there was no sign of injury. "Rashi, breathe," he snapped, pushing black hair away from Rashi's face.

Rashi groaned and turned towards him, his eyes dark and unfocused. "Cal," he gasped. "Attacked."

Haru cursed and picked Rashi up before stalking out of the bedroom, through a sitting room, to another door. When he opened it, he found two elves standing guard down the hall, on either side of the stairs. He was in no mood to be told they were still prisoners and loosened the tight hold he kept on his magic, ready to fight his way past if necessary. The guards' eyes widened, but they didn't move away as he'd hoped. He might have been impressed by the caliber of the guards, if not for Rashi's labored breathing.

He cursed the Fate bond, and himself for letting this happen. The bond shouldn't be so powerful, but it was incomplete and compensating for the absence of a bond between him and Cal.

He moved for the stairs, where one of his Fate strings stretched below them, towards the other side of the palace, and snarled softly when a nearby door opened and an elf rushed out.

Rashi's ears twitched forward. "Fa-Faelan," he croaked.

The elf spun towards them with wild eyes. "Rashi! Are you hurt?"

"Cal," Rashi said, and panic flickered in Faelan's eyes before the elf took a deep breath.

"Juls too. This way."

Haru fell into step behind them, unsure if Faelan was male or female. Elves were all the same to him. Nothing but delicate limbs and deceitful beauty.

They'd started down the long flight of stairs when Rashi groaned in relief and slumped in Haru's arms. "I think the healers are there now."

Some of Haru's tension eased when the echo of pain faded, but he didn't put Rashi down. They reached a lower floor and hurried across a large foyer, through a set of ornate doors, and directly into chaos.

Humans, elves, and a few other creatures filled the large room with curved tables spiraling out from the center, but even the guards stepped out of their way as they cut a path through.

Rashi tipped his head back, exasperation sparking along their bond. "Your face is scaring everyone."

"Good," Haru replied, tightening his grip when Rashi huffed a laugh against his shoulder, the quick puff of warm breath comforting and familiar.

Faelan led the way across to the far side of the chamber, where a group of guards surrounded a cluster of healers and prone figures. The guards shifted to let Faelan through, then tried to block Haru, so he loosened his hold on his magic a bit more. Fear rippled through everyone within a few feet of him, their primal instincts reacting to the presence of something far more powerful than them.

He pushed through while they were still reeling and surveyed the injured. Four elves with various internal and external injuries, most likely caused by the backlash. The smallest one had ugly bruises and burns around their throat.

Rashi made a soft sound of distress and shifted in his arms.

Haru instinctively tightened his hold, unwilling to let him go with so many elves nearby. He eyed those lying prone again, spotting the thread stretching between himself and the one with a crown, before stepping closer. None of the guards appeared eager to stop him, a few even taking a step back, and he revised his opinion on their caliber.

He set Rashi on his feet, watching as the fox sank to his knees at Cal's side, opposite a healer. A closer examination of the elf's injuries showed two cracked ribs and deep bruising that was slowly fading. The elf who'd been with Cal in the prison had a broken shoulder. The other elf had blood on their face and matting their hair from a head injury. The healers seemed to have everything under control, even if their skill and ability were lacking compared to Rashi's.

Haru stood behind Rashi, itching for his weapon and his own clothes as the rot of magic in the city crawled along his senses. It was the same fetid violation of magic that had run rampant at the end of the war, just after the destruction of the Shadow Throne created a backlash through the ley lines themselves, and the Wound ripped across the continent.

He'd seen that cataclysmic event himself, drawn from the safety of the high mountains when he felt the corruption in the very essence of magic. Even then, the rest of the dragons chose to remain in the mountains and deepest parts of the earth, letting the realm continue to believe dragons no longer existed.

He'd watched the human armies from afar, but the distance couldn't hide the vile feeling of what their shadow magic had become. Feeling it growing again now made him want to take Rashi and retreat into the forest or mountains, but with the Fate string connecting him to the elf with the crown, he knew that wouldn't be possible.

Fate might be a cryptic wench, but She refused to be denied. What She expected from an elf who couldn't even prevent backlash from knocking them unconscious, Haru couldn't begin to fathom.

A sudden flurry of movement had him tensing and turning to the elf with the damaged throat. They were struggling against a healer holding them down, their eyes wide with terror on their face.

The healer made a shushing sound that wasn't soothing in the least.

The elf let out a sharp, broken keening sound as a human reached for them with a vial of purple-black liquid. It resembled any other potion, but the twisted magic emanating from it was the same rot infecting the rest of the kingdom.

"Stop!" He tore himself away from Rashi's side, shoving past the startled guards, but the human ignored him. "That's poison!" he yelled, snarling as a guard grabbed his arm. His magic flared as every instinct screamed to throw the guard off and kill the human before they killed the injured elf. He'd already survived the prison once. He could do it again if necessary. So long as Rashi wasn't there, he might even manage to raze it to the ground.

"Freeze!" A sharp voice cut through the commotion and terrified keening, magic underlying the command.

The spell hit him with the force of a rampaging girallon, but whatever subconscious intentions were woven into it deemed him not a threat.

The two healers and the guard holding Haru stopped moving as the spell locked them in place, only too late. The vial was already against the elf's lips and the liquid spilled out of it, the latent spells activating as they mixed with saliva.

"Rashi," he called, but Rashi was already moving, urged into motion by Haru's desperate helplessness. If he hadn't hesitated, he could have stopped this, but his magic was useless when it came to healing, much less stopping a spell designed to destroy someone from the inside.

Rashi dodged another guard that reached for him and crashed to his knees beside the elf, and Haru immediately slammed a solid shield of ice around them both to keep anyone from interfering. The shield wrapped close against both of their bodies and then expanded, pushing the healers and the vial away from them.

"What the fuck."

Haru looked up at the tall guard hurrying towards them and froze despite being free of the spell. Sorceress. They were a rare species as wholly borne of magic as dragons were. They could be born from anyone and took after the species of their parents, but they were marked by a pair of tiny black horns on top of their head. Their ability to harness every element made them some of the most fearsome creatures he knew of. Her magic essence was the deep shades of blues and reds of a female sorceress, shot through with the flickering lines of pale gold of most elves.

She stopped near the frost barrier with a frown, following the magic to its source. Her eyes widened in shock when she spotted Haru, mouth dropping open with a sound like she'd been punched in the chest.

They stared at each other, one rare creature and one that was all but myth.

"Right, then," she said, recovering far quicker than he'd expected. "Poison?"

Haru nodded to the human still holding the vial, and the sorceress plucked it free. There was still some liquid inside, and she gave it a little shake. He sensed the gentle pulse of magic as she studied it closer, and he breathed a sigh of relief when she swore, sealed it with a spell, and tucked it into a pouch at her hip.

She turned a hard look over the rest of the healers still working on the other elves. Another spell slammed into and over Haru, similar to the first one, but no one else froze.

Whatever their goal was, it seemed the two healers were working alone.

Haru pulled free of the frozen guard. The spell released them as soon as Haru was no longer being restrained, and Haru moved closer to Rashi as the sorceress turned her attention to him.

Rashi's soft, deep green magic glowed bright and strong as he fought to keep the poison from spreading.

"Lower the barrier," the sorceress ordered.

Haru narrowed his eyes at her and braced himself for an attempt to break through his shields.

She returned the glare with an annoyed scoff. "Expand it, then. These two aren't moving, and no one else here is a threat."

Haru glanced at the others, reluctant to let an elven-born sorceress any closer, but Rashi made that decision for him.

"Haru, I need her help," he said, his voice strained. "I don't know what this is. He's going to die."

Haru snarled and slammed magic into the barrier, forcing it out farther to enclose the small group of healers, injured elves, and the sorceress.

She strode forward and sank to her knees across from Rashi, the young elf between them. Here," she said, opening a connection and allowing her magic and Rashi's to flow together. "I'll take care of the poison. You protect his heart and lungs."

Rashi gave a sharp nod, some of his tension easing as she took over controlling the poison's advance, their magic threading through the elf in a delicate weave.

Long moments passed as Haru watched the tainted black essence of poison and the blue-red magic that encased it, slowly drawing it back out. Rashi's deep green magic wrapped around the elf's heart and lungs in a solid, protective aura that never wavered.

His attention flicked to the crowned elf when he stirred with a pained groan, but he didn't see anything serious enough to be concerned about, and turned back to Rashi.

Another long moment passed before finally, a black substance trickled out of the elf's nose and mouth. Haru bared his teeth with a growl at the unnatural feel of concentrated, rotting magic.

The sorceress wrapped her own magic around the ooze and lifted it into the air, collecting it into a floating black ball that grew to the size of her palm before the elf stopped leaking. "That should be it." She pulled an empty bottle from her pouch and guided the black ooze into it, earning Haru's approval when she set several protective and sealing spells on it before putting it away. Once that was done, she let out a deep breath, listing a bit to the side before righting herself, but not before the immobility spell wavered.

Haru instinctively threw another barrier into place, encasing Rashi as well as the elf's head and part of his torso, protecting them both from the healers.

The one who'd held the elf down to begin with made an aborted move for the nearby satchel, freezing again as the sorceress threw a hand out towards them. "Who are you working for?" she snarled.

The healer sobbed, tears streaming down their face. They opened their mouth, but no sound came out until they said, "He'll kill them." And then they were screaming as magic flared around their wrist. Dark shadows writhed and pulsed with veins of violet, spreading to envelop their entire body.

"Get down!" the sorceress yelled, a moment before Haru felt the spell ignite.

He didn't have time to get Rashi to safety. He didn't even have time to try. He threw both hands forward and called on all his magic to form a third barrier around the screaming healer, and then another on top of that one, and another, as unnatural violet-black flames ate through each layer. Just the touch of that magic against his own burned like living fire along his senses, seeking a path to his own body to burn him alive too. Which should have been impossible.

What little he'd ever learned of the humans' twisted magic could never have prepared him for this. The purpose of any spell might be infinite, but its target was finite, constrained by the caster's subconscious intentions. Once the spell attached, it couldn't transfer itself. Except that was exactly what this one was doing, as if it were its own caster.

Too late, he realized this was the true danger of this magic returning to the realm. Whatever the humans had done to their shadow magic, it had changed the very essence of it. Infected it with some semblance of sentience with their greed and desire for power, with their need to destroy.

He continued layering barriers over barriers, but the flames weren't slowing, and he couldn't maintain this forever. His magical reserves were a fraction of what they should have been after the prison, and he was already nearing magical burnout. He doubted he could even keep this contained long enough for anyone here to get to safety.

His control wavered as the corrupted magic coiled through the spaces between his barriers, violet-black smoke rising above them. He dropped to his knees as the explosive force of flames pushing against his magic suddenly vanished. His barriers shrank to nothing around the burned-out husk of ash that was all that was left of the healer.

There was a strange ringing in his ears, but all he could focus on was the relief of no longer straining his magic, of no longer reforming a dozen barriers against a spell intended to kill everyone around him. It wasn't until the violet-black smoke still hovering in the air moved as if to strike that he realized the ringing sound was partly Rashi screaming his name, and partly the thrum of magic lingering for far longer than it should.

The two shields he'd cast initially were somehow still intact, which was all that truly mattered. His instincts surged, summoning another shield in front of himself, but it flickered before it fully formed, bursting into tiny puffs of cold air and snowflakes.

This was it, then. And he hadn't even exchanged a proper greeting with the crowned elf.

A second later the smoke slammed into him, except there was no searing agony as it burned through his chest. No force of impact. Nothing.

He blinked against the darkness of his vision, only to realize the darkness was from the shadows encasing him, held at bay a mere sliver of space from his body.

It took another moment for him to fight through the onslaught of magical exhaustion to realize his personal shields still held. Shields that he'd held in place without conscious thought for centuries. He could only assume they held because they weren't actively fighting against the smoke, and they were far more solid than any hastily cast shield could be.

The shadows moved around him as if alive, points of violet flickering in front of his face like blinking eyes. As disturbing as that thought was, he accepted it as a good thing. So long as the shadows were focused on him, they wouldn't go after anyone else. His barrier around Rashi still held, kept in place by the desperate desire to keep him safe when initially cast. At the moment, that had to be enough.

He gritted his teeth against the pain of magical burnout and lowered himself to the floor.

# CHAPTER 6

CAL WOKE to chaos and the sharp, bitter tang in the air that came from working powerful magic. His body ached, but the agony from simply breathing was gone. He recognized the healer beside him, even though the other elf's attention was no longer on Cal.

He pushed himself upright to focus on the blinding spot of magic and… Rashi and Haru? "What?" he started to ask, before taking in the glittering shields around them with a detached fascination. His head ached, and everything felt fuzzy around the edges, a sure sign he had a head injury and had been given strong pain suppressants. But something was going on and he needed to be coherent.

He looked around again, spotting Duaia next to Haru, and the terror on her face was enough to clear the haze in his head, his heart hammering with a surge of panic. The last time he'd seen that expression on her face was fifteen years ago, when an assassin infiltrated the guard, killed his mother, and took his sister captive.

Duaia still blamed herself, even though it hadn't been her fault. It'd been Cal's.

He shoved those memories away and struggled to his feet. When he focused on the powerful spell contained by more shields, he saw the shadows seeping through them. He sucked in a breath, sure he was seeing things that weren't there, because that wasn't possible. Shadows had belonged to the humans, and that magic no longer existed.

And yet the shadow-like flames grew darker and larger, rising above them. Instinctively, he stretched his arm out, calling on his magic.

"Don't!" Duaia yelled.

Cal hesitated, his chest twisting with fear when the flames swarmed towards Haru a moment later. He stumbled forward, pressing a hand against the barrier beside Rashi. Duaia's magic wrapped around the shadows, but the spell fractured as she tried to pull them away from Haru.

He cursed and spun around, searching for anything that could help them. His eyes landed on Liria. She was struggling to sit up, blood smeared across her face, but her sunstone was next to her. It was old and powerful, passed down through her family for Ages.

He snatched it up, holding it with both hands outstretched towards the shadows. The crown grew warm on his head as he called on the Sun and his connection to all the elves nearby.

Shadows couldn't abide the light. That was what the elders always said, though any techniques or spells for dealing with the shadows were all but lost, reduced to what few records had been written before the end of the war.

Still, he had to do something. Trusting the Sun to guide him, he let his magic flow into the sunstone. It warmed in his fingers, growing brighter and hotter by the moment, until it blazed like the sun itself. The flare of pain in his hands quickly turned cold, then numb. The shocked yells around him faded behind the high-pitched ringing of condensed magic. A whisper of *enough* cut through everything else, and he released the magic. Pure white light exploded from the sunstone, lancing towards the shadows and slicing through them with far more force than he'd intended.

The ringing in the air turned to a horrible screaming, as if the shadows themselves were alive and in pain. He had only a moment to dwell on that before the light coalesced around the remnants of the shadows and then retracted towards him. The sunstone absorbed the light and shadows both, and then exploded.

The force of it sent him flying back, crashing into another shield behind them with a grunt. "Fuck," he gasped, his already sore body protesting. He was fully awake and present now, even if his legs felt like overcooked vegetables.

"Report," he ordered, needing to know the damage. Other than a pile of black ash and Haru's prone form on the floor, everyone looked dazed but whole.

A palace guard rushed forward from the other side of the chamber, and he felt dread coil in his gut. "My King," the guard said, pressing a fist across his chest as he continued speaking. "Justice is missing."

"What do you mean missing?" he snapped.

The guard winced and dropped to his knee. "The two who were assigned to guard the door said a page arrived with a missive directly from you, ordering them to release Justice to his quarters. I personally checked his rooms. He's yet to be found."

Cal closed his eyes and took a deep breath. One thing at a time. The immediate threat was dealt with, but the next one could happen at any moment.

"Find the page," he said, opening his eyes as he straightened, forcing his legs to hold steady. "Bring them to me. Lock down the palace. Search every room until the page and Justice are found. And send the order to activate all the sunstones in the kingdom."

Most of their sunstones were kept at minimal power even at night, the permanent ones lighting the streets enough to keep them safe. The larger ones fixed to the tallest buildings were a wartime measure that kept the entire city lit as if at high sun. They were one of the only precautions that had kept the humans from completely overrunning them during the war.

The guard bowed lower in acknowledgment before turning to carry out Cal's orders.

He waved his healer off and pointed to Haru. "Tend to him," he said, before kneeling next to Julius. He was awake but looked dazed, struggling to sit up despite a nasty gash on his head. He started to squeeze Julius' shoulder before remembering the state of his burned hands. "Stop giving your healer grief and let her work," he ordered, then he left Julius to Faelan and the healer as he turned to Liria.

She scowled at him. "Did you have to destroy my sunstone?"

Cal winced and did a quick sweep of the floor, hoping to find even a piece of it, but it had exploded into fine dust and magic residue. "I'll find you another one."

"A better one."

He held up his hands in surrender. "Yes, I'll find the oldest sunstone and ensure it's spelled against spontaneous explosions," he said, quickly moving on before she could get started on a lecture.

When he reached Rashi, he slowly sank to the floor. The post-battle fatigue was setting in and he was starting to feel pain in his hands again. "Are you all right? What happened?"

Rashi leaned against the barrier separating them. "We're all right," he said quietly. "One of the healers tried to kill him," he said, nodding to where Kithiel was sprawled on the floor and across Rashi's lap.

"What?" he asked sharply. He looked at Duaia, the grim set of her lips confirmation enough.

"Slave collar," she said tightly. "On her wrist."

Cal swore before letting out a controlled breath. What the fuck had he set in motion? He shuddered to think that all of this was connected. The prison, Justice, slave collars, and now the return of shadow magic? The timing couldn't be a coincidence, but why now? More importantly, to what end?

# Chapter 7

It was deep into the night yet again by the time the healers finished with them. Neither Justice nor the missing page had been located, but Duaia found the ring acting as a slave collar on the other healer and deactivated it without triggering any more traps.

Haru recovered enough to lower the barriers, though Kithiel clung to Rashi and refused to let go. The worst of his injuries were taken care of, but he hadn't spoken a word, and there was a haunted air about him that hadn't been there before they'd removed his collar. Before the explosion and assassination attempt.

Since there was little else he could do without a functional Truth Seeker, and without some proper rest, he left Zaos, Duaia's second in command, in charge, a battlemage who'd served as his personal guard until Julius came of age. By some unspoken agreement, the eight of them ended up in Cal's sitting room.

He sank into his favorite, overlarge armchair and fought the sudden, intense urge to simply pass out as the others settled in chairs and the long sofas. He rubbed his forehead and hissed in pain. The healers had done what they could for his hands, but the burns had been severe, and he'd insisted they focus their efforts on the others.

He dropped his hands to his lap with a sigh. Not even two days wearing the crown, and he'd uncovered the first threads of some sinister plot, survived magical backlash, and stopped an attempt to murder at least one elf with shadow magic that shouldn't even exist anymore.

Cal glanced up in confusion when Rashi appeared in front of him.

"Can I see your hands?"

He tilted his head before lifting his hands, watching as a soft green energy surrounded Rashi's fingers. "Oh," he whispered, surprised. He knew most beastkin had some form of life or nature magic, but it was his first time seeing pure healing energy. Even their own healers mostly used light magic to cleanse and improve the body's ability for self-healing.

Rashi's magic was fundamentally different, restoring Cal's skin to its previous state as if erasing the burn damage altogether. That certainly explained Haru's miraculous healing.

"What in darkness is happening?" Liria demanded, sounding more angry than anything.

"I have no idea," Cal murmured, looking up from his hands to those gathered. His inner circle, he realized, with the exception of Kithiel, who still refused to be separated from Rashi. Which was understandable, considering Haru and Rashi were the only reason he was still alive.

"It's the rot," Haru said from where he stood near the door, as if standing guard.

"Haru," Rashi chided as he smoothed his palms over Cal's hands. They left a gentle tingling and perfectly healed flesh in their wake. "It's not a rot."

Haru huffed and crossed his arms, his brow furrowed. "The *shadows* then. It's infecting the entire city."

"What do you mean?" Cal asked, leaning forward. "There's more than what was unleashed tonight?" How was that possible? No one had reported unusual magic, and as far as he knew, this was the first sight of shadow magic since the war.

"You can't feel it?" Haru turned from Cal to Duaia, his frown deepening into a scowl. "How can you not feel it?"

Irritation and offense flared hot in his chest, aided by three days of no sleep, and Cal took a slow, deep breath before he could act on it. "Feel what?" he asked tightly.

Rashi perched on the arm of his chair, his fingers lingering on Cal's palm. "The magic here is… strange."

Cal raised an eyebrow at Duaia, who gazed back at him in confusion. He closed his eyes and breathed deep again, reaching out to the magic surrounding them rather than calling it to him. Ylrendorei was built atop one of the biggest ley lines, the deep pool of raw magic resting beneath their feet. That nexus fueled their throne and was one of the reasons the kingdom had survived for Ages.

As a child, he'd sprawled out in the gardens, under the shade of the thousands-of-years-old dawntrees, hidden in the shade of their long branches with their rich golden-orange leaves. He'd let his magic seep into the ground, past the foundation of the palace and the roots of the trees, deep into the earth, then farther, where the ley lines pulsed with the lifeblood of the realm. That source of magic was what sustained all life on the surface.

Whatever had happened during the war, it had severed part of that connection, resulting in the Wound that lay between his kingdom and the forests, but the magic itself felt the same now as it'd been when he was a child. If the infection had been there all that time, it'd been there for far longer than he'd been alive.

"It feels the same as it always has," he said, opening his eyes to look at Haru. He wasn't expecting the play of emotions his answer caused—disbelief, anger, horror, and then devastation as Haru slumped against the wall.

"You've—" Haru started, his mouth moving without sound before he frowned. "Thirty-five years and you've never noticed anything?"

Cal decided he was far too tired to take offense to that accusation. He rubbed his eyes with his free hand, only then realizing Rashi still had hold of his other one. He could feel the echo of worry along their bond and gave Rashi's fingers a light squeeze.

Then his attention shifted to Kithiel, curled up in the corner of the large sofa closest to Rashi. "Do you know why they tried to kill you?" he asked softly.

Kithiel flinched and tried to disappear into the cushions, but Rashi was the one who spoke.

"No," he said firmly, getting to his feet without releasing Cal's hand. "Everyone is exhausted and still in shock. You need sleep," he added with a pointed glare at Cal. "Even I can't heal sleep deprivation."

Cal eyed him with a sullen glare, but he didn't have the energy to argue. Despite the stress and not knowing when the next attack could come, he was struggling to stay awake. A quick glance at Julius and Liria showed they were no better. With a sigh, he stood, reluctantly letting go of Rashi. Somehow, he knew no one would be willing to go back to their own rooms, so he motioned to the spare bedroom he had available. "You can fight over who gets the bed," he said, turning for his own room.

He stayed coherent just long enough to remove his boots before he fell face first into his bed.

# CHAPTER 8

RASHI PERCHED on the arm of the plush sofa as he watched Haru, weaving layer after layer of spellwork into the threshold of Cal's sitting room. "I'm not sure he'll appreciate this," he said.

"I don't care," Haru replied, not even slowing in his casting.

He shook his head with a soft, exasperated huff. Even if Cal didn't like the added safety, it was needed. What little bit of a threshold existed was old, the spells weak and faded, as if no one had bothered to acknowledge their existence in years. He hadn't felt a solid threshold anywhere, certainly not one strong enough to keep out someone with ill intentions. At best, they seemed to only be used to keep privacy, and he wondered if it was another bit of magic and knowledge the elves had lost during the war.

When the Wound appeared, it ripped through the battlefield where the humans fought against every other species aside from dragons. The rich valleys and endless plains between the northern forests and southern seas all vanished, taking the majority of the human armies, as well as the elven warriors and elders. Or so the stories went.

Haru might have been old enough to remember those times, but Rashi was only twenty. The war was ancient history for him, but he suspected the stories held some truth, considering no one here seemed to find the magic within the city unnerving.

As soon as he and Haru had passed through the Wound, he'd felt the shift, like something lurked in the depths of the ley lines.

"What do you think of him?" Haru asked, pulling Rashi out of his thoughts.

Cal, he guessed. He shrugged at Haru's back as he considered, glancing towards the bedroom where the elf had been deep asleep since two nights ago. He felt the bond shift between them and knew Cal was finally awake, lurking in his bedroom and fully aware of their conversation. Well, he certainly wasn't going to change his opinion because Cal wanted to eavesdrop.

"I'm not sure," he said. "He feels a bit… lost sometimes." Which he supposed was to be expected. Cal's father died just a few weeks ago, long before his time, and from what Faelan had said, it sounded like there were some who thought his death was anything but natural. "I know we're bound for a reason, but I'm not sure how he's supposed to help with restoring the Wound with his city under attack."

"They're connected," Haru said, then cursed as one of his spells refused to set. Tiny sparks of bright white snowflakes exploded around the door.

Rashi snickered, catching a snowflake on his palm before it faded, leaving only a tingle of cool magical residue behind. "You tried to make it refuse entry to anyone you don't know," he said.

Haru huffed, shooting an annoyed glare over his shoulder. "It worked on our room."

Rashi rolled his eyes, biting his tongue before they could get into a debate on intentions in relation to threshold ownership. Haru was stubborn enough to think that because he was an all-powerful, mystical dragon, he should be able to control any space he inhabited, while Rashi understood that Cal didn't view his guestrooms as his own space, but the sitting room belonged to him as much as his bedroom, so Haru's intentions couldn't override Cal's when it came to the main threshold.

He glanced towards the bedroom when movement caught his eye, smiling at a sleep-rumpled Cal. "Good morning, Your Majesty."

Cal paused at the edge of the room, watching Haru with curiosity thrumming along their bond before turning to Rashi. "Good morning. And it's just Cal," he said, moving to sit in the chair he'd taken the other night. He didn't pretend he hadn't been listening as he asked, "How are they connected? And where are the others?"

"We haven't seen them since lunch yesterday." At Cal's confusion, Rashi added, "You slept all of yesterday and last night. Julius wanted to wake you, but I convinced him that you both needed more rest. Aeliria said she wanted to find her brother, and that she expects a replacement stone when she gets back. And Duaia looked like she was going to tear the entire palace apart."

Cal sighed and rubbed his forehead. He still looked tired, but not as if he was still suffering from the soul-deep exhaustion from the other night. He tilted his head as another layer of spells snapped into place, a soft thrum of magic reverberating through the room. "What are you doing?" He sounded more confused than alarmed, and Rashi wondered if he'd misjudged how Cal would react.

He hoped so. A ruler who couldn't accept help was worse than one who wouldn't ask for help to begin with.

"Strengthening your threshold," Haru answered.

"Oh," Cal said, his eyes widening slightly. He glanced around the room before giving a brief nod. "Thank you."

Rashi smiled to himself when Haru stilled before glancing over his shoulder with a slight nod of his own. When they both remained silent, he realized he would have to be the voice in this relationship. "How are they connected?" he repeated.

"The shadow magic," Haru said, stopping with his hand lightly pressed against the door. "The corruption only exists here. What are the chances that a human has gained access to magic for the first time in three hundred years, near the land where they lost it, and where this rot has apparently been trapped and festering ever since?"

"Maybe they can help fix the Wound."

Cal snorted. "Not likely. Even if Justice weren't trying to kill every magical creature, he'll be executed as soon as he's found for using slave collars."

Rashi shuddered with disgust. Of all the magic they seemed to have lost, the most barbaric survived. "Well, then we'll have to find a way on our own. Maybe start where the shadows are most concentrated."

"Beneath the palace."

Both Cal and Rashi looked at Haru, and he turned to face them, sliding his palms along his arms in a familiar gesture. Except he didn't have his own clothes with the voluminous sleeves to hide his hands in.

Haru's lips twisted in annoyance, and he dropped his arms. "Our belongings were taken in the prison. I would like them back."

Cal winced. "Yes, of course. I'll go there today and retrieve what I can, if you can give me a list."

Before Haru could respond, someone knocked on the door. He tensed and turned to open it.

Rashi leaned to the side and spotted a servant with a cart. "Oh, breakfast," he said with a grin, hopping to his feet and moving to help pull it inside.

The young man watched him with wide, startled eyes before flicking a wary look at Haru. He cleared his throat, then flushed when he spotted Cal. "Your Majesty," he said, ducking his head in a bow.

"Good morning. Did Duaia send you?" Cal asked dryly.

The servant bobbed his head with a quick smile. The coy glance from beneath his lashes that followed almost made Rashi growl before he caught himself. "Yes, Your Majesty. She also said I might find Kithiel here?"

Haru drew himself up to his full height and stepped forward. "And who are you?"

The servant paled and scrambled back. "A-Aster."

Rashi pressed a hand against Haru's arm. "Scary face, love," he murmured, despite being secretly pleased. "He thinks you're going to eat him." He grinned when Haru shot him a scowl that would have made the jorogumo flee. He patted Haru's arm and turned to Aster. "I'll ask if he's up for seeing you, but he still isn't speaking," he warned, before moving to their guestroom.

Kithiel had laid claim to the sofa and was curled up in the corner beneath a blanket. He had a closed book in his lap and a blank expression as he stared across the room at the window.

"Hungry?" Rashi asked quietly, smiling at Kithiel when he slowly turned his head towards him. "Aster is asking to see you. A friend?"

Kithiel's expression turned wary as he glanced at the door.

Rashi stepped into his line of sight, crouching in front of the sofa. "You don't have to see anyone. I'll tell him you're asleep." He couldn't blame Kithiel for being scared. The very healers who were supposed to help and protect him had tried to kill him. They didn't even know where this Justice person was, or if there were more like him. He'd prodded as gently as he could for information, but Kithiel either didn't know much, or he was too scared to say anything.

"Should I tell him you're asleep?"

Kithiel hesitated, swallowing hard before nodding.

"All right." Rashi squeezed his hand and stood. "I'll bring you a plate."

He found the others where he'd left them and shook his head. "He's still asleep, but I'll let him know you asked after him."

Aster frowned like he wanted to argue, but a quick glance at Haru changed his mind and he nodded instead. "Thank you." He backed out of the room and closed the door with a soft click.

"I don't like him," Haru said.

"You don't like any humans," Rashi replied, though he couldn't help but agree. He filled a plate of food for Kithiel, only realizing after he'd piled it high with food that the king should have taken his share first. He turned to Cal with an apology spilling from his lips, but Cal waved him off with an amused smile.

"It's fine. I'd prefer not to be treated like a king in my private chambers."

Rashi relaxed, liking Cal more and more. He took Kithiel his food, then filled another plate to hand to Cal. Then another for Haru, before filling his own and settling on the sofa.

"How is he?" Cal asked, nodding towards their guestroom.

Rashi wrinkled his nose. "I healed his throat last night. He's fully recovered, but he won't speak."

Cal sighed. "Likely scared that if he says anything, someone else will come after him." He took a few bites before adding, "I'm more worried about how many more people might be collared. We haven't had problems with collars in years. We've been too lax if even our healers are compromised."

"We'll keep Kithiel safe," Rashi said. "You worry about protecting the city. We'll try to find a way to cleanse the magic."

He wasn't sure if Cal knew the Wound was spreading, but he didn't think the extra worry was needed if he didn't. It was surely creeping closer to the city, as surely as it had already destroyed some of his village's good farmland. That was part of why they'd come, besides the Fate strings leading them here.

He wasn't at all surprised that their strings bound them to the new elf king. If reconciling dragons and elves wasn't part of Fate's plan, he wasn't sure where else to start.

# CHAPTER 9

THERE WAS too much to do, not even taking into account the daily tasks and people needing to be addressed to get the government working again, and Cal had lost an entire day to sleep. Not that he wasn't grateful for it. His ears were no longer ringing, and his eyes no longer felt like someone poured firesand into them. He flexed his fingers, still amazed by Rashi's magic. No blemish or scar or even a lingering blister.

He paused at the bottom of the stairs near the throne room, keenly aware of the weight of the crown on his head despite the spells making it nearly weightless. No matter how inadequate he might be, this was his city now, his kingdom, and he had to protect it. With a deep breath, he stepped inside and found Duaia waiting for him. The dark look on her face wasn't encouraging, so he turned and led the way to his office, bracing himself for bad news as he sat on the edge of his desk.

She didn't bother with pleasantries. "We found three more collars in the palace."

Less than he'd expected, but still too many. "Only three?"

Her expression soured further. "At this point, I'm sure any we missed have been ordered to stay away."

"Not surprising," he murmured, especially considering how quickly Justice had managed to escape and send someone after Kithiel. It was more surprising they'd found any at all. "Have any of them said who collared them?"

"They're not saying much of anything," she said in annoyance. "They're scared. Not just for themselves, but for their families. I sent a few guards to check on their homes, but it will take time to track them down. We can't even find the family of the healer who was killed."

This was a scenario he hadn't anticipated. Justice held plenty of sway in the palace, even among the magical community, and had taken full control of the prison, but his reach was far too great for a human official, even one who'd been expanding his influence and popularity for years.

"What about the rest of the city?" he asked.

Duaia raised an eyebrow, staring at him like he'd spoken in an ancient fae tongue. It was an expression he was too familiar with, so he simply stared back until her eyes widened.

"Fuck," she whispered, turning as if to march off and issue orders for guards to descend upon the city, before realizing that wasn't possible. "I don't have that many men to spare."

He nodded, already aware they could barely contain the threat in the palace. The kingdom had been at peace for centuries, effectively cut off from the rest of the realm by the sea on one side and the Wound on the other. The edges of the kingdom saw some skirmishes along the western borders near the desert, but nothing their local patrols couldn't handle. Most of their skilled fighters were taken by the war and the Wound. They had no standing army. Their largest fighting force were his kingsguard and the palace guards, a few battlemages, and Duaia, their resident sorceress. The rotating guards that stood at the city gates were all well-trained, capable of handling the occasional thief or brawl, but there weren't enough for a city-wide search.

Not for the first time, he wished there were more Truth Seekers at hand, but the combined sun and blood magic was something barely afforded the branches of the royal family. There wouldn't be a civil war if he tried to expand that law; his sister would simply become queen after he was murdered.

"We need to secure the palace first," he said. "Spread the word through messengers to the city workers to be watchful for gold collars or rings." A new surge of slave collars was something his father had dealt with every couple of decades, as new generations of humans rose up, still carrying the beliefs and old prejudices of their parents.

Duaia shook her head. "Won't work," she said, pulling a small collection of jewelry from her pocket and dumping it on the table beside him. An earring with a small red orb of ysazicite, a thick gold band too large for a finger, a delicate silver chain interwoven with tiny pieces of ysazicite and sunstones. None of them looked like a slave collar.

He reached for the band, only for Duaia to flick his hand away.

"You don't want to know what that was attached to," she said with a twitch of her lips.

Heat crept up his neck, and he cleared his throat. "These were all spelled as collars?"

She sobered with a nod. "It was only a matter of time before this happened. Collars draw too much attention, but no one would even notice these, other than how pretty they are," she said, tapping the delicate chain. It wouldn't have been out of place on a young noble's wrist. "I only found these by using seeking spells."

"How powerful of one?"

"Not very, why?"

"How difficult would it be to cast it over the entire palace? Or sections of the city?"

Duaia made a face but then appeared intrigued after a few moments of thought. "Not difficult, but I'd need someone to ground the spell so we could track them down." She eyed him as a sly smile curved her lips. "That tall man of yours is quite powerful. I'm sure he could help if you want the palace secured today."

Cal nodded, pleased to find a way for Haru and Rashi to help, if they were willing. "He is, isn't he?" he said softly, heat creeping into his face again. He may not have witnessed the entire event, but from overhearing others while the healers had been working on them, he knew Haru was not only powerful, but willing to protect an innocent even at the risk of his own life.

Duaia chuckled and squeezed his arm, her smile softening to something fond. "I'm glad you finally found them."

He returned the smile and lightly clasped his hand over hers. "Me too." Once she left, he turned his attention to the jewelry on the desk. He knew Duaia would have removed any of the spells, but when he picked up the earring, he felt a bit of magical residue. How many others were wearing innocuous pieces of jewelry that kept them under another's control? How many had been forced to give a ring or necklace to someone, knowing it would enslave them too?

Rage simmered through him, and he took a slow, deep breath to calm himself. There may have been peace with humans now, but there were always those who feared magical creatures. Even when humans had magic themselves, they fought against those they deemed vile or unnatural. Maybe if dragons had still existed then, things would have ended differently. Maybe they could have stopped the Wound from forming or erased humans from existence.

With a sigh, he swept the items into a drawer and locked the room behind him. He had too much to do to worry about what could have been, starting with finding a replacement sunstone for Liria before she returned and castrated him.

THE VAULT sat underground, with multiple spelled doorways that only a few people could pass through, specifically those with royal blood. Sunstones set into the walls lit his path as he moved down a narrow, winding staircase. Cal wished he could rip one of them out and give it to his cousin, but they were too small, and the same spell had been sitting in them for Ages. Far too long for them to be worth the trouble of turning into a Truth Seeker's tool.

When he reached the bottom of the stairs, he strode across the root of the ylren tree that had been smoothed and shaped into the floor. Large, ornate doors carved from a dawntree stood at the end of the short hall leading to the Vault. The rich wood was the color of autumn leaves and was polished to a high shine, a soft glow still emanating from it despite its age. A sun motif sat in the center, the phases of the moon carved along the sides and across the curved top.

He spoke the entry phrase in ancient Elvish and pressed his magic into the sun.

The doors swung open without a sound, a burst of cool, stale air rushing out. Thankfully he didn't smell rot or damp, the spells to keep out pests and water still functioning.

The size of the Vault always amazed him. Even with sunstones flaring to life around him, he couldn't see into the depths of darkness in the distance. Pictures hung on the walls near the entrance, and pillars lined the long chamber, pedestals arranged neatly every few paces between them. Old currencies not seen in thousands of years, priceless jewels, spellbooks, and ancient magical artifacts from less peaceful times all littered the pedestals. Even family heirlooms, including the scepter used by Ysildea, the first Sun Queen. The staff was carved from ivory and dawntree wood, with a large, perfectly round sunstone on top.

He paused as he considered it. His history lessons said the scepter was used to tame the lands of the kingdom, turning wild plains to farmland and protecting against the old horrors that used to haunt the night. He wasn't sure if it was suitable for truth seeking, but he hefted it up and continued the search.

The treasures were older the farther he went. Mythril armor, darkstone swords, ironwood bows. Then farther still there was a unicorn horn, glinting in the low light, a somber melancholy emanating from the pearlescent spiral. A pile of glimmering siren scales, shifting between a hundred hues of colors, some he had no name for. A sphinx paw, tawny fur still soft to the touch. The frail, delicate wings of a sylph, locked in a cage of spelled glass to keep them from blowing away.

He turned away from the evidence of slaughter with a grimace, but his eyes caught on a larger pedestal holding a dragon skull. Despite the lack of hide or scale covering the bone, it still felt as if the empty eye sockets were staring at him, accusing him of its death and imprisonment. The teeth were still attached, as sharp as if the dragon had died yesterday. The largest was longer than his forearm. Beside that pedestal was another covered in light blue scales that glittered like solidified drops of a cloudless sky. Lying on top were two long horns that were closer to deer antlers than something that belonged to a scaled creature. They were light brown and covered in what looked like fine velvet fur.

Nausea twisted his stomach. This had been one of the last dragons, betrayed by the elves and struck down for glory, for use in spells to add elements not accessible to the caster. Not long after that, all records of dragons stopped.

He stepped back and slowly turned, regarding the hundreds upon hundreds of pedestals around him, filled with pieces of creatures long forgotten by the realm. "This is my legacy?" he whispered, shaking his head and blowing out a harsh breath.

He stalked towards the other end of the Vault until he found what he needed. Sunstones weren't rare, but the large ones, the pure ones needed to work spells rather than provide light or store simple enchantments in jewelry, took centuries to form. Most had been mined and stored here during Ysildea's reign, then again three Ages ago, before the mythical creatures began disappearing.

Along the wall were several rows of neatly stacked sunstones, varying in size from as large as his torso to as small as the palm of his hand. Even unpolished they gleamed, absorbing and reflecting the ambient magic in the air. He lightly brushed his fingers over the smaller ones, not quite sure what he was looking for, but he paused over one that felt clearer than the others. The magic reflecting through it was like fresh air after a storm, and when he pulled his hand away, he realized the magic in the Vault was thick and cloudy, like a fog rolling in from the sea.

Was that what Haru meant by a rot in the magic? He'd always thought the stifling pressure here was due to the remains of so many magical creatures, but when he focused on the older sunstones, the ancient magic in them felt cleaner. Even the scepter felt pure compared to what he was used to. If that was how magic should feel all the time, he could understand why Haru called it a rot.

He reached for the sunstone again and picked it up with a surprised grunt, the weight far heavier than he expected. He considered choosing a lighter one, but Liria could come down here herself if it was too heavy for her. He turned with his spoils and made for the exit, stopping when a chill, shivery sensation traveled the entire length of his spine, his heart suddenly racing. He glanced back, coiling sunlight tight around himself as he scanned for the source of his unease.

A whisper of sound turned him around, another rippling shiver running over his arms. He distinctly felt like he was being hunted and couldn't help but wonder if some old creature hadn't been completely dead when his ancestors dragged it down here. Pulled forward by something deeper than instinct, he found himself in front of an iron pedestal with a chunk of stone small enough to fit comfortably in his palm. Rough edged, like it had been broken from a larger structure, and strangely void of a magical presence, considering the soft purple haze surrounding it.

Sure he would regret it, but unable to leave it, he picked it up, surprised yet relieved when nothing happened. He slipped it into his pocket, intending to give it to Duaia, and left. He sealed the Vault and began the long trek back upstairs, careful not to strike the scepter against the narrow walls. He'd barely made it through the last door before Julius accosted him.

"Oh, good," Cal said, and before he could break whatever horrible news he had, pressed the heavy sunstone into Julius' chest. He made sure the last door was locked and sealed before saying, "I need to go to the prison."

Julius' face twisted like he'd bit into a sour and rotting lemon. "Later," he said, before his expression turned almost smug, and Cal knew exactly what he was going to hear before Julius said, "Your sister is on her way back."

# CHAPTER 10

HARU STALKED along the boundary of the sitting room, testing the threshold and every spell he'd put in place. It still wasn't enough, not with the rot in the magic sitting on the back of his tongue every time he breathed. He was fully aware of Rashi's irritation and took only a little pleasure in riling him up. He couldn't help the need he felt to set proper protections in place, and he knew that wasn't going to fade. This wasn't his home. This wasn't even his city. This was a kingdom of elves, with humans and a smattering of other creatures for a mockery of balance.

Elves who had betrayed his kin and were ultimately the reason his kind had gone into hiding. And now he was bound to their king because Fate thought She had a clever sense of humor, when She was really a crafty, cruel wench.

"Haru," Rashi said, his voice sharp enough that Haru stopped and turned towards him, only then realizing he'd affected the temperature of the room enough for frost to crust over the window.

"Sorry," he murmured, breathing out and releasing the magic he'd pooled around him, the air immediately regaining its warmth. A whisper of cloth was the only warning he had before Rashi was a solid weight against his back, lithe arms wrapping around his stomach.

"What's wrong?"

He bit his tongue before he could say "everything." That wasn't fair to Rashi. Haru may have agreed to come here, but it hadn't really been a choice. He'd known he would have to leave his mountain home yet again when Cal's Fate bond appeared thirty-five years ago, but after the harrowing experience that came with his first bond, he'd refused to follow the string to the other end. And then, twenty years ago, a second string appeared, brighter than the first, and he knew Fate wouldn't allow him to ignore them both.

He realized he'd been silent too long when Rashi bit his arm. He hissed, but he didn't pull away. His entire being rebelled at the thought of ever pulling away from Rashi, and he hated that he knew Cal would take the fox away from him. Nothing he could do would prevent it.

"Stop that," Rashi murmured against Haru's back. "I can feel… whatever that is. I'm not going anywhere, love." His arms tightened, and Haru let out a soft sigh.

"I almost lost you," he whispered.

Rashi snorted. "I was fine. Kithiel was the one in danger."

Haru shifted enough to turn and face Rashi, gripping his arms and breathing through the fear he hadn't allowed himself to feel before now. Before they were safe. Or as safe as he could make them, surrounded by a threshold that wasn't truly his. "You didn't feel it," he said, his voice tight as he choked back the knowledge that he could have died if his personal shields had failed. "Whatever that spell was… it was old. Older than me. And it felt alive. If it had gone after you…."

He trailed off, knowing there was no possible way he could have saved anyone else if the magic had gone for them. Only his shields and the sorceress' magic had saved him.

Rashi cupped Haru's face in his hands and pulled him down to press a gentle kiss to his lips. "I'm safe. You're safe," he said softly. "Kithiel and Cal are safe, thanks to you."

"Thanks to *you*," Haru murmured, still raw from terror at the thought of their Fate bond snapping to pieces between them. "No one else could have helped pull a curse out of someone while protecting them from it."

Rashi preened at the praise and planted another kiss to his lips. "We make a good duo," he said before giving Haru a sly look. "We'll make an even better trio," he added, laughing at Haru's scowl. "You need to give him a chance."

"He's an elf."

Rashi rolled his eyes, propping his chin on Haru's chest with an exasperated stare. "He's too young to even know anything but stories about dragons, let alone the feud between your species."

Haru knew better than to argue with a fox. All of them were too clever for their own good, and Rashi was stubborn enough to win any argument, with spite if he had to. So he hummed in response and let Rashi interpret it as agreement.

Rashi sighed and pinched him. "Ass," he muttered, pulling away and stretching.

He hummed again, softer, as he let his eyes roam over Rashi's lean body. The borrowed clothes were snug in all the right places.

Rashi grinned over his shoulder, fluttering his lashes as he wiggled his hips. Before either of them could act on it, someone knocked on the door.

Haru growled as he stalked across the room to yank it open, coming up short when he found the sorceress on the other side.

Duaia raised an eyebrow. "Everything all right?"

"Yes," he answered, then belatedly stepped back to let her inside when she eyed him expectantly.

She stepped into the room, both eyebrows going up as she crossed the threshold. "That's new."

Rashi wiggled his fingers in greeting from where he'd sprawled across a sofa. "Any luck finding the asshole?"

"No." She scowled, perching on the arm of Cal's chair, one of the few places that would let her see all points of entry into the room. "But that's why I'm here," she said, focusing on Haru. "I need your help with a spell."

Duaia's plan was simple enough. The spell wasn't too dissimilar from dowsing, except the spell sought out the unique magical signature of enslavement spells instead of ground water. Easy enough to cast over someone in the same room, where the focal point and targets were the same, but tracking magical signatures over a larger distance required a moving target as a focus. One that was powerful and skilled enough to maintain the spell while moving.

Rashi was all too happy to volunteer Haru to the task, seeing him out with a kiss on the cheek, cheerful wave, and muttering about finding some peace and quiet.

He growled at the door as it closed between them, turning on Duaia when she chuckled.

"Adorable," she said, turning down the hall. "Let's go."

Haru sighed and slid his hands along his arms, biting back a snarl when there was no cloth to cover them. He missed his sleeves, missed his own clothes and the protection they offered, and he especially missed all his personal belongings hidden in the magical storage space inside them.

When they reached the bottom of the stairs, Duaia led the way through a series of halls and rooms until they reached a small alcove near one of the gardens. It looked like a reading nook, with a large chair and table in the corner, plush rug, and pillowed seat on the ledge beneath the window.

Rashi would absolutely love the room, with its view of a large dawntree and patches of brightly colored flowers, the teasing scents of mint and lavender in the air.

"Have you told him yet?" Duaia asked.

Haru turned to find her standing in the center of the rug. On closer examination, he saw the pattern woven into the wool was one that would enhance the strength of a spell, though he couldn't fathom why she thought either of them needed it.

"What?" he asked.

Duaia huffed. "Cal. Have you told him what you are?"

He tensed, straightening to the full height of his borrowed human form, though she continued watching him as if she weren't impressed or concerned about being alone in a room with a dragon. "No," he said tightly.

If he'd had any choice in the matter, he never would have come across a sorceress who could see him for what he was, much less tell Cal, the king of elves, that he was Fate bound to a dragon.

She hummed softly, easily conveying how idiotic she thought that answer was. "You have two days to tell him before I do it myself," she said, lifting a hand when he stepped forward with a soft growl. "I understand why you don't want to, and maybe if we didn't have someone trying to destroy this kingdom from the inside, I might say to take your time. But he needs to know the true state of all his pieces on the board."

She gave him a hard look as she stepped forward and dared to poke a sharp nail into his chest. "More than that, he deserves to know. You're Fate bound for a reason," she said, easily dodging when he slapped at her hand.

"And he's a good person," she added quietly. "Too kind to be king, but I don't think that's a bad thing. And if you can't even trust him with this truth, you don't deserve him." She stepped back to stand on the edge of the rug.

Haru bit back a snarl as he tried and failed again to hide his hands inside sleeves that were no longer there. "Are you done?" he snapped.

It was the same argument Rashi made, but that didn't make the choice any easier. His entire life, he was told elves were the enemy, that they couldn't be trusted, would stab anyone in the back the moment they had the chance. Dragons weren't easy to kill, nearly impossible for anyone who didn't know their weakness.

Despite the ease with which the shadow curse had cut through his shields, most magics couldn't damage him. A sorceress might be able to best him in a fight, but killing him required destroying his heart, and after the elves' betrayal, every dragon he'd ever met had numerous shields layered over their bodies, and more surrounding their hearts. Short of hitting him with enough magical power to destroy an entire mountain, or stabbing him with the claw or tooth of another dragon, he wouldn't die easily.

Which made it all the more frustrating that he could feel the echoes of his lost kin. Somewhere in this city, the bones of a slain dragon cried out for home.

Duaia studied him in silence before nodding. "Let's free some slaves."

# Chapter 11

Cal's day could not get any worse.

Not only had he not made it to the prison to find Haru and Rashi's belongings the day before, but word of his sister's return had spread faster than sunlight slicing across the dead, empty landscape of the Wound.

His sister had gone into mourning after the burial five weeks ago. With her return, people were given permission to end their grieving of his father's death, and he couldn't deny that hurt. His father may have failed in some of his duties to the kingdom, but he was Cal's father. Now that he was gone, his sister and cousins were the only living members of the royal family.

Resources that he needed to be searching for Justice or his allies had been reallocated to cleaning the palace and decorating for the night's impromptu feast. Irritation was a living sensation beneath his skin, made worse by the fact he hadn't seen Haru or Rashi since yesterday morning. Both had still been asleep when he rose for the day, hours before the sun kissed the horizon. He knew where his duties and responsibilities lay, but he had been waiting over thirty years to meet his bondeds, and he'd barely stolen a few hours alone with either of them.

He sighed in relief when the last of the city planning advisors left, closing the large tome of notes and figures from the last several years with more force than necessary. The heavy book shut with the sound of sturdy leather and paper against solid wood.

Julius shot a knowing smirk at him from his post near the door before moving to take a seat across from him. He studied Cal for a moment, striking to the heart of the matter as usual with, "The city needs this."

"I know," Cal said tightly. Even if he still felt the sharp ache of loss beneath his ribs, he couldn't expect the living to mourn someone they didn't truly know.

Julius nodded and moved on. "Synne should be here in a few hours."

The nickname was apt. Sometimes he was convinced Calaesynne existed only to cause mayhem. If she was due to arrive soon, she'd have just enough time to wash off the dirt of travel before the feast.

"Also," he drawled.

Cal frowned and focused on Julius, sure he wasn't going to like whatever he had to say next.

"Rumors of your guests are starting to get ridiculous."

He groaned and scrubbed a hand against his face. "What are they saying?"

Julius fought back a grin, but he gave up a moment later. "My favorite is that they're both runaway princes who were forbidden to be together, so they've come to pledge loyalty to you. Along with their bodies."

Cal muttered a fervent curse under his breath. "How do the nobles not have more important things to do?"

Julius laughed. "What could be more important than the king's love life?"

He shot a glare at his closest confidant through his fingers. "And you bring this up why?"

"You should bring them to the feast and properly present them as your bondeds."

A soft growl escaped him before he could stop it. He'd barely spent any time with them, and now Juls wanted him to share? As much as he hated it, he knew it was a good idea. It would give them both status and ensure them some protection amongst the court.

"Fine," he muttered, pushing his chair back to stand, "but that will require going to the prison and finding their possessions."

Julius scowled, but he didn't argue. "Let's get this over with, then." He stood and turned for the door. "We should clear it out and tear it down. What do we need with an old iron-and-silver fortress these days?"

Cal couldn't argue with that, especially since the prison sat across several city blocks. Tearing it apart would take months, if not years, but he'd always hated the sight of it. A monument to a time lost even to most memories. The only remnants of the creatures that were burned by iron or silver were locked in the Vault, protected by spells that kept them from decaying to dust.

Once they found Justice and stopped whatever he was planning, he could focus on his plans to improve the city again.

He just hoped a civil war wouldn't destroy it first.


THE PRISON was as oppressive as the first time, but the guards who greeted them now were members of his kingsguard.

Elwin, a feline beastkin, pressed a fist over his heart and dipped into a brief bow before offering a tired smile. "Don't worry, all the prisoners have been treated and fed, and promised that their crimes will be investigated again."

"Thank you," Cal said, a bit of the weight on his shoulders lessening.

"Oh," Julius said, clearing his throat when Cal eyed at him with suspicion. "Liria also sent word that she found Aelin, and they're heading back to 'help tear out the evil that's taken root in our city.' They'll likely get here in time for the feast."

Cal tipped his head back with a groan. Just the thought of his entire family at the same table as his bondeds filled him with dread. "You weren't going to tell me, were you?"

Julius didn't answer, instead turning to Elwin. "We're looking for Haru and Rashi's belongings. Where were personal effects tossed?"

Elwin winced, and Cal wished, just once, he could hear some good news. "As far as we can tell, most of them were burned shortly after a prisoner arrived. We found a room where valuables were kept. Seems like the guards were free to take whatever they wanted."

Cal flexed his fingers to dispel the magic coiling around them. He dearly wanted to blow a hole through every wall until the entire prison caved in, but he set that plan aside for when it'd been evacuated. Of prisoners and his kingsguard, at least.

He was starting to think that everyone involved in this atrocity should share the same fate as Justice: a public execution. The despicable crime of using slave collars was one of the only crimes that still held that sentence, but the corruption in his kingdom ran far deeper than he ever thought possible.

Julius' hand on his shoulder brought him back to the moment, and he shook his fingers again before straightening. "Show me."

Elwin led them to a room near the warden's office. Shelves lined the walls, most of them bare aside from empty bags and purses. It was obvious that countless pieces of lives had been stolen from here, and he added yet another task to the ever-growing list of things needing done. Most of which would benefit from a Truth Seeker handling it. If he wasn't so attached to his balls, he'd be desperately tempted to beg Liria to marry for the sake of continuing the Seeker line.

He stopped in the center of the room and turned, spotting a pack in the corner that appeared untouched. He prayed for the Sun to finally take pity on him and reached for it.

"I wouldn't touch that," Elwin said. "There's some spell on it. Burns like acid and sparks like flames if you try to open it."

Somehow, that sounded exactly like something Haru or Rashi would do. He shared a look with Julius and smirked faintly at his friend's resigned sigh. He wrapped his hand in what protection he could and touched the bag. Nothing happened. That was all the convincing he needed, sure the spell was set to protect against those its owner didn't know or trust. He picked it up and held it out to Julius, laughing softly when that earned a scowl.

"Good to see you're finally in a good mood," Julius said dryly.

He didn't dare test the fire spell by trying to open it and slung the pack over his arm as he turned back to Elwin. "Where was everything burned?"

"This way." Elwin led them across the prison to a small courtyard that once served as a garden, if the dead and barren strips of soil were any indication. In the center was a large pile of ash and half-burned clothing, the stone beneath it charred black from years of fires.

"What was the point of this?" Julius whispered, but Cal didn't want to understand the twisted logic behind it.

He stepped around the pile, letting his magic settle around his fingers before guiding it lower, heating the air hot and quick enough to change the air pressure. A self-contained wind picked up, circling the enclosed space and scattering the ashes. He wasn't sure what he expected to find, but if his bondeds had spelled their pack, surely their clothes would survive a fire. Sure enough, once the top layer of ash blew away, brilliant white cloth appeared, untouched by either fire or the ash covering it. He coaxed his magic faster and hotter, sending another several layers of ash and pieces of cloth into a wild swirl.

He bent and picked up the pristine clothing left behind. A large white robe with voluminous sleeves and ice blue accents, a matching set of pants, a deep green silk tunic with pale green stitched into a forest motif, and black silk pants. The hefty weight and quality of the materials were surprising. Both sets of clothing were finer than what some of the nobles wore. "Did they burn the shoes too?" he asked, draping the clothes over his arm.

"No, seems the shoes were sold off to the cobbler down the street, and then sold at market once repaired."

"And there's your allotment of luck for the month," Julius murmured under his breath.

Cal ignored him and thanked Elwin before heading out of the prison. He didn't put his faith in luck. Not when he seemed to have Fate as a puppeteer.

HANDING THE clothes and pack over was the single brightest moment of happiness Cal'd had in weeks. Rashi's entire being lit up with delight as he took the pack, and even Haru looked at him with gratitude and relief. When he told them of Julius' suggestion of presenting them at the feast, Rashi readily agreed, on the condition that Kithiel join them, and elbowed Haru until he grunted his agreement.

Then Cal left them to get ready and headed down the hall to his sister's room. She'd arrived shortly before they returned from the prison and had retired to her room to rest. Apparently, she'd left her entire guard behind and ridden ahead with only Vesryn by her side.

The elven guard opened the door when Cal knocked. "Your Highn-Majesty," he corrected, his gaze flicking quickly to the crown on Cal's head. There was a complicated play of emotions across his expression before he met Cal's eyes again. He moved back to let Cal inside, lifting one arm in a familiar invitation, and Cal couldn't resist taking it.

He stepped into Vesryn's solid comfort like he'd done a thousand times before. Without warning, the grief crashed over him with the same intensity as it had the day his father died. His father was gone. He'd had a month to accept that, and the chaos of the past few days had given him something to focus on, but he hadn't seen Vesryn or his sister since the burial, and their return brought that day back in their wake.

Vesryn didn't say anything. He didn't need to. They'd known each other longer than Cal had known Julius. Vesryn had been one of his father's kingsguard and served him until Synne was old enough to walk. Other than Cal, Vesryn was the only one who could ever find her when she slipped her own guards, so he'd been placed with her permanently. He'd been watching over the heirs since the day they were born.

Cal drew in a last shaky breath and finally found the strength to step away.

Vesryn let go without comment, giving Cal a sheepish smile despite towering over him by half a foot. "I did try to stop her, Your H-Majesty," he said, tilting his head towards the sofas.

He smiled back, grateful for the easy manner between them. "I don't doubt it," he replied. Even their father had given up any hope of controlling Synne. When she was six, she ordered a noble boy to give her a horse to ride, because she'd been forbidden from riding out to watch the celestial lights and shooting stars filling the skies over the Wound.

Cal sank into a chair, the twin to the one he preferred in his own rooms. "How is she?"

Vesryn stood behind the sofa across from him, running a hand through his sea-kissed golden hair. "Grieving still," he said quietly, "but I think the time away helped." He glanced at the door to Synne's room. "I can't deny I'm glad to be back, though."

"You've been missed."

Vesryn turned back to Cal with a faint, rueful smile. "Not so badly, I trust. I hear your bonded has finally found you."

Cal winced. "Yes," he admitted, wishing he could have been the one to break that news to Vesryn, even if he was relieved to be free of that conversation.

"No, none of that," Vesryn said, pointing a finger at Cal as if scolding him. "Your string was never a secret, and I harbored no fantasies of ever being more than what I am." He sighed and sat on the arm of the sofa. "I will miss the sex, though," he said, at the same moment Synne's door opened.

"Oh for—" She glowered at them both, her cheeks flushed, though Cal knew it was from one of her too-hot baths and not the conversation she'd walked in on. "I do not need to know about my brother's sex life."

"Don't worry, it's been nonexistent since you left," Cal replied dryly, standing and wrapping his arms around her in a tight hug. "Welcome home," he murmured, breathing in the familiar scent of orange blossoms in her hair.

A knot in his chest loosened at seeing her safe and sound, though the moment only lasted until she punched his arm.

"What's this I hear about your bonded being a prince?"

Cal tipped his head back with a groan. Was there no one who hadn't heard the rumors? "Not a prince," he said, ignoring her raised eyebrows and sinking into his chair again. He was sure he could have found some work to be done, but Duaia and Haru had found the last few people wearing collars yesterday, Justice had disappeared so completely he may as well have been lost at sea, and any spare workers in the palace had been delegated to feast preparations. Progress could be made tomorrow, especially if his cousins returned tonight.

"I'm fairly certain they're not princes," he amended when she continued staring at him. "I haven't exactly had much time to speak with them."

"You don't *know*?"

Cal looked at Vesryn for help, but the guard was of no use and seemed more amused than sympathetic.

"Wait, what do you mean *they*?" she demanded, and when she sat across from him with an expectant stare, Cal filled them in on everything that had happened while they'd been gone. "Well," she said when he finished, "this is a mess. And you not knowing a thing about your bondeds is unacceptable. You can rectify that tomorrow." When Cal opened his mouth to protest, she lifted her chin in challenge and he shut it instead. "I can handle court for a day. I certainly sat with Father enough times."

"It's not your responsibility," he said.

"This is *our* kingdom," she said with their mother's scowl. "I'll not sit aside and watch it destroy you like it destroyed Father. If there's a snake to be found, we'll defang it together. Besides," she said with an impish smirk, "you're terribly insufferable when you haven't been recently ravished."

Cal growled and threw a pillow at her face. Her delighted cackle as she caught it was as aggravating as it was satisfying.

# Chapter 12

"WHY DO you keep rubbing your chest?" Synne demanded, smacking Cal's hand as if he could ruin his clothes from touching them too much.

Cal scowled at her and dropped his hand, hardly realizing he'd even been moving it. "Nerves," he said, knowing she expected an explanation. He wasn't worried about Haru or Rashi so much as how the court would react to them. Fate bonds were a gift, but to have two was unheard of. And to have a bond between elf and beastkin? Even elf and human bonds were rare.

Synne flicked the back of her hand against his arm, eyeing him with completely unjustified suspicion before shrugging. "It'll be fine," she said. "And if it's not, we can tar and feather some nobles."

He was about to offer a less messy solution when her mouth dropped open with a soft "Oh."

Cal turned to see what she was looking at and sucked in a breath of shock.

Haru and Rashi descended the stairs with Kithiel leading the way. Rashi and the half-elf were similar enough in height and build that the green silk tunic Cal had recovered from the prison fit Kithiel well, and Cal found he could still be surprised by how seriously Rashi took his promise to look after Kithiel.

He met Kithiel's uncertain gaze with an encouraging one of his own, before his attention was drawn to Haru and Rashi.

Instead of the borrowed clothes they'd been wearing for the past few days, they were finally dressed in their own attire. Haru wore a robe in similar fashion to the white one Cal had found in the ash pile, this one black with silver accents. His hands were tucked into the long, billowy sleeves, and the odd gestures he'd caught Haru making the past few days finally made sense. His long silver hair was pulled back with an ornate hair pin, and when they reached the bottom of the stairs and drew closer, Cal saw the jade at the top was shaped into a dragon.

Where Haru was dark, Rashi was a burst of color, his tunic shifting colors according to the light, turning from rich oranges to deep reds, reminding Cal of the fallen dawntree leaves in autumn. Crimson kohl at the corners of his eyes brightened their green to emerald, and his lips glinted with some kind of gloss.

Cal realized he'd been staring too long when a sharp elbow dug into his ribs. He shifted away with a hiss before clearing his throat. "This is my sister, Princess Calaesynne. Synne, this is Haru and Rashi, my bondeds."

Haru politely inclined his head, but Rashi stepped closer with a grin, reaching out to clasp Synne's offered hand between both of his. "Finally, someone closer to my own age," he said.

Synne snickered, shifting to loop her arm through his. "Yes, my dear brother acts like he's centuries older than he is," she said, leading Rashi into the dining room, Vesryn and Kithiel behind them.

"Let me tell you about the time he bored our lorekeeper to tears," Cal heard, before they were lost to the din of the court.

He let out a long-suffering sigh and tipped his head back, wishing deities truly existed, even if there could never be enough of them to grant him the patience needed to deal with his sister. Then he realized Haru was still standing next to him. He smiled and motioned to the dining hall, and Haru fell into step beside him. "Were any of your things missing?" he asked. "Besides the shoes."

"No, everything was there. Thank you for returning them."

Cal nodded, relieved he could at least solve one of the endless problems on his list. "You really had only the one pack between you?" he asked. The pack had felt light, and small enough it couldn't have fit much more than a few sets of clothes for each of them. He felt Haru's gaze on him before he stopped walking, and Cal turned, curious.

Instead of answering, Haru lifted an arm and with his other hand pulled a sword partway out of his sleeve.

Cal breathed a laugh, stepping closer but stopping himself before he tried to touch either Haru or the sword. The fact they hadn't touched and completed the Fate bond was a constant awareness beneath his skin, especially when he was near either of them. Where Rashi was a steady thrum of energy at the back of his mind, the place where Haru should have been was a void, only sometimes filled with an echo from the bond Haru shared with Rashi.

"Amazing," he said, staring at the sword in awe.

A few of the elders still possessed items with such magic woven into them; Cal even had a few himself, but the spells to create more had been lost. Even their lorekeeper had only found references to the spells with no instructions, as if it had once been such commonplace knowledge, no one ever thought to write it down.

Haru studied him for a moment before carefully sliding the sword back into his sleeve. There was a faint twist of magic before it seemed to vanish completely, the fabric as loose as it would be without a sword weighing it down.

"What all do you have in there?"

Haru's lips twitched into a smirk. "Everything."

Cal felt warmth on his neck, even though nothing about that had implied any innuendo. He cleared his throat and continued into the hall. He could exchange meaningless pleasantries with any of a hundred courtiers, but he found himself at a complete loss when it came to Haru. The sense of being in the presence of a predator was still there, scratching at the back of his mind, but it wasn't so different from how he sometimes felt near Duaia, knowing she could reduce him to dust without much effort.

"Your sister seems delightful."

It was Cal's turn to smirk. "Say that again at the end of the night and I may believe you mean it."

"Should I be worried?"

Cal laughed and led Haru to a chair next to his own at the head of the main table. "Absolutely."


THE FORMAL presentation of a bonded was excruciating, but it was far worse when it involved someone of the royal line. There was the reading of their lineage going back five generations, which Haru and Rashi had given Faelan earlier, the foreign names odd to hear outside of history records. Then came the endless procession of nobles, courtiers, and officials, claiming their few moments of glory to speak directly with the three of them.

Hours passed with delicious food, inane conversations, and a blur of faces, until the courtiers finally had their fill and contented themselves with each others' company. At some point, Synne had moved to sit beside

Haru, leaning into his space and watching him in utter fascination. Haru remained as placid as usual, though the slight shifting in his seat gave Cal the impression of nervousness. It was almost amusing. It was certainly endearing, seeing his sister so enamored, but the wine had gone to his head two glasses ago, and he felt barbs of irritation in his chest at Haru paying attention to his sister and not to him.

He reached for his glass and tossed back the last large swallow of wine. Was it late enough he could leave without causing yet more rumors in his wake? Maybe he could start a tiny fire in the center of the dancing courtiers and end the feast. Feeling eyes on him, he glanced up to find Rashi watching him with a discerning eye.

Rashi shifted where he leaned against the back of Haru's chair, murmuring something into Haru's ear before holding a hand out to Cal. "Come dance with me."

Eager to have something to do before he drowned himself in more wine, he took Rashi's hand and followed him to a corner of the dance floor. The music was a mellifluous rhythm beneath the never-ending chatter of the court. He found both easy to ignore the moment one of Rashi's hands settled against the back of his neck, the other resting comfortably in Cal's. He pressed his free hand against Rashi's back and let his feet guide them in a simple pattern that kept them distanced from the other dancers.

Rashi grinned at him, one ear twitching towards the table where they'd left Synne and Haru as he said, "Your sister is devious."

"Yes," he agreed. "What'd she do now?"

"I think I agreed to be a decoy so she could sneak out of the palace for the festival without an escort."

"Oh," he said, making his tone as severe as he could manage after six or seven glasses of wine. "Endangering the heir is a very serious crime."

Rashi's eyes squinted as he grinned, revealing white teeth and sharp canines. "Are you saying you'd have to punish me?" he asked, a suggestive purr to his voice.

Cal drew in a sharp breath as want flooded him. He pulled Rashi closer until their chests pressed flush together, dipping his head until their cheeks brushed. "I wouldn't call it a punishment."

"No?" Rashi teased, sliding his fingers into Cal's hair and curling them into a light grip.

He closed his eyes with a shiver, managing to swallow a moan before he embarrassed himself. He could feel Rashi's delight and spark of desire along their bond, and it was captivating. He'd imagined what it would be like to finally be with his bonded for years, but he hadn't been prepared for the certainty of it. Of holding Rashi in his arms and knowing with every shred of his being that they belonged together. Of feeling that certainty echoed back to him.

Rashi somehow pressed closer, wrapping both of his arms around Cal's shoulders and burying both his hands in Cal's hair. His breaths were hot against Cal's neck, and his skin smelled like vetiver and lemongrass, with his natural forest scent beneath it.

Cal held Rashi tight and gave up any pretense of moving to the music, content to simply stand there and lose himself in his bonded's presence. Minutes or hours could have passed before Rashi's nose nudged his ear.

"I was promised that you'd spend tomorrow with us," he said softly.

"Yes," he agreed, refusing to feel guilt for taking a few hours for himself. His sister could handle the court. Everyone had their orders and knew what needed to be done. If anything significant happened or a new problem arose, Duaia knew how to find him. He lifted his head and reluctantly took a step back.

"We can have breakfast on the balcony. Or lunch." He wasn't sure how late it was, but he suspected late enough that they'd sleep through breakfast.

Rashi nodded, then looked past him as a commotion rippled through the court.

Cal turned and spotted his cousins striding across the room. They weren't heading for him and Rashi, though, and he was relieved when they moved straight for Synne, since that meant nothing dire had happened in the last few hours. He had a bit too much wine in him to be making decisions for the kingdom.

He didn't miss the way Haru straightened and turned towards them, only relaxing when he spotted Rashi, though he still seemed ready to flee. "He doesn't like parties much, does he?"

Rashi snorted, leaning into Cal's side and threading their fingers together. "He doesn't like crowds. He's a very solitary creature," he said dryly.

"And you?" Cal asked, leading them back to the table.

He glanced up with a coy flutter of his lashes. "I'm a very tactile creature."

"Why do I feel like you and my sister are going to find new and terrible ways to torment me?"

Rashi's laughter was not reassuring in the least.

THEY ESCAPED the dwindling court shortly after his cousins had a chance to eat. Cal made another round of introductions for his cousin Aelin, Liria's twin, before his inner circle followed him back to his room. With the addition of his sister, Vesryn, and Aelin, that made eleven people all crammed into his sitting room. He caught Synne's eye as she surveyed the limited seating and knew what she was going to suggest, but he shook his head. Even if it had been used by every ruler before his father, moving into the sovereign suite was not something he was willing to do just yet.

The issue was solved by Julius and Faelan carrying in the small sofa from the second guestroom, while Haru and Rashi moved the one from theirs. The walking space was severely diminished, but they could all sit comfortably.

He left them to get situated while he retrieved the staff and sunstone from his room, unsurprised when Liria immediately accosted him. Though when she realized exactly what he held, she let out a sound like an excited banshee.

"By the Wound, where did you find this?" she hissed, snatching the staff from him and cradling it like a fragile piece of crystal and not a thousands-of-years-old weapon.

"In the Vault," he replied, eyeing her warily. He had a feeling maybe he should have left the staff where he'd found it, but if anyone was going to be trusted with it, it would be his cousins.

"And why does she get a priceless artifact and not me?" Aelin demanded, grinning from where he'd taken up part of a sofa.

"I broke hers," Cal said, sinking into his chair.

"You broke… her sunstone?" he asked incredulously, looking around at everyone gathered in the room. "What the fuck have I missed?"

IT DIDN'T take long to fill Aelin in on the important things, and tossing him the spare sunstone mollified him enough to stop his complaining about not getting a new weapon.

When everyone had finished adding their own details, Aelin let out a low whistle. "And here I was convinced I had the more disturbing news."

Cal tensed and wished he had another glass of wine, since he was already sobering up. "Please tell me that whatever it is, you already resolved the situation."

"Sorry, no. That murder in Syll Taesi you wanted me to investigate, there were seven others."

Duaia leaned forward with a snarled, "What?"

Aelin held up a hand as if to ward her off. "The strange thing is, six were humans, but they were all…." He trailed off with a grimace. "They looked like they'd been torn open by wild animals, but no animal I know of would tear out someone's throat and their stomach and not eat them. And they were all missing their left ear."

Duaia flinched, and Cal remembered Justice's words. "Trophies," she whispered.

Cal swallowed hard, sure he already knew the answer as he asked, "What about the seventh?"

"Right, yeah…." Aelin flexed his fingers around the sunstone from the Vault, the magic inside it sparking as it reacted to him. "There was a beastkin living there. A canine, I think. The villagers blamed him for the murders and stoned him to death."

The wounded sound Rashi made wasn't nearly as painful as the lance of sorrow and anger that filled their bond.

Duaia swore as she got to her feet, pacing in the scant space left on the outskirts of the room. "This is what his plan is? Murder and fearmongering? How is it even possible he has this much reach?"

"He's had thirty years to make his plans," Julius said.

Cal let out a slow breath and tried to think through the lingering wine. "Finding him and stopping him has to take priority," he said. "Now that you're both here and properly equipped, I need one of you sorting out the innocents from actual criminals in the prison, and the other getting what information you can from those who were collared."

The twins shared a long look before Aelin shrugged. "I'll take the prison. Am I free to use my own judgment on releasing them?"

Cal sighed, knowing his cousin would release a thief if they were only trying to feed themselves. "I'll have Elwin sit with you. He can help make sure no one ends up back in prison in a week."

"He's the one with the nice ass, right?" he asked, grinning when Cal let out an aggrieved sigh.

"Haru's is better," Synne offered, much to Rashi's delight.

"Haru's is the best," Rashi agreed. And that was the end of any further official business, the next few hours filled with comfortable conversation.

Cal found himself watching and listening, not even offering more than token protest when someone brought up an embarrassing memory of him. He couldn't help but notice how Synne had taken up one of the small sofas with Kithiel beside her, or how Kithiel finally seemed to shed some of the fear he'd worn like a cloak the past few days. He leaned towards Synne like a flower seeking sunlight, and Cal couldn't bring himself to begrudge him that.

A quick, pointed glare from Synne kept him from even attempting to warn Kithiel of the pandemonium he was courting. They could figure it out themselves. There was always the Vault to toss them into if they caused too much trouble.

# CHAPTER 13

RASHI SAT with his legs crossed on the bed, leaning back on his hands as he watched Haru dress for the day. They'd slept well into the morning after falling into bed a few hours before sunrise, but he didn't mind the lack of sleep. He minded even less when Kithiel had slipped out shortly after Synne retired. Even if he still refused to speak, at least he wasn't standing in Rashi's shadow any longer.

He'd missed being surrounded by family. The journey across the Wound had taken three weeks, and only Haru's ability to create water with his frost magic had kept them alive through part of it. And then the prison....

He shoved those memories away with the same deliberate intention as he had when he gave his tunic to Kithiel. Those humans had targeted them because of him, because his clothes were expensive and he appeared weak. All of his clothes were of the same quality, and that tunic had been his favorite, one he'd chosen to wear in the hopes of finding Cal that night. But just the sight of it reminded him of the prison and of Haru being tortured to keep him safe.

He must have let the memories too close to the surface, because Haru turned, sitting beside him and folding him into a tight embrace. "I'm fine," he murmured into Haru's shoulder. "You're the one with the problem today," he added, tipping his head back to meet Haru's eyes. "You have to tell Cal the truth."

Haru glared at him, only pulling away when Rashi gave him a firm shove.

Rashi glared back. He didn't need coddling.

He tilted his head when he heard the main door open and Cal thanking someone, before the sound of a cart moving across the floor followed. "Come on," he said, rolling off the bed and snagging Haru's hand on the way out.

Rashi grinned at Cal and intercepted him to press a quick kiss to his cheek in greeting, then followed him to the balcony. It was still early enough that they'd been sent breakfast, and he immediately filled a cup with strong tea, adding a generous amount of cream and honey before sitting back to watch them.

He'd considered himself the luckiest fox in the realm when he learned he was bound to a dragon, and now he was bound to the elf king who sat on the Sun Throne. He knew Fate required them for something, and with the amount of magical power between the three of them, that something terrified him. What if they failed? What if he lost one or both of them? What if he lost himself?

He blinked as Cal and Haru both stopped to look at him, shrinking into his seat from the intensity of *two* stares on him. That would take some getting used to. He set his tea aside and scooped some eggs onto his plate. If Haru thought he was going to use Rashi's drifting emotions as a distraction from having to tell Cal the truth, then he didn't know Rashi well at all.

"Your family is delightful," he said, since neither of them seemed keen on starting a conversation.

"I believe you think so," Cal replied with a faint smile.

"There are lots of strings between them," Haru said, picking up a small yellow berry and examining it. He tensed when both Rashi and Cal turned their attention to him.

"What do you mean?" Cal asked, and Rashi couldn't find much sympathy for Haru when he winced. It was his own fault for not telling Cal what he was before now.

Haru cleared his throat, avoiding Cal's gaze as he answered, "I can see them."

"Fate strings? You can see the Fate strings of others?"

"All strings."

Rashi shook his head faintly, keeping his mouth shut as he added some fruit to his plate. He shrugged at Cal when the elf looked at him, refusing to offer an explanation on Haru's behalf.

"What other kinds of strings are there?"

Haru adjusted his plate, turning it a bit before picking up some more berries. "Silver strings. They tie together those who are destined to be saved by or save the other."

"And you saw some?"

Haru hesitated before nodding. "Your sister and her guard share a silver string."

Rashi took a bite of eggs as he watched Haru, knowing he saw far more than that single string. The fact Haru was refusing to look at either of them might have concerned him, if he didn't know that Haru feared speaking of them, in case doing so tempted Fate into meddling further.

Cal shifted, fear disguised as anger shivering across their bond.

Rashi reached out to rest his hand on top of Cal's. "If there were a black string on anyone in your family, Haru would say so," he said gently. If any of them were to die by another's hand, Haru would do whatever he could to prevent that death. It was almost laughable how Death was more easily thwarted than Fate.

Cal focused on Rashi with the expression of one who intended to argue, before he sighed. "And black is death?"

Rashi pointedly shoved another bite of eggs into his mouth.

"Yes," Haru answered, though Cal didn't seem convinced. One of these days, Haru's taciturn answers were going to get him punched.

Cal sighed again and turned his attention to the food.

Rashi finished eating his fill and finished a second cup of tea without either of them saying anything else. How was it possible he'd been bound to two silent men? He was used to Haru's quiet presence. Even their bond was quiet until there was danger, or Rashi filled the silence himself, but Cal's silence was only external. The shift and pull of his emotions as he likely sought answers for issues that had been brought to him was a steady thrum of energy along their bond.

Rashi decided he didn't like it, much like he didn't like the irritation he'd felt from Cal when Synne held Haru's attention last night. He'd been promised Cal would spend the day with them, and he expected to have Cal fully present. He refilled his cup again, staring at Haru, who was deliberately ignoring him. He narrowed his eyes, considering kicking Haru under the table, before settling for the trick he knew would work without fail.

He stretched his senses along their bond and focused very hard on imagining himself spread across their bed, naked and moaning Haru's name.

Haru straightened as if he'd been slapped with magic, focusing on Rashi with heat in his gaze.

Rashi sipped his tea, hiding his smug smirk behind his cup. What he didn't expect was to find Cal giving him the same look, but he considered that a gift. He raised his eyebrows at Cal, affecting his most innocent expression.

Cal glanced from Rashi to Haru and back again. "You two are close."

Rashi smiled. "I *have* known him almost my entire life."

Cal poked at the remains of the eggs on his plate, sounding wistful as he said, "You know I almost went in search of you."

"You did?"

"When I was about fifteen," he said, trailing off as he gazed out over the city. "It felt like I was dying. There was a pressure in my chest, like something squeezing and pulling me apart. Like I needed to be somewhere."

Haru nodded faintly. "I felt it too. When Rashi was born."

Rashi winced and tightened his fingers around his cup. "I never told you this, but… I almost died at birth," he said, flinching against the intense sparks of alarm on both their bonds. Haru had never mentioned that feeling, but if they both experienced the same thing, there was only one explanation. "There was a storm the night I was born. A bad one. It turned the sky black and green, and the elders tried to delay my birth, saying it was a bad omen. But my mother wanted me to have the blessing of being born under the full moon of the last harvest."

He shifted in his seat and tilted his head towards Haru. "The cherry blossom tree in the field behind the house? The crack through its core is from when I was born. Mom said there was a surge of power, like she was caught in backlash from two directions. It ripped through her and the tree, and when I was born, I wasn't breathing. Every member of the village came and shared magic with both of us, to revive me and keep me alive through the night. Supposedly, that's why my magic is so strong. When the storm finally eased and the backlash faded, they knew I would live."

Cal let out a harsh breath, scowling across the table. "The Fate bonds nearly killed you."

Rashi laughed softly and shook his head. He had no doubt that he would have died that night without Cal and Haru's bonds as anchors. "No, they saved me."

# Chapter 14

HARU WAS no happier than Cal about learning of Rashi's birth. He'd had Cal's Fate string attached to him for fifteen years before Rashi's appeared. He'd known something was different about it. The desperate need to get to him hadn't been there when Cal's bond appeared, but he never imagined it was because he'd nearly lost the fox before even knowing him.

When he saw Rashi's pointed stare, he knew if he waited much longer, he could lose Cal in a different way. It would be worse to wait until after they completed their bond. If Cal decided he couldn't accept a dragon, they could continue as they were now, with the Fate string present, but not connecting their souls.

He cleared his throat. "While we're sharing truths," he said quietly, "I need to share my own."

"Did our bond nearly kill you too?" Cal asked, only for Rashi to throw a berry at him. It bounced off his cheek and rolled off the balcony.

"No," Haru said, refusing to be distracted. If he didn't say this now, he wouldn't say it at all. "I'm a dragon," he said, watching Cal for any sign that he might attack.

Rashi sighed loudly, which he ignored.

Cal stared at him. "What?" he asked with a soft laugh of disbelief.

Haru returned the stare, gripping the arms of his chair as he removed the glamour he'd wrapped around himself. When he'd realized the Fate strings were leading them across the Wound to Ylrendorei, he'd adjusted his appearance to be more human, unable to stomach taking the form of an elf. Now, he let those changes vanish, letting Cal see the form he'd used for the last few hundred years.

Long white horns stretched for three handsbreadth above his temples, and seemed to be the sole focus of Cal's attention. The silence stretched between them for long, excruciating moments.

"Fuck," he finally said. "A dragon… I just… need a moment," Cal whispered, standing and stumbling inside.

Haru tried not to be disappointed. It certainly could have been worse.

Rashi sighed again. "You could have been a *little* more delicate than that."

Haru shrugged, watching the door for a moment longer before looking at Rashi. "Either he can accept it or he can't. He reacted better than your family."

Rashi nearly spit his tea. "You had *no* glamour when you walked into my village with me in your arms. They thought you were going to spirit me away!"

"I should have," he muttered. "Your mother is terrifying."

Rashi laughed. "She knows it too. She'll be smugly telling everyone she has a dragon as a disciple until the day she dies."

"I am not her disciple," Haru said, ignoring Rashi's snicker.

"Believe what you want, love," he murmured, picking up a few of the remaining berries. He ate two before throwing one at Haru.

Expecting it, he caught it in his mouth.

"Cheater," Rashi grumbled.

Minutes passed with no sign of Cal returning. Haru didn't think even a few hours would be long enough. He should have waited. This was their first chance for the three of them to spend more than a few stolen moments together. Sharing the fact that he could see strings should have been enough secrets revealed for the day. When he'd seen everyone together last night and felt the grip of Fate tightening around them, he'd gotten curious enough to let his sight slip into his magic, revealing the connections between them all.

He'd never seen so many strings between so few people before. The silvers were the brightest, the events that formed those connections drawing closer in time, and they linked all of them. Synne to both her guard and Kithiel, Rashi and Duaia to Kithiel, himself to Aelin, and Cal to everyone. Not just to his family and those in the room. Countless silver threads stretched out across the expanse of the city, all of them wrapped tight around Cal.

If he'd had doubts that their purpose to stop the spread of the Wound was connected to what was happening in this city, the brilliant light of a tapestry of silver wiped them away.

Then there were the reds, nearly lost beneath the silver, but they glowed just as brightly. The three between him, Rashi, and Cal. Between Julius and Faelan. Between Synne and Kithiel.

And the blacks, shadows beneath the brilliant glow of the rest. A single black thread stretching from Kithiel into the city, and several around Vesryn, reaching in various directions. The ones around the guard were faint, their time lost in the distant future. Those concerned him less than the one attached to Kithiel, a deep black as dark as the silvers were bright.

He blinked as a berry struck his nose and gave Rashi an unimpressed look.

Rashi stuck his tongue out. "I'm going to go talk to him."

Haru sighed and got to his feet to follow, but they didn't even make it inside before the main door flew open and Duaia rushed in with a shout of "Cal!"

There was a heavy thump and harsh curse from Cal's bedroom before he stumbled out. "What's wrong?"

"Liria finally learned who put some of the collars on people."

# CHAPTER 15

CAL MANAGED a quick apology to Rashi and Haru with a promise to talk later before he escaped after Duaia. He knew very well he was being a coward and told himself his kingdom had to come first. The fact he had a *dragon* in his city, bound to him by Fate, would have to wait. He could only focus on one crisis at a time.

Julius was waiting for them with horses as they exited the palace. Cal took a brief moment to stroke his mare's face with a soft murmur of greeting before mounting.

"Edge of the farmer's district," Julius said. "Third house on Sunrise Path."

And then they were off, taking the less crowded alleys and servant paths. As they rounded a turn and nearly crashed into a merchant's cart, Cal wondered if maybe he shouldn't be the one running headlong into potential danger anymore.

His father had slowly drawn back from investigating the concerns of the people, especially after Cal's mother died. He'd stopped venturing into the city even to attend festivals. But this city needed a king who was willing to protect the people, not a figurehead.

His family had proven ineffectual enough for countless innocents to be imprisoned and tortured, others to be enslaved, and a distasteful human to have possibly gathered enough influence to start a new war. He wouldn't be remembered throughout history as the elf king who lost his kingdom to a human.

The air shimmered as Duaia threw a protective barrier around them and continued on, their hoofbeats reverberating in the narrow alley between buildings. The streets opened up as they reached the farmer's district, larger buildings giving way to shorter homes with space between them. The streets were empty; this late in the morning, everyone would be in the fields.

They slowed their horses to a brisk walk, and Julius stopped in the yard in front of the third house. "This should be it. He didn't report for duty this morning," he said, dismounting.

They tethered their horses to a post in the yard and converged on the front door, Duaia's barrier still distorting the air around them.

Julius beat a fist against the door. It swung open with an ominous creak under the force. They shared a look of unease before Duaia stepped inside first, slowly moving forward.

"Taegen Adwynn," Julius called. "Are you home?"

Cal took up the rear and followed Julius. The house was quiet, and there was an odd smell of old fish and sour fruit in the air. The farmer's district was one of the oldest areas in the city, built during Ysildea's reign. Despite the age, he didn't see any cracks or distortions in the faded gray wood, but the walls were bare. No ornaments or paintings. The sitting area only held a low table, chair, and sofa, with a thin layer of dust over them. "Are you sure someone lives here?"

Duaia cursed from the next room, and they hurried in, coming up short as the smell grew worse.

Cal gagged and covered his nose, breathing shallowly through his mouth as he stared at the elf in a chair at the dining table. His skin was grayed with death, a dagger protruding from his chest, dried blood soaked through his shirt and on his chin. Cal turned away, his other hand moving to the same spot on his own chest, pressing against the phantom echo of pain.

"By the Wound," Julius murmured, taking a step forward, but Duaia motioned him back.

"Out. Both of you," she ordered.

They retreated without protest, leaving her to her work. If anyone could find a trace of what happened, it would be her.

Cal stumbled out the door and heaved a deep breath of fresh air, bending forward and bracing his hands on his thighs. The urge to gag still sat at the back of his throat, but he pushed through it until he could speak. "He didn't fight," he said, unable to get the sight of Taegen's body out of his mind. He'd sat in that chair, his hands folded in his lap, and let someone stab him.

"He had a collar," Julius said. "Somewhere."

Cal closed his eyes and focused on breathing. "Justice did this? Why? Because we found and freed his slaves?" The families of those they'd freed in the palace had been found, safe and unharmed, and they'd all been moved somewhere Justice would hopefully never find them.

"Do you know how old he was?" Julius asked, his voice soft enough it caught Cal's attention and forced him to look up. "Nearly three thousand. He was one of the twelve remaining elders who were alive before the war. He was a soldier. He *fought* in the war."

"Then how the fuck did Justice collar him?"

Julius shook his head, his expression tight as he stared into the distance. "If he's really trying to take power, we interrupted whatever he was planning. He doesn't have the palace at his fingertips anymore. He has no one to give him information on our movements."

"Then why kill Taegen?" An elder and a soldier, he would have likely been part of the guard. He would have access to the palace, could still get information to Justice about what their plans were. Unless he didn't need that information anymore. If he was giving up on taking power through his position as one of the most trusted officials, he'd now have to rely on force.

Cal's breath stuttered as he stared out across his city. The farmer's district was built at the start of an incline, with the crops planted farther up in terraces to aid in irrigation. From here, he could see most of the city, the palace rising near the western wall, the ancient and massive ylren tree towering above everything else, its high branches filled with blue-green leaves and casting moving shadows all the way past the city gates. The seven younger ylren trees, only a fraction of the height of the palace, but still towering over all the buildings. The prison's large black stain on the other side of the city, its iron walls seeming to capture and hold even light captive.

And beyond the walls of the city stretched the Wound, as far as he could see. Between them were countless buildings and lives who depended on him to keep them safe. He couldn't help but fear he was going to fail them worse than his father had. How many would die before Justice was stopped? How many were already under his control?

He'd never fought in a war. How could he possibly win one against his own people?

"Haru is a dragon," he said, the words slipping out before he realized he was even going to speak.

Julius spun to face him, staring in silence, obviously expecting him to admit it was a jest. When Cal tore his gaze away from the city and looked back at him, Julius swore. "He actually told you that?"

"Just before D came to retrieve me."

"And what does he want? Revenge? To raze the city to the ground and bathe in its ashes? Like we don't have enough fucking problems."

"They came to fix the Wound." Even as he said it, he knew how ridiculous it sounded. Their best mages had spent decades after the war trying to restore the land, but even blades of grass coaxed to life by magic withered and died within moments. A quarter of all the land on this side of the sea sat barren, slowly wasting away to dust. "He said it's all connected. Justice and the corrupted magic and the Wound."

"How?"

Cal shook his head. If they knew that, maybe they could have stopped this by now.

"Sounds like a heavy burden," Julius murmured. "The stuff of legends. Of heroes, like Alais," he added with a taunting smile.

Cal frowned at him. "Are you saying I'm not a hero?"

Julius shrugged. "If any elf can get to the bottom of this and possibly restore the Wound that not even D has been able to coax life into, it'd be you," he replied. He tilted his head after a moment to add, "But you might need a dragon to help do it."

Cal sighed, unsurprised that Juls accepted the existence of a creature that hadn't been seen in Ages so easily. "Are you saying to trust him?"

"I'm saying you're tied by Fate for a reason. Besides, you're tied to Rashi too, so I doubt Haru will eat you. It'd make Rashi cry."

"Thank you," he said dryly, wishing he had something to throw at Juls' smug face.

The door swung open behind them and Duaia stalked out, her red hair even more of a wild mess than usual, fanning the air around her head from the residue of powerful magic. The dark glower on her face quickly doused any good humor Cal had scraped together. As did the quick spell she cast, lighting the sky above the house with a glowing red sigil that would summon the healers to retrieve the body.

"Did you find anything?"

"This," she said, holding up a gold bracelet. "That fucker made Taegen sit there while he pushed that dagger into his chest." She drew in a shaky breath. "Taegen trained everyone in the guard, including me," she said, blinking rapidly as she shoved the bracelet into her pocket. She shook her hand and flexed her fingers, dislodging sparks of magic.

Cal swallowed against an echo of pain beneath his ribs. "We'll find him," he said softly.

"Yes," Duaia said, her voice hard. "And when we do, I'm going to kill him myself."

# Chapter 16

Haru wasn't surprised when Cal left, but he couldn't help the annoyance that the elf had run away. Even if it was better than the alternative. Just because Cal hadn't attacked him now didn't mean he wouldn't later. Or after they succeeded in Fate's grand plan. And how was he supposed to trust an *elf* with his life? With Rashi's? At any moment Cal could turn on him, stab him in the back like his ancestors had done.

He heard Rashi's sigh as he paced the boundary of the sitting room, sparing him a quick glance before resuming his pacing. He desperately wished he could shift forms and fly, something he hadn't been able to do since before they'd left the forest. He'd intended to fly them across the Wound, but the moment he'd taken his dragon form, whatever curse lay on the land began eating away at his very magic.

Condensed into a smaller size with a human glamour wrapped around him, he'd been unaffected by the Wound. He still didn't understand why, since Rashi had been unaffected even in his fox form, but he was sure the reason held the answer for restoring the Wound. And once they did that, they could leave this kingdom and return to Rashi's village with his terrifying mother. Or maybe he'd take Rashi back to his own home. His grandsire would want to meet his mate.

Whatever happened, he was sure an elf king wouldn't fit into their future.

He stumbled as his musings were interrupted by a pulse of desire along his bond with Rashi, accompanied by the same image he'd been assailed with during breakfast. He scowled and turned to stalk into the bedroom. "That is a dirty trick," he started, though whatever else he was going to say was forgotten when the sight on the bed nearly matched the image in his head. The only difference was that Rashi had dropped his glamour and his three fluffy black tails were spread out against the sheets.

He growled softly as he shut the door, flipping the lock and adding a shield for good measure.

Rashi fluttered his lashes at him, stretching on the bed with a languid flex of muscles and smooth brown skin. "I guess I'll get dressed then, if you're not interested," he said, pushing himself up and laughing when Haru pinned him back down.

"You're insufferable," Haru grumbled, stretching out on top of Rashi and grazing his teeth against the bared flesh of his neck.

"Thank you," he said, sounding far too pleased with himself, but when he buried both hands in Haru's hair and gave a firm tug, Haru couldn't bring himself to care. It might have only been a few weeks, but it felt like months since the last time they'd had any time to be together like this. Not since before they started across the Wound. They hadn't wanted to chance the distraction at first, and then they'd lost a pack of supplies in a rotting marsh and had to focus on surviving.

"You're not naked," Rashi complained, wiggling a hand into the folds of Haru's clothes. When he found skin, he slid his palm against Haru's chest and stomach with a drag of blunt nails.

"Haru," Rashi whined.

It was Rashi's own fault for working himself up alone, but Haru kept that observation to himself. He sat up enough to strip, letting the silk slide to the floor as he enjoyed the sight of bare flesh in front of him. He would have preferred to take his time and reacquaint himself with Rashi's body, but the fox's impatience thrummed along their bond.

He snagged the open bottle of oil from the bedside table and poured some into his hand while Rashi shifted to wrap his legs around Haru's hips. With the new position, he was able to see exactly why Rashi was so impatient; his skin was already slick and glistening with oil. That didn't stop Haru from pressing two fingers inside.

Rashi gasped, arching on the bed and rocking against the intrusion, his tails flicking wildly on either side of him. "Yes," he moaned, his clenched hands twisting the sheets. "In me," he said, pushing into Haru's hand. He latched on to Haru's bicep and tugged, his other hand gripping the back of Haru's neck with a fistful of his hair. When Haru leaned down far enough, their lips met in a messy kiss. Their tongues clashed and teeth clicked from Rashi's desperation.

Haru fumbled the oil as that desperation seeped deep into the bond, his arousal bordering on painful. When Rashi grumbled and sank sharp teeth into his shoulder, Haru hissed, finally having enough. He pulled back and gripped Rashi's hips, flipping him to his stomach and forcing the fox's thighs apart with his knees.

"Haru," Rashi whined, trying to roll back over.

He gripped the back of Rashi's neck to pin him in place, coated his cock with an excessive amount of oil, then gripped Rashi's hip to hold him still before pushing into him.

Rashi keened and shoved back against Haru as much as he could, trying to take him deeper and faster.

Haru pressed his body along Rashi's and bit his shoulder with a growl, pleased when Rashi groaned and went pliant beneath him. He knew what Rashi needed and had every intention of giving it to him. In due time.

He dragged his tongue along Rashi's neck and across his shoulders as he slowly pressed into him, breathing in the familiar scent of forest and musk, until he was buried to the hilt inside him. He slid his hand from Rashi's neck into his hair, tugging his head to the side enough to claim his lips again. His other hand moved down Rashi's arm to his wrist, then threaded their fingers together.

"Haru," Rashi whined, arching beneath him. "Please."

"Patience," he murmured, giving a shallow thrust of his hips.

"Fuck patience," Rashi hissed. "Rather, fuck me," he added with a growl, squeezing Haru's fingers tight as he clenched his lower body.

Haru groaned and dropped his head to Rashi's shoulder. "Foxes and their dirty tricks." He slammed his hips forward, and once he started moving he couldn't stop, thrusting in earnest.

Rashi let out a breathless laugh and rocked back to meet his thrusts. "Finally," he groaned, before they were both reduced to gasping and moaning, their bodies coming together with the sound of sweat-slicked flesh.

"Yes, yes, fuck, Haru," Rashi chanted. "Close. Fuck. Harder!"

Haru grunted and shifted back on his knees, grasping Rashi's hips and lifting him off the bed to do just that.

Rashi yelped, planting a hand against the headboard for balance as he eagerly got his other hand on himself and started stroking. It didn't take more than a few more thrusts before Rashi tipped his head back with a long, growling moan. His body shuddered and tightened around Haru with his release, and after another few thrusts, Haru followed him over the edge.

He dropped his head to Rashi's back as they panted for air, finally shifting to pull free and letting Rashi stretch out on the bed with a satisfied groan. There was a towel on the floor, and he snagged it to clean them off, grimacing as he found the oil had spilled all over the sheets. He set it back on the table and ignored the mess as he stretched out beside Rashi, pulling him in close to bury his face in unruly black hair. He breathed deep and let himself relax, Rashi's scent and warmth grounding him like nothing else could. Enough that he could breathe through the stench of rot creeping through everything.

He hummed as Rashi's fingers combed through his hair and caressed the bases of his horns, relaxing further. "Never told me you nearly died," he murmured, pretending he wasn't as sullen as he sounded.

Rashi laughed and tugged Haru's hair before stroking through it again. "You're nearly four hundred. How many times have you nearly died?"

"I'm a dragon," he replied with a huff.

"So just the other day, then?"

Haru closed his eyes and remained silent. He'd given up enough secrets for the day. He didn't have any inclination to visit unpleasant memories.

Rashi didn't prod for more, and they lapsed into a comfortable silence filled with only their breathing, Rashi's heartbeat a steady, calming rhythm against Haru's cheek.

He was on the verge of dozing when Rashi whispered, "I want to be with him."

His fingers twitched against Rashi's hips, but otherwise he managed to hide his unease. He didn't dare admit his fear that Cal would take Rashi away from him.

Rashi had been bound to both of them his entire life. He'd never known a time he wouldn't belong to someone, let alone two of them.

Cal's bond may have been there first, but Rashi was the one he'd spent the last decade with. The one he'd watched grow from a gifted kit into a brilliant fox. Haru couldn't lose him, but he knew he would if he tried to keep Rashi and Cal apart.

"You don't need my permission," he murmured.

Rashi snorted and gave a sharp tug to Haru's hair in clear admonishment. "Yes, I do. Just because we're all bound doesn't mean you like him."

"I like him fine," he muttered. That wasn't the issue.

"You haven't even touched him."

"I'm not going to complete the bond without knowing he can accept that I'm a dragon," he snapped, rolling away from Rashi and getting up.

"Haru...."

He ignored Rashi as he headed into the bathroom and quickly cleaned himself up. Foolishly, he hoped Rashi would drop the conversation when he returned, but the fox was sitting in the middle of the bed, his hair and ears askew, tails puffed up where they rested against his crossed legs.

He watched Haru dress with a frown, tail tips twitching like an irritated cat. "You're shutting me out."

Haru tensed at the accusation, but he couldn't deny that he'd pulled away from their bond.

"Because of Cal?" Rashi asked, growling softly when Haru shook out a clean pair of pants and pulled them on. "Haru, talk to me. I can feel how scared you are even though you're trying to hide it."

"I'm not scared," he snarled, nearly ripping the silk beneath his fingers in his haste to dress. He spun to glare at Rashi and deflated at the hurt and loss in his expression.

"I'm terrified," Haru whispered. He didn't resist when Rashi grabbed his hand and pulled him back to the bed. He sat and took a deep breath as Rashi tucked into his side.

"Terrified of Cal?" he asked softly. "Because you think he won't accept a dragon?" He sighed when Haru shrugged. "We're Fate bound. Why would you think he couldn't accept you given time?"

Haru squeezed his eyes shut but quickly opened them again as bloody memories surfaced. "Because it's happened before."

Rashi straightened, his grip on Haru's arm turning painful. "What? You were bonded before?" he demanded, before yelping and jerking away from Haru, frost coating his fingertips.

Haru swore and stifled his magic until the air warmed again. This was the last thing he would ever want to talk about. He'd rather tell Cal he was a dragon again. It'd been nearly three hundred years, but after he watched the Wound appear, he'd returned to the mountains, convinced his kind had been right to distance themselves from the rest of the realm. But stepping off the mountain to begin with had been a mistake, because Fate decided to use him.

"When were you bonded?" Rashi asked, carefully resting his head on Haru's shoulder.

"Just after the Wound appeared."

"You would have been young. Not even a hundred?"

Haru nodded, his throat constricting enough he could hardly breathe. "It was a human," he choked out, finding Rashi's hand and squeezing. He let out a shuddering breath, glancing down to find two of Rashi's tails in his lap. He buried his other hand in soft black fur, focusing on the silky feel against his fingers. "I waited a year before following it," he murmured. "To a crude settlement at the edge of the Wound. It led me directly to a young man," he said, smiling faintly when Rashi made a confused sound.

"I didn't understand either." A bond shouldn't have appeared and attached him to someone already born, much less an adult, but after the Wound appeared, magic had become strange, at least for a while.

He still remembered the explosion that shook the mountains, the backlash of magic that lit up the skies with purples and greens and yellows like a horrible bruise. The way black lightning crackled to the earth, turning healthy plants into rot with its touch. Magic itself had felt foreign, like a living thing full of wrath, intent on destroying anything it touched.

For two days, magic fought to destroy all living things on the surface, and when the storm finally faded, the Wound was a barren wasteland, humans were bereft of magic, and strings had become more numerous than ever.

Once the realm returned to some semblance of normal, he followed his red string to a young man leading a small village, too close to the Wound to properly grow or raise anything, but they'd been unwilling to leave.

"You stayed," Rashi said with certainty.

"Yes... I helped clear land far enough away to grow crops and ensure they survived the winter."

Rashi leaned into him, curiosity more than alarm humming through their bond. "What about your bonded?" he asked gently.

"He was…." Haru trailed off. It was hard to remember what Sorren had been like in the beginning. "Angry," he finally said. "They were all angry at the loss of magic and their homes. They blamed their Shadow King for losing the war…."

He fell silent, focusing on one of Rashi's tails and stroking along the length of it over and over again in a slow, soothing rhythm. "I never told them what I was but… we were together for less than a year before they realized I wasn't human.

"I'd never used magic near them, but then there was a fire. One of the cooking pits…. It spread to the trees and around their entire settlement, and there was a child." He fell silent again, barely feeling Rashi's hand rubbing his arm. All he could see was orange flames and charred wood, and the tree toppling to the side, and the child crying in the center of a swirl of smoke. "I used a barrier to shield him. Another to snuff out the flames."

And after he'd saved their homes and their child, the humans all stared at him as if he'd been the one to start the fire.

He'd been prepared to leave then, but Sorren thanked him. Convinced the others they were lucky that he had magic. Convinced him to stay.

But then he'd overheard them arguing. "I was everything that they'd been fighting against in the war and couldn't be trusted. I told Sorren I would leave, but he said I could help. That he knew how to fix the Wound, could undo the ritual that had created it."

Of course he'd agreed.

He drew in a deep breath, but he felt like he was suffocating, choking on smoke and the stench of blood and rot.

"There was no ritual," Rashi guessed.

Haru shook his head. "There was. But it required a sacrifice. A magical creature powerful enough to undo the damage."

"He was going to kill you?" Rashi snarled, climbing into Haru's lap and cupping his face with both hands. "Tell me you killed that bastard first."

Haru swallowed, unable to meet Rashi's eyes. "Not just him," he whispered. He hardly remembered the actual moment. Sorren had come to him with a curved dagger that still resonated with shadow magic and the blood of some powerful creature. The fight had been quick, and he could still remember the feel of fresh blood spilling hot over his fingers, the sound of Sorren's curses through wet, labored breaths.

His feet had dragged him back to the village despite knowing he wouldn't be welcome there. When they saw the blood, they knew, and they attacked him. "Killed them all," he whispered. Every single human in that village had tried to kill him, even the children, driven by some deep hate or fear he'd never understand.

"You did what you had to do, love."

"You weren't there."

"No," Rashi agreed, brushing his thumbs against the bases of Haru's horns. "But I know you would have left them alive if you thought they wouldn't hunt you down. Or find another creature to try again."

Haru shuddered, burying his face in Rashi's neck. "They were children."

"Yes," Rashi murmured. "Children raised by people who would sacrifice their own bonded. For what? Was he really trying to fix anything? Or finish what they started."

Haru shook his head. He'd wondered himself what Sorren wanted to accomplish.

Rashi kissed his temple and coaxed him into lying down again.

Too exhausted to resist, he let Rashi hold him and stroke his hair until he fell asleep.

# CHAPTER 17

Waiting for the healers to collect Taegen's body was excruciating. Every one of Cal's instincts screamed at him to be doing something, anything, to find Justice before he killed again. But Duaia's tracking spells were having no luck. Even now, she stalked the perimeter of the house, searching for where Justice had entered, for any clue that might show them where he was hiding.

"Why did he live out here?" he asked, watching Duaia from the corner of his eye as she made another pass.

Julius tilted his head from where he'd propped himself against the post with the horses. "I think his wife worked the fields, before the war."

"Wasn't she a battlemage?"

"I'm not sure. I think so. She's listed as dying in battle." Julius tilted his head. "Why?"

Cal shook his head, unsure why it mattered. "Most of the guards live in the barracks close to the palace or the gates."

"Most of the guards are younger than two hundred and still act like horny adolescents when not on duty," Julius replied dryly.

"Fair enough," Cal murmured, though something still bothered him, even if he couldn't identify what. Justice oversaw the enforcement of the laws. Most of his duties would have kept him near the palace or prison, and he'd lived in a small room in the palace as part of his station. Maybe that was why Justice followed Taegen all the way home to kill him. Few around here might recognize him, especially if he was no longer wearing the clothes denoting him as an official.

"What's wrong?"

Cal sighed and shook his head. "I don't know. Something feels strange about this."

Julius nodded before his lips pulled into a slow smirk. "Sure it's not just because you ran away from your dragon in the middle of an important conversation?"

Cal glared. "How the hell can you accept the fact we have a *dragon* here?"

Julius shrugged. "I guess I always believed they still existed. You can't read the old stories and think we really killed them all. In fact, the only evidence we have of any dead dragon is the one in the Vault, right?"

Cal frowned. "I suppose so." He'd lost interest in the legends and old stories years ago, after he'd first been allowed into the Vault and found that not only had those creatures truly existed, but they'd been slaughtered. Pieces of them taken as prizes, their parts used for spells and potions.

The horrible thing was, Justice's fearmongering was effective because it had some truth to it. The only difference was, it was never humans that were killed for trophies.

Julius let out a long-suffering sigh, clasping a hand on Cal's shoulder. "I love you as a brother, so sometimes I wish I could strangle you and not be hanged for treason."

"I wouldn't let them hang you," Cal replied with a smirk. "I'd exile you to a fishing boat for a week."

Julius scowled. "You know I hate the ocean."

"You'd rather be hanged?"

"It would certainly be better than getting eaten by a giant squid."

Cal laughed and shook his head, straightening when he caught sight of the carriage heading towards them. "You really think I can trust him?"

"You haven't seen the way he looks at you."

"Like he wants to stab me more than you do?" he guessed.

"Like he wants to trust you, but he's not sure he can. I'm guessing that you leaving after he told you his most guarded secret didn't help."

Cal winced, stepping to the side as the carriage reached them and pulled as close to the house as it could get. He let out a slow breath, watching Duaia lead the healers inside. "The ones who killed that dragon aren't even alive anymore," he murmured, more to himself than Julius. "If anyone is going to repair the broken trust and bring dragons back into the realm, it has to be us."

Julius slapped Cal's back with an approving nod. "Now go tell him that."


As MUCH as he wanted to return to Haru and Rashi, Cal remained with Duaia until they'd escorted the healers back to the palace. The healers removed the dagger and handed it over to her before preparing Taegen for burial. Duaia stayed to oversee it, searching Taegen's clothes for anything that might help, but there was nothing.

Cal eyed the dagger in Duaia's hand, clutched tight between nearly bloodless fingers. He shared a look with Julius, who grimaced before lightly touching her arm.

"We should leave the healers to their work," Julius said softly.

Duaia shuddered and slowly turned towards him, as if she'd forgotten they were there. She took one last look at Taegen before nodding, letting Julius guide her out of the room.

Cal followed behind as they headed to a private sitting area nearby. It was lit by small sunstones, as there were no windows, with comfortable chairs, a short table with an assortment of books, and a few plants. He closed the door, reaching for the threshold to prevent anyone from listening. He took a seat across from them, watching Duaia clean the blood from the blade with a spell. "Can you get anything from it?" Cal asked softly.

"Just that it was a man who held it," she said, turning it over between her fingers. The silver glinted in the light, the blade simple and the hilt plain. No adornments or markings. Something a commoner would have.

As far as he knew, Justice wasn't a noble. He'd been born a commoner, but he'd been vocal on enforcing laws equally across species and status, especially against magical creatures. Vocal enough that the humans elected him as their voice, eventually earning him his place as an official. And he'd used his position to staff the prison with only humans, procure cuffs and bits of iron spelled to suppress magic, and ensure the torture of any magical creature he could get his hands on.

Unable to keep still, Cal stood and paced the small room. He'd found a noticeable decrease in the magical population when he'd started reviewing the records. Each census over the past few decades showed a dwindling number at inconspicuous rates. The Wound was blamed for most things when it came to magical issues. The way it seemed to absorb even ambient magic had been used to explain many of their problems over the past three centuries, but what if there was something else to blame? Or someone?

How many creatures had been tortured to death in the name of Justice? Cal had always thought the name sounded pretentious, but now it carried an ominous weight. How many humans knew what was going on and believed this was exactly the kind of justice they deserved? How had Justice done this for years and not been stopped?

"Someone has to be helping him."

"No one in the palace would," Julius said.

"No," he agreed. "Liria confirmed none of the officials knew anything."

"The only collars found have been on servants, healers, or guards," Duaia added quietly, turning the dagger between her fingers again. "Your father may have figured it out...."

Cal stopped pacing and spun to face her in confusion. "What? Then why didn't he say anything?"

"Maybe he didn't get the chance."

"What are you talking about?" His stomach twisted when they both refused to meet his eye.

"Julius," Cal snarled, but he didn't need them to say it. He already knew. He'd suspected from that first day and refused to acknowledge it, but when Julius finally looked at him, the black pit of grief inside him cracked open even further.

"Your father was in his prime. How could he have died of natural causes?"

Except there'd been no wound, no sign of attack or poison or even an accidental injury. He'd been found in his bed when he was late to rise, as peaceful as if he'd still been sleeping.

He stared at Duaia, the sorceress who was as much an older sister to him as she was to Julius. Who'd protected him and his sister since they'd drawn their first breaths.

"You knew," he whispered, the hurt of betrayal sparking into anger. "You've had proof. For weeks, you've watched me grieve, knowing I should be seeking his killer, and you've said nothing!"

"I don't have proof!"

Cal scoffed. "The gift runs in your family," he sneered. "Julius Sees the future, and you can discern the truth as easily as my cousins. When have your instincts ever been wrong?"

She flinched and looked away. "Just the once," she said softly.

Cal's lungs squeezed tight as if caught in a winch and he braced himself against the back of a chair, its worn leather growing warm beneath his fingers before it started smoking. He tried to stifle his magic, but it was no use. He could barely even breathe.

Duaia's instincts may have been wrong that day, but his mother's death was his fault. If he'd trusted Julius, if he hadn't tried to change the vision, his mother would still be alive. Maybe Justice wouldn't have managed to sabotage them so completely with his mother there to support his father. But the moment Julius told him that Synne would be betrayed by one of her guards, Cal had gone to his mother to warn her. Instead of Synne being taken captive for a few hours, his mother confronted the assassin herself, unprepared for the spelled and poisoned dagger of his partner.

The stench of charred leather filled his nose, and he tore his hands away from the chair. "Who else?" he demanded, pacing again. "Who else knows my father was murdered and that we've done *nothing*? The rest of the palace? By the Wound, does Synne know?"

Cal froze as horror crashed through him. "Kithiel."

If Justice was behind even his father's death, Kithiel would know. Or was involved. And what better way to strike another blow at them than from the inside?

He turned to rush from the room, the door slamming into the wall as he threw it open.

"Cal," Julius called, but Cal ignored him until Julius grabbed his arm.

He followed the momentum of the tug, bringing his other hand up to slam his palm into Julius' chest with a burst of condensed magic. The force threw him into the wall with a loud crack.

"Do not. Touch me," he hissed. "You've lied to me for weeks."

Julius slipped as he tried to regain his footing and stay upright, one hand pressed to his chest with a grimace of pain. "You've known the truth," he spat back. "You just didn't want to admit it. You've never wanted the crown. You've been scared of it since your mother died. Admitting your father was murdered too would mean you had to take his place and do the fucking job you were raised for."

"Fuck you," Cal snarled, but Julius didn't back down.

"And now you're trying to put the blame on anyone to ease your guilt. What exactly do you plan to do when you find Kithiel? He was collared. Justice tried to kill him, and you think now that he's free he has any loyalty to that bastard?" Julius pushed off the wall and stalked forward. "Do you really intend for your first defining moment as king to be punishing or executing a man who's as much a victim as you are?"

Cal desperately tried to hold on to his anger, but Julius was right. If Kithiel meant any of them harm, he surely would have done something before now. The loss of anger left him empty enough for the grief to swamp him again, and he closed his eyes, fighting the ache in his chest for shallow breaths.

He wasn't suited to being king. If he'd accepted the crown in the beginning, maybe they could have stopped Justice weeks ago. Synne or Liria would have made a better ruler than him.

Julius grasped both his shoulders and gave him a shake. "We will figure this out," he said firmly. "D and I will go talk to Kithiel. Maybe your sister has softened him up enough he'll finally speak."

Cal cracked his eyes open enough to give him a baleful glare, but Julius only winked and let go.

"Why don't you go deal with your dragon? We're going to need him soon," he said, and the hint of power in those words caught both their attention.

Julius' gift didn't always show itself in visions. Sometimes he Spoke a truth of the future. They shared a look, and Julius stepped away with a wince.

"Go see a healer," Cal murmured.

Julius snorted. "You didn't hurt me that badly. Go see to your dragon." He glanced at Duaia where she lingered near the door of the room. "We'll make sure Synne is safe."

Cal let out a slow breath before nodding. He stood there as they moved past him, heading for the spiral staircase that would take them to the royal apartments. He set aside the lingering anger and buried his grief, hoping it would be less when it found its way to the surface again.

He was too raw to return to his rooms yet, and he was sure Haru wouldn't believe he'd accepted the fact he was a dragon so quickly. Not without some kind of proof.

He headed for the kitchens, requesting dinner for him and his bondeds be brought to his rooms in an hour, then let his feet guide him until he found himself at his office. He truly needed to move into his father's much larger office, but he liked this one. It was cozy despite the messy stacks of papers on the desk. Dozens of books filled the bookcase and shelves lining the walls, with a flowering plant in the corner of the window. The trinket box in the shape of a pile of books with a white dragon on top, its tail coiled around the edges, was a gift from Juls. The ornate mug that was spelled to keep its beverage warm, with a giant black spider carved into the bottom, was a gift from Synne. By the Wound, he hated that mug. He should have known there was a trick the moment Synne offered him a warm drink.

He stopped in front of the bookcase and spotted the large chest tucked into the corner beside it. The chest gleamed with the brilliant bright color of dawntree wood. He opened it to find it empty, one of the chests he'd used to move part of his book collection into the office. When he ran his fingers along the edge, the spellwork shimmered, strong and intact. Spells for durability, protection from the elements, light weight, increased storage, and a dozen others that would ensure anything inside remained in precisely the same condition as when it was stored.

He picked it up and left, moving deeper into the palace, through spelled doors, down narrow stairs, and into the Vault, where the remains of a dragon sat on a pedestal.

The skull was heavier than he expected, and it took a few spells and a lot of maneuvering to get it into the chest. Packing up the rest was easy enough; the legs were a bit lighter and mostly intact, though a few of the talons were missing. He used the cloths on the pedestals to form a pouch for the scales and to wrap around the horns. When he was sure he'd gotten everything, he closed and secured the lid, taking a steadying breath before lifting it and making the long journey up to his apartments.

The sitting room was empty, but the door to the guestroom was closed, with the faint thrum of a spell over it. He set the chest on the table and moved to knock on the door. "Haru, Rashi?"

There was a long moment of silence before Rashi replied with, "Yes?"

"I'd like to speak with you and Haru if you have a moment."

"Or just Haru?" Rashi asked.

"If he'll speak to me."

"He'll be right out."

Cal hated the flutter of nerves in his gut as he stepped back. He forced himself to sit on the arm of his chair instead of pacing the room, shoving his hands under his thighs and focusing on his breathing. When the door finally opened a small eternity later, his head snapped up, and he found he was disappointed to see Haru's glamour back in place.

Haru stepped forward far enough to close the door behind him, then stood there with a wary, expectant expression.

Cal cleared his throat. "I'm sorry," he said quietly. "For leaving so abruptly this morning."

Haru inclined his head. "It sounded important."

"Yes, but…." He shook his head. "I promised myself if I ever wore the crown, I wouldn't let it come between me and those I care for. My duty has to come first, but I can't hope to take care of the entire kingdom if I can't even take care of my family."

He took a deep breath and pushed to his feet. "I can't deny that you surprised me." He offered a faint smile that Haru didn't return, but he hadn't expected otherwise. He cleared his throat again and motioned to the chest. "This should have been returned to you years ago. Perhaps if we'd known dragons still existed…." He trailed off, reaching over to open the chest when Haru took a hesitant step closer.

The moment Haru saw what was inside, he sank to his knees beside the table, gripping the edge of the chest, his breathing ragged.

Cal felt a distant echo of sorrow and relief and glanced up to find Rashi standing in the doorway, watching them with wide eyes.

He mouthed a thank-you to Cal before sitting beside Haru and slipping his arms around the dragon.

Haru immediately leaned into him, never taking his eyes off the chest. "This was the son of my great grandame's sister," he whispered.

"I'm sorry," Cal said softly, hating that part of Haru's family had been sitting in the Vault for more than three Ages. "I know my family betrayed him, but I never understood why."

Haru nodded faintly, lightly dragging his fingers along the edge of the chest, as if afraid to touch what was inside. "She never speaks of it."

"She's still alive?" After all they'd lost since the war, it was hard to imagine living to his true lifespan, much less for several Ages.

Haru glanced up with a wry smile. "I think she'll outlive us all," he said, letting out a slow breath before closing the chest with care. "Thank you," he added softly.

Cal nodded and stepped back. "Of course. I hope this is enough for you to believe I don't wish you harm. I've always regretted that my people were responsible for the loss of dragons in the realm."

Rashi kissed Haru's cheek with a grin. "I told you there was nothing to worry about."

At Haru's soft huff, Cal relaxed enough to take his first real breath in what felt like days. "Thank you," he said, sinking into his chair, "for telling me the truth."

He tilted his head as he studied Haru, his silver hair pulled back in an intricate braid along the side of his head. "You don't have to use that appearance if you don't want to. I wouldn't mind if you didn't use any glamour at all," he said, his breath sticking in his throat as Haru's amber eyes focused on him with a piercing look.

He caught the movement as Rashi ducked his head, thought he saw the hint of a smile pressed into Haru's shoulder, but he didn't dare look away from Haru to be sure. He'd run away once already, he wouldn't back down now. If he was going to accept Haru, it couldn't be halfway.

"All right," Haru whispered, nudging Rashi away before standing. His throat worked as he swallowed, and then there was a ripple of magic as the glamour faded. Haru's appearance shifted, the human ears replaced by ears with pointed tips and two grooves along the back. His brow and the area beneath each eye were ridged, the texture resembling snakeskin. Dusting his cheeks, throat, and peeking out of his sleeves were bright white scales edged in palest blue, fading into smooth pale skin like melting snow.

"Beautiful," Cal whispered, pretending not to notice the flush of warmth around the scales of Haru's cheeks.

Rashi chuckled and stretched out on the sofa, and only when Cal glanced at him did he catch sight of the long, serpentine tail curled around Haru's feet. The scaled appendage ended in what looked like a delicate fan of long white-blue crystals. That alone would certainly ensure that word of a dragon's return to the realm spread across the kingdom within hours.

A knock at the door drew his attention, and he stood to answer it, smiling at Aster and stepping back to let him in.

Aster placed the cart and bowed, before glancing around the room. He paused as he spotted Haru and his new appearance, a frown briefly creasing his brows, before he looked at Cal again. "Is Kithiel still here? I was hoping I could finally see him."

"Sorry," Rashi said, before Cal could answer. "He still hasn't been feeling well. I'll tell him you asked after him again."

Aster nodded, irritation crossing his features and fading so quickly Cal thought he must have imagined it. "Thank you." He bowed again and backed out of the room.

Once the door closed, Cal pushed the cart out to the balcony, activating the sunstones for light as the sun dipped below the horizon. He glanced up with a smile when Haru and Rashi joined him. "I do want to know you better," he said, setting out the plates of food. "Both of you. But it may be difficult until after we've found Justice."

Rashi dropped into a chair, snagging a plate of crispy vegetables as if to hoard them for himself. "What can we do to help?"

Cal shook his head. "I'm not sure. Why don't you tell me what your skills are?"

# Chapter 18

IN THE end, the decision of how they could help was made for them. In the morning, a new bundle of problems was brought in with their breakfast.

"Kithiel wasn't responsible or involved," Julius said, leaning back against the balcony, his eyes straying to Haru before flicking away, only to be drawn back again a few moments later.

Haru hadn't put his glamour back in place, and it was clear for anyone who actually looked to see exactly what he was.

"But?" Cal prompted, knowing he wasn't going to like what else Julius had to say, and that suspicion was confirmed when Julius made his sour-and-rotting-lemon face.

"But he remembers Justice gifting your father a gold ring when he was younger. Maybe ten years ago."

Cal lost his grip on the creamer, hardly noticing as it spilled across the table. The knowledge that his father had been murdered was horrible enough, but the thought that he'd been wearing a slave collar was unbearable. It should have been impossible. The king, the entire kingdom, under someone else's control? It made sense in a sickening way. It certainly explained how Justice had seized the prison without any protest.

The ache in his chest was familiar, but it wasn't until a warm flurry of magic swept through him that he realized he'd been fighting for anything more than a shallow breath.

Rashi's hands were warm on his cheeks, his bright green eyes close enough for Cal to see the flecks of gold in them. "It's all right," he said softly.

Cal swallowed hard and forced a deep breath into his lungs before nodding. "We have to be sure," he said, looking at Julius.

"D's already gone to the crypt," he replied. "But there's also a more pressing issue."

"Of course there is," Cal muttered.

"The autumn festival is in a week."

."Apparently, the supplies that had been set aside for it were used for the feast instead."

Cal closed his eyes with a groan. "There should still be plenty stored." He'd just met with Afamrail the other day to verify how much their granaries held. They had enough food to get them through the brief winter and into the spring when they could start planting again, especially with the last harvest that should be done in the next few days.

"Yes, except the crops have turned… strange."

"Strange?"

Julius pulled a cloth from his pocket and set it on the edge of the table before unfolding it. Inside was a leaf, except instead of the bright green of a healthy plant, this one was a shimmery purple with veins of black, splotched through with pale green.

"Fuck!" Rashi stood quickly enough his chair toppled over.

Cal and Julius both eyed him in surprise, and Cal found himself on his feet, reaching for Rashi as dread crashed through their bond. "What's wrong?" he asked, wincing as Rashi's fingers dug into his arm hard enough to bruise.

Rashi let out a shuddering breath, sharing a quick look with a grim-faced Haru before focusing on Cal. "It's the Wound," he said. "It's infecting the land beyond it, like it's infecting the forest in the north." He stared at the leaf again as his weight slumped into Cal's side. "This is what our crops have looked like the past few years."

"Incredible," Julius muttered. "Like we really needed another potential spark for civil war."

Cal ignored him. "Is there anything we can do?"

Rashi sighed. "Maybe. I can't promise I can heal them all, but I can probably save some."

Haru growled quietly, the sound clearly that of a dragon. "You are not overextending yourself this time."

Rashi scoffed and waved a hand at him. "I'll be fine."

Cal decided not to get involved in what was obviously an old argument. Instead, he righted Rashi's chair and guided him to sit back down. "Is that the last of your terrible report for the morning?" he asked dryly.

Julius gathered the cloth back up. "I suppose that depends on if Liria deciding to help Aelin sort out the prison is terrible or not."

Cal stifled another groan. "You know what. As long as they don't release a murderer onto the streets, I don't care. I take it she didn't get any useful information from those we freed of the collars?"

"Not much we don't already know. Most of them didn't know who collared them, the jewelry pieces were left for them like secret gifts, but the guard with the ah, ring on his privates. He said it was a servant who put it there."

"Wait," Rashi said, his ears twitching forward. "He used a ring as a slave collar and put it on their cock? That's... almost ingenious."

"Which servant?" Cal demanded, but Julius shook his head.

"Said he didn't know his name, and yes, it's exactly how you think. Liria already got the truth from him, and he's been sent to the prison." Noticing Rashi's confusion, Julius explained, "He apparently had a habit of cornering the younger servants and demanding sexual favors."

Rashi's ears flattened, and he bared his teeth with a growl that rivaled Haru's.

Julius smiled faintly at the reaction. "Hence why he's been sent to the prison. He'll rot there for the rest of his life. And yes," he continued, glancing at Cal. "Before you ask, Liria looked into the rest of the guards. They're all clean."

Cal nodded, deliberately breathing out the tension that had taken root in his body. "Thank you," he said, beyond grateful he had people he could fully trust to handle these situations exactly how he wanted.

Julius slipped the cloth into his pocket before clasping Cal's shoulder on his way back inside. "By the way, your sister wants a word," he called as he slipped out the door and quickly closed it behind him.

Cal groaned. "Bastard," he muttered.

"Why is speaking to your sister a bad thing?" Rashi asked, affronted.

Cal reached for a slice of bread and slathered it with butter and fresh preserves. "Juls and D may have interrogated Kithiel," he said, managing not to flinch at the burst of alarm along the bond.

"Because of your father," Haru said.

Cal glanced up to meet his eyes before looking away again. "Kithiel has been Justice's personal servant since he was a boy. If anyone might be involved or know what Justice's plans are, it would be him."

"He was collared," Rashi snapped. "That healer tried to kill him."

"Yes, but the question is why? If he doesn't know anything and he's not part of the plan, why kill him?"

"This Justice doesn't sound like someone who'd accept his slave being freed," Haru offered.

"Maybe not," Cal conceded, taking a bite of his bread. Justice had certainly been an unpleasant human; it wouldn't surprise him in the least if that was the only reasoning he needed to kill someone.

He finished his bread and stood. "Let me deal with Synne, and then I'll show you to the crops?"

Rashi nodded, quickly swallowing his mouthful of eggs. "Tell her she's not allowed to damage your goods."

"Yes, that's exactly how I'll start the conversation," he replied dryly, though on second thought, maybe that wasn't such a bad idea.

The walk to his sister's rooms was too short by far, and when he stepped inside, Synne was sitting in a chair with a cup of tea, Vesryn a silent presence in the corner of the room. Kithiel was curled up on the sofa, a light blanket draped over him. Even in sleep, he seemed terrified, with deep shadows beneath his eyes.

"How dare you accuse my guest of murder," Synne snapped, pitching her voice low enough it wouldn't disturb Kithiel.

Cal raised an eyebrow. "Your guest now, is he?" he replied mildly, lifting a hand to stop her when she opened her mouth to argue. "I won't apologize for ensuring the safety and peace of this kingdom, and I'm sure Juls and D were far gentler with him than anyone else suspected of conspiracy or treason could hope to expect. He refused to speak even after his throat was healed. I'm sorry he was attacked. If we had the time to wait for him to recover on his own terms, we would, but we don't. Does that address all your arguments?"

Synne set her cup on its saucer, holding it in front of her as she stared him down. The expression was so similar to their mother's that for a moment, a fresh wave of much older grief surfaced. After a drawn-out silence, she lifted her chin. "We share a Fate bond."

"No," he replied immediately.

She set her tea on the table and clasped her hands in her lap. "You of all people know you can't argue against Fate."

Despite his flinch at the accusation, he replied, "You cannot take him as your consort."

"Because he's only half elf?"

"By the Wound," Cal breathed, pinching the bridge of his nose. His sister could barely be considered an adult. He certainly wasn't going to start arranging a consort or marriage ceremony for her.

"Wait," he said, focusing a glare on her. "Since when do you have a string?"

She shrugged primly. "As far as we can tell, it appeared when your fox saved him."

Cal stared at Vesryn, sure this was some elaborate plan for revenge, but the older elf gave him a sympathetic shrug. "That's not how strings work."

"It's how this one worked," she replied, and Cal recognized the tone. She'd set her mind to something, and even Fate Herself would be mad to try and change it.

He lifted his hands in surrender. "He's your responsibility, then. But he won't be an official consort for at least five years."

She rolled her eyes and stuck her tongue out, proving his point, and he turned to leave.

"When this mess is dealt with, we'll figure out who he is," he added over his shoulder.

Rashi and Haru were waiting in the sitting room and stood when he returned. It didn't take them long to fetch horses from the stables, and Cal led the way down one of the main streets, hoping to give them a better impression of his city.

Already there were preparations for the festival underway, the year's worth of dirt and grime being scrubbed off the buildings. Windows washed until they sparkled, giving the sun every speck of space to reflect light as the days grew shorter. Tiny pieces of sunstones that would have spent the height of summer absorbing sunlight were being strung over the streets from one roof to another. They wouldn't have nearly the same power as the larger sunstones that lit the streets, but they would sparkle like stars once night fell.

Between his father's death and the threat of Justice, he'd forgotten about the festival. The feast thrown for his sister's return may have lightened the hearts of the nobles, but the festival was for the city.

"What's all this for exactly?" Rashi asked, pointing at a sun catcher someone had hung from their roof, the slices of dried oranges hanging in a cascading spiral.

"It used to be a festival to release the sunlight harvested through summer, to get us safely through the shortest days. But that was Ages ago, before even the dragons disappeared. After the Wound formed and humans fled to us seeking help, it became more of a celebration of the end of the war. A time for new beginnings."

Rashi hummed softly, the sound dubious.

"What is it?"

"The humans celebrate too?"

"Of course, why?"

Rashi reined his horse to a stop and nodded towards a door adorned with a sun painted in black, a smear of red across it like blood. "Seems like it could be seen as celebrating all they lost."

Cal stared at the symbol, turning in his saddle and finding two more on other buildings nearby. "That's—" he started, but he didn't get a chance to say more as an arrow struck his shoulder, another whizzing by and spooking his horse into rearing.

"Fuck," he snarled, keeping his seat only thanks to Julius' mad insistence on him training to ride a wild horse. Some distant part of his mind recognized that was likely because Julius had Seen this exact moment, but the rest of him was scrambling to make sense of the sudden screaming and chaos on the street.

"Cal!" Rashi shouted, staring at him with wide eyes as arrows *thunk-thunk-thunked* against a barrier around them.

His horse stomped all four feet and tossed her head with a snort. "Go," he ordered. "Straight ahead, left at the Dawntree Inn."

Cal glanced at Haru as Rashi's horse surged ahead, trusting Haru to protect their backs as he took off behind Rashi.

He hadn't seen the attackers, but up ahead was someone in a black cloak, their hood pulled down to obscure their face. When they lifted a bow, he caught a glimpse of a black sun on their chest and he cursed. Sunlight answered his call, bursting around his fingers in a brilliant glow that lit even the shadows of the alleys as he threw it forward, catching the attacker in the face.

They fell back with a scream, fire licking the edges of their cloak. Even as they raced past, Cal spotted at least five more melting out of the shadows ahead, as if humans still possessed magic, with another standing from their spot on a roof.

"Haru!" he yelled, knowing he'd be unable to take them all. He pointed to the one on the roof even as he summoned more magic, but on a galloping horse, he'd be lucky to hit two of them.

They all lifted their bows at the same moment, and the unnaturalness of it sent a shiver of unease down his spine. They didn't have magic or they would have used it by now, but a thrashing, injured horse could cause just as much damage as a spell, especially with the chaos of people rushing for cover on the street.

"Rashi, down!" he called, aiming several more light spheres at the nearest three as Rashi crouched low over his horse's neck. One he caught in the face again, another the chest, and the last he got in the shoulder as they were releasing their arrow, sending the shot high enough it sailed over his head. Or it would have, if Haru's barrier hadn't stopped it first.

More thunks of blocked arrows echoed beside him, and at the same time a long white shard shot past him from behind, piercing one of the remaining attackers through the chest. They rushed by the last one, their arrow again deflected by Haru's shield, but as they rounded the corner by the inn, a line of cloaked figures spread across the street greeted them.

Their horses skidded to a stop, and as they turned, more figures melted from the shadows of the alleys to block them from behind.

Haru drew his sword with a guttural growl, turning his horse to stand between them and the attackers at their backs, the glimmer of his barriers surrounding the three of them on all sides.

"Death to the Vile," the figures chanted as one, lifting their bows. "Death to the Elf King. Death to the Sun."

"Oh, fuck this," Rashi snarled.

"Don't!" Haru shouted, but Rashi ignored him, an aura of green magic erupting around him. The earth trembled beneath them, making the horses toss their heads, eyes showing white as they spooked sideways.

Cal felt the gathering energy in the way the hairs on his arms stood on end.

"Rashi," he warned, catching the echo of Haru's dismay on the bond. That kind of power required more than a few moments to channel it without harm, and Rashi was still gathering more, his eyes glowing nearly white. "Rashi!"

Rashi tipped his head back on a scream, and the ground shuddered. Roots sprang from the ground, whipping through the air like beheaded snakes before lashing at the cloaked figures. They wrapped around legs and torsos, dragging the attackers to the ground. There was a spray of blood as one pierced through a neck like a sharp blade.

Between one breath and the next, the dozen figures were dead or restrained, and as the magical backlash shook the buildings around them, the roots retreated back into the ground, dragging corpses and thrashing bodies with them.

Rashi groaned and slumped forward, listing to the side, his ragged breathing loud in the sudden, echoing silence.

With a curse, Cal pulled his horse around, reaching out to steady him.

"Grab him," Haru ordered, and Rashi's body went lax a moment later. Cal hauled the near dead weight of the fox to his own horse despite the screaming agony in his shoulder. "Now move."

They needed to get back to the palace, but it was too far away, and going back the way they'd come meant they'd be easier to track. He pulled Rashi in close and took off down a side alley, getting off the main streets. There were fewer people here, though that was likely due to the terror and panic finally spreading enough to get people clear.

The stench of magic burning filled the air, and black smoke billowed above the buildings, but he couldn't stop to worry about that yet.

Either the attackers hadn't planned for them to move off the streets, or Rashi's magic was enough to warn them off, because they slipped free of the central trade district with only one more cloaked figure to stand in their way, which one of Haru's white shards took care of.

Cal didn't slow until they passed the tavern near the docks, turning onto the last street before stone could give way to the wood-plank paths and sands of the beach. He stopped in front of the barracks, guards shouting in alarm when they saw him. Several rushed forward to grab their reins. "Get a healer," he snapped, refusing to release Rashi to any of them. Only when Haru appeared beside him did he lower Rashi into his arms.

He slid from his horse, taking a stumbling step after Haru, before turning and lifting a hand to the sky. He closed his eyes, forcing the pain and worry aside enough to breathe deep and focus. He shaped the spell in his mind, carefully visualizing the old Elvish words. When he released the spell, fiery light spilled into the sky in bright script. *Black Sun in city.*

Then he turned towards the barracks with a quick glance to the horses and a subdued feeling of surprise at the sight of all three of them. Either Rashi's horse had followed, or Haru had grabbed it in the rush.

He tripped on the step leading inside, catching himself with a hand on the doorjamb. With the shock of the attack wearing off, his body was rebelling, fine tremors starting in his legs and hands, but he pushed through them and moved inside.

Haru had apparently claimed a table by sweeping a card game to the floor before laying Rashi on top of it.

"How is he?" he asked, freezing as he got a look for himself. Rashi's face was smeared with blood, though not from any injury he could see.

Haru wiped it away with a cloth he'd procured from somewhere, but more replaced it, oozing from Rashi's closed eyes and the corner of his mouth.

"What the hell is this?"

"Backlash," Haru said tightly, pressing his fingers against Rashi's forehead, and even Cal could feel the cold radiating from them.

Two guards hurried towards them, and he recognized Zaos with a flare of relief. "Your Majesty," Zaos said, pressing his fist across his chest in a quick salute. "What in darkness happened?"

"Atta—" Cal answered, blinking as his tongue refused to finish. "A-ta-er," he slurred. Only then did he realize that not all of the cold he felt was coming from Haru. It was spreading through his back and into his neck.

Haru turned towards him, eyes widening in alarm. "Cal?"

"Heh." He stumbled into Zaos with a soft laugh. "Frrrssst," he managed to get out, barely finishing the thought that Haru had finally called him by name for the first time, before he blacked out.

# CHAPTER 19

HE WAS burning, his entire body engulfed in flames. Smoke clogged his throat, and he couldn't cough, couldn't move, couldn't even draw breath to scream. Terror ravaged his mind. His skin blistered and burst as the flames grew hotter. His lungs caught fire, and then the flames were gone, along with everything else.

CONSCIOUSNESS WAS slow to return, and with it came a horrible headache. Cal turned his head with a groan and carefully cracked his eyes open, blinking in confusion when he found Vesryn sitting in a chair beside him.

"The fuck?" he croaked, grimacing as his tongue felt like it was about to crumble into sand.

"Oh, good morning to you, too, Your Royal Majesty," Vesryn replied, sounding testy, which meant he'd been sitting there a long time. He pressed a cup of water to Cal's lips, and he drank it all before closing his eyes to get his breath back.

When he looked at Vesryn a moment later, he was gone, replaced by Haru. "Am I dead?" he asked, wincing as he tried to sit up, only for his shoulder to give out on him. "Fuck, what did they poison me with?"

Haru gave him an unimpressed look, which was somehow more terrifying than the predatory ones he was getting used to. "You weren't poisoned."

Cal squinted at him, sure he had to be lying. "Then what was on the arrow?"

"Nothing. No spell, no poison. The edges were serrated. The healer said you must have passed out from blood loss."

That didn't sound right, but he knew how futile it was to argue against the healers. "How's Rashi?"

Haru blew an annoyed breath through his nose. "Recovering faster than you."

"Good," he said, taking a deep breath. This time when he sat up, he made it far enough to pitch himself to the side, supporting himself on his left shoulder. He fought the blankets until he got his legs free, then pushed into a sitting position. It put his back to Haru, but he didn't feel the need to look over his shoulder, since Haru moved to the door and stepped out.

He heard a murmur of voices, but he was too focused on getting to his feet to listen. Someone had dressed him in the simple cotton shirt and pants he usually slept in, which was better than being naked, especially since he wasn't sure he could dress himself without a bit more healing. His shoulder throbbed and ached with every breath, but it wasn't cold anymore. Now it burned, and he would have preferred to have the numbness back.

When he finally made his way out of the bedroom, he found Faelan sitting on the sofa.

Faelan stood and poured a cup of tea, offering it to him after Cal sank into his chair.

"Thank you," he murmured.

Faelan nodded and sat on the edge of the sofa. "Juls and Duaia are on their way back."

"From?" he asked, taking a sip of the tea.

"Justice was spotted near one of the old temples, right before you were attacked yesterday."

"Yesterday?" Cal glanced out the window. It'd been morning the last time he woke, he was sure, but now it was nearing high sun, a full day after the attack. "Did they catch him?"

"No. They've been searching ever since, but with the chaos and the murder—"

"Murder?" Cal hissed. "Who died this time?"

Faelan clasped his hands together. "The elder historian," he answered softly. "Yrasne."

Cal nearly lost his grip on his cup. He'd spent countless hours in the city library with Yrasne as a child, pestering her for books with the best stories and legends. She wasn't as old as their elder lorekeeper, whose role was to record and remember those stories, but she was still an elder and should have had sufficient protections from any kind of an attack.

"How?"

Faelan shook his head. "I just know it was during the attack, when people were fleeing the streets and seeking safety anywhere they could."

The guestroom door opened, distracting him from asking more questions.

"The sorceress will have more information by now," Haru said, shifting to help Rashi shuffle into the room. The fox was pale, leaning all his weight into Haru, but at least he wasn't leaking blood anymore.

Cal breathed a soft sigh of relief, lifting his free hand towards Rashi, hissing as his shoulder punished him for the movement.

Rashi shuffled faster, detaching from Haru to topple into Cal's lap.

"You even think of trying to heal him, I am letting the sorceress put you to sleep for a week," Haru growled, before sitting across from Faelan on the other sofa.

Rashi grumbled under his breath and tucked himself against Cal's chest.

Cal pressed his face into Rashi's hair, rubbing his cheek against a soft ear. "You were reckless," he murmured, letting Faelan take his tea so he could settle both arms around Rashi.

"He's always reckless," Haru said, still glaring at Rashi as if he expected the fox to try to heal Cal.

"Only when I need to be," Rashi replied, and Cal had a sudden, vivid portent of how his life could be.

They managed to enjoy a few minutes of quiet before the door was thrown open and Duaia stalked in, Julius and a healer close behind.

Cal shuddered with relief when the healer moved towards him, letting out a slow breath when the deep ache finally began to ease.

Duaia stood near the table where she could see everyone and explained what he'd missed.

Just before the attack, they'd received word that Justice had been spotted going into the old temple, but before Duaia could gather enough guards and investigate, dozens of robed figures had filled the streets all across the city. They'd shot arrows at anyone within range, humans and nonhumans alike, inciting panic as they echoed the same chant.

*Death to the Vile.*

"It's the Black Sun," Cal said softly, his tension easing a bit as the worst of his injury healed, the pain fading to an unpleasant throb.

"Yes," Duaia said, and Cal could feel the malice radiating off her.

"What's the Black Sun?" Rashi asked.

"It's what the Shadow King called his most loyal followers," Haru answered.

"Those who were willing to pledge themselves to the shadows," Julius added. "It let him seize control of their minds."

"What, like slave collars?" Rashi asked, face twisting with disgust.

"We're pretty sure that's where the idea of slave collars came from."

Duaia nodded. "Except only the blood of the Shadow King should be able to control them."

Cal tensed. "Is Justice a descendant, then?"

"No," Haru said firmly. "The king's line is dead."

Cal nudged one of Rashi's ears aside with his chin so he could see Haru. "How are you sure? Draekor's body was never found. Neither was his son's."

Haru flexed his fingers over his knees. "I killed Sorren myself."

Rashi jerked upright with a sharp "Oh." He scrambled out of Cal's lap and crashed onto the sofa beside Haru, reaching over to clasp his hand. "I didn't know that's…."

"I didn't realize until later," Haru said quietly, tensing when he noticed everyone's eyes on him. He stared at Rashi's hands on his for a long moment before explaining how, three hundred years ago, a Fate bond appeared.

Cal listened with quiet horror forming in his gut. If he'd doubted that Fate saw them as Her playthings before, he was certainly convinced of it by the time Haru finished. "So not only did Fate intervene to ensure his bloodline ended, She also forgot there was another heir somewhere?" he growled.

What other explanation could there be? There were no signs of other humans using shadow magic.

Duaia cleared her throat. "Not that this isn't information that I'm glad to have, but we need to focus."

She glanced at the healer, still hovering beside Cal, and he realized his shoulder was as restored as it could be without Rashi's magic. He trusted Duaia to have ensured the healer was no spy, but they couldn't afford to take any risks.

Julius caught his eye and straightened where he leaned against the sofa behind Faelan. "How's the shoulder?"

The healer startled. "Oh, it should be good now," she said, before motioning to Rashi. "Do you need assistance as well?"

Rashi waved a hand at her. "I just need rest," he said, ignoring Haru's snort as he gave the healer a serene smile.

Once she slipped out of the room, Cal focused on Duaia in time to see her sway slightly on her feet. She looked even more exhausted than Rashi, dark smudges under her eyes belying how little rest she'd been getting.

He reached for the threshold, surprised by how quickly it responded to him, as if it were eagerly awaiting his intentions. He barely needed more than a thought about wanting the room sealed for privacy before several spells flared and hummed to life, blocking sound and magical interference. Even obscuring sight from outside the windows.

He glanced at Haru and didn't miss the brief, smug expression before he focused on Duaia again. He wanted to order her to sit down, but he suspected being upright was the only thing keeping her awake.

"What else happened?" he asked. "Faelan told me about Yrasne."

Duaia's lips thinned. "Did he tell you about the fires?"

When he shook his head, she took a breath as if bracing herself.

"Some of the attackers had spelled arrows. They lit them on fire and attacked the north river granary. The flames burned through the protection wards, along with over half of its stores."

"He intends to starve us out? What about the Waterside granary?"

"They emptied it out the night before the attack."

"Fuck," Cal whispered. Between that and the crops failing, winter was going to be harsh even if they called off the festival.

"Not just that," she added, though Cal's bitter laugh interrupted her.

"How could there possibly be anything else?"

She continued as if he hadn't spoken. "Over a quarter of the human workers didn't show up today, and not a single one to work the fields."

"They left the city?"

"Seems that way. They may have been part of the Black Sun, but they might have just been scared and left."

Cal rubbed his forehead. "You said fires," he murmured. "Where were the others?"

When Duaia didn't immediately answer, he looked up. Her light brown skin had turned almost ashen, and she blinked too-bright eyes, but it was Julius who answered.

"The library is gone."

Even preparing himself for the worst, the news left him breathless.

The city library was built in the second-largest ylren tree in the kingdom, second only to the palace, and nearly as old. Both had stood for over seven Ages, since before Ysildea founded the city and claimed the Sun Throne. He'd gotten lost in the library's bookcases and the biggest tomes he could find every chance he could, and now all those books, all those stories, all that history, was gone.

The palace library had copies of the most important, most vital books, and the Vault had originals or diaries with guarded secrets, and courtiers would have some of the more interesting or entertaining ones in private collections. Others in the magical community would have copies of their own histories, but he knew only a portion could ever be rebuilt, and the loss of the entire history of their culture was like losing his father and mother all over again.

"Cal," Rashi whispered, his warm fingers running through Cal's hair. "It'll be all right."

He blinked his eyes open, though he didn't remember closing them or hunching over his knees. His chest and stomach ached, and he could barely draw breath through his constricted throat.

"It can't be gone," he gasped. "*How?*" The library should have had even more protections than the granary, wards that should have prevented even a candle from catching fire inside.

"In the chaos, so many were rushing to get off the street, Yrasne was taken," Faelan answered. "They paralyzed her, collared her, and forced her to lower the wards and protections. Some of those who first saw the fires said robed figures were throwing bottles onto the shelves that erupted into walls of flames."

"We don't know what they paralyzed her with," Julius said, sinking onto the sofa and slumping into Faelan, looking decades older. "They left her there…. She was so badly burned they wouldn't have even found the puncture if not for the way the skin on her back wasn't touched by the flames."

"She burned to death," Cal echoed, remembering the nightmare after he blacked out. It had felt real, in the way all nightmares felt real, but then there was Taegen and the dagger in his chest, in the same spot he'd been pressing against before the feast.

"Fuck," he whispered. When he'd performed the ritual to ascend the throne, there'd been that moment when he was connected to all the elves in his kingdom. If he could sense their lives, why wouldn't he sense their deaths?

"I felt her die." He clutched Rashi's hand as it settled over his own. "I felt them both die."

Had his father felt it when elves died? How many had disappeared into the depths of the prison, never to be seen again? If his father had known, he would have put a stop to it, unless….

"The ring Justice gave my father," he said. "It was a collar, wasn't it?"

Duaia didn't need to answer, the glower on her face was confirmation enough.

Justice truly had managed to collar the king. Then tormented him for years as he slowly decimated their community. Now he'd somehow re-formed the most abhorrent faction of humans and destroyed the pillar of their entire civilization.

And what had Cal done to stop any of it? What could he do? Short of forcing every human out of the city, into the Wound, or farther up the coast? The city was large, and the roots of the ylren trees formed countless caves and tunnel systems in the underground. Justice and his Black Suns could be anywhere, and now they had the supplies to stay hidden for weeks.

That couldn't happen. Justice had been steps ahead of them for years, but that ended now.

"Liria is still helping Aelin?" he asked.

"Yes. They're making good progress," Julius said.

"Which temple was Justice seen in? Waterside?" he guessed, unsurprised when Duaia nodded; it was the only one built into one of the smaller ylren trees, with access to the elaborate tunnels beneath.

"You're to take the rest of the day and rest. That's an order, for both of you," he said, pointing at Duaia and Julius. "You're no help to anyone if you burn out. I don't care if you're a sorceress. Magic cannot replace sleep." He ignored Rashi's amusement along the bond as he repeated the fox's own words.

"And what do you plan to do?" Julius asked, watching him suspiciously.

"I'm getting Liria from the prison, and we're going to the temple. Maybe find some of those attackers who were dragged underground with your reckless spell," he added to Rashi.

"We already found them," Duaia said. "Two are even still alive."

That made things easier, though he wasn't counting on that luck holding out.

"You're not going to the prison alone," Julius said, narrowing his eyes when Cal started to protest. "No."

"We'll go with him," Rashi said.

Cal shook his head. "You need to rest too."

Rashi leaned back where he'd sat on the arm of Cal's chair. "I wasn't asking permission."

Cal hissed softly and glanced at Haru. He didn't appear any more pleased than Cal felt, but he didn't try to persuade Rashi otherwise. "Only to the prison," he said, pretending Rashi agreed instead of giving him a placating smile.

Within the hour, Duaia and Julius were dead asleep in the guestroom, Faelan watching over them from the sitting room, and Cal was in a carriage with Rashi and Haru, once again on his way to the prison. This time with six of his kingsguard riding beside them.

After the attack, Duaia had called most of them back from the prison to take up their rightful duty. The unrest in the city echoed inside him as they passed through empty streets. The stench of smoke still lingered in the air, and he swallowed against the bile threatening to rise up his throat. So much destruction and loss, and for what? Centuries old hatred and prejudice?

This was supposed to be an Age of peace, despite the Wound sitting as a stark reminder of the price paid for that peace on both sides.

"What are you needing Liria for?" Rashi asked.

Cal pulled his thoughts away from the city and his failures and turned to the fox. "I'm hoping there's something in the temple we can use to track Justice. Or if we need to interrogate his men, they'll give up some information."

"And when you find him?" Haru asked.

"He'll be executed." Despite how much he hated executions, he couldn't find any dismay about ordering one. Justice had more than earned the punishment, along with anyone who helped him.

The carriage finally bounced from cobblestone to gravel and came to a stop a few minutes later. Two of his kingsguard were posted at the entrance, and when this mess was finally over, he'd need to give them time off duty.

One of his men led them inside to his cousins, where they'd set up in an office near the kitchens, sitting beside each other at a table. Elwin stood a few feet behind them, wearing the expected expression of someone forced to endure Aelin flirting with any creature who breathed for days on end.

A centaur stood across from them. Her hands were clasped in Aelin's, his sunstone glowing with soft gold light beneath their fingers.

"And you didn't step on Lord Whatshisface's foot and break it?" he asked.

"Oh, I did do that. He called me an over-bred horse and suggested he could show me a better time with his tiny human cock. I've seen worms that are bigger," she replied with a familiar cackle.

Cal stared at her in surprise. Kephine was a well-respected centaur, and the only one of her kind that he knew of to ever love the sea enough to captain a fishing vessel. It'd gone missing a few months ago, rumored to have been taken by a summer storm. She'd lost weight, and there were pale scars marring her glossy ebony flanks, likely from a whip, but she was still the raunchy pirate-turned-captain he knew.

"Well, I'd say he deserved it, then," Aelin said, releasing her hands as the glow faded. "And the true crime has been your deep-sea urchins missing from the market." He grinned and winked, and Cal fought back a groan, moving forward to interrupt.

"Kephine," he greeted. "It's good to see you again. I'm sorry I ever believed you were lost at sea."

A fierce scowl crossed her dark features. "Aye, that's a load of bollocks. A siren would sooner drown afore I let a storm take my ship."

"We'll do what we can to see it returned to you."

"Thank you, Your Majesty," she said with a bow, before following Elwin when he motioned for her. She paused as she noticed Rashi and Haru behind him, her eyes widening as she stared at the dragon. Her ears flattened and her back hoof twitched as if instinctively trying to move away, before she deliberately planted it.

"Kephine," he said gently, "I'd like you to meet Haru and Rashi, my bondeds." He shifted so he could face the three of them, lightly resting his hand on Rashi's shoulder. "This is Kephine, captain of the Fleeted Hoof."

Rashi's eyes lit up with a smile. "I've never been on the sea."

Kephine's wary gaze remained on Haru a moment longer, before she looked at Rashi. "We'll have to change that, soon as I find my ship," she replied. "Glad to see you finally found your bonded. I shouldn't be surprised that if anyone were to bring dragons back into the realm, it would be you," she added, carefully stepping around them with a quick dip of a bow.

She clasped Elwin's shoulder, demanding he point her to her nearest crewmate on their way out.

"What's going on now?" Aelin asked once the door closed. "Don't tell me the city's been flooded this time. Or maybe you've found a unicorn?" he added, glancing at Haru with a grin.

Cal knew better than to let Aelin provoke him, so he ignored the teasing completely. "No. I need to borrow Liria for a few hours."

Aelin shifted from his chair to sit on the edge of the table, propping a foot in his vacated seat. "And why does she get to go on some grand adventure and not me?"

Cal raised an eyebrow. "Would you prefer to come instead?"

"No, but it would be nice to be asked first," Aelin replied with a sniff. "Besides, the next prisoner is some wolf beastkin. I don't want to miss hearing his tale."

Liria tipped her head back with a soft groan and shot Cal a look that pleaded for rescue.

"There's a wolf here?" Rashi asked, his ears twitching forward with interest.

"I'm sure they'd have put a fucking siren in here if there was a pool," Cal said with a soft snarl.

Aelin winced. "There is, and we've already freed them. Why they thought they could get away with imprisoning a siren when the sea is *right there*," he muttered, shaking his head.

"Well, you enjoy listening to more stories of how the humans have thoroughly proven to be worse than monsters. I'm going to go get blown up. Again," Liria replied brightly, swinging her scepter around as she stood and accidentally on purpose catching Aelin's knee with the end, before neatly side-stepping his retaliatory kick.

Cal ignored the comment and the antics and turned to leave.

"Tell the wolf I'd like to meet him," Rashi called as he followed.

"Sure, I'll send him right to the palace," Aelin replied.

Cal stifled a groan, knowing he actually meant that.

When they reached the carriage, he motioned Rashi and Haru inside, but Rashi stopped and stared at him with a frown.

"You're not planning on getting in."

"No, I'm going with Liria to the temple," he replied, lightly resting his hand against the side of Rashi's neck when he lifted his chin to protest. "You need rest. We still need you to fix the crops if you can, and you can't do that if you you're still burned out."

Especially if they were attacked again and Rashi responded with that same level of magic. Not that he wasn't grateful, but if Rashi used that spell again soon, he likely wouldn't recover.

"I do not appreciate being handled, Callith," Rashi replied, pushing Cal's hand away. "But fine. I could use a nap." He climbed into the carriage and slid to the far side to make room for Haru beside him.

Haru stopped and leaned in close enough to whisper, "Bring back something sweet and he might forgive you," before settling in the carriage with a smirk.

Cal sighed and closed the door, watching as it took off for the palace with two of his kingsguard as an escort, while the other four remained with him.

"So, to the temple, then," Liria said, lightly brushing her fingers over the sunstone on her scepter. "Hoping to find something I can use to track them?"

Cal nodded, accepting the reins of a horse and pulling himself up. "Let's go."

# CHAPTER 20

THE TEMPLE was the smallest ylren tree in the city, though the four granaries weren't much larger. With the loss of the library, the only other ylren tree besides those and the palace was the academy, which was half the size of the palace. Both the temple and academy grew in valleys of the greater ylren tree's roots, which had been shaped and trained with magic Ages ago to provide shelter and guide rainwater to sustain the smaller trees.

Outside of the winter solstice festival to celebrate the sun's slow return, the temple was used as a sanctuary. A place of quiet solitude available to anyone in the city. The temple was empty now, their footsteps echoing in the deepest recesses of living wood.

The scent of smoke lingered, and there was a heaviness in the air Cal had never felt before. His skin prickled with disquiet and he flexed his fingers, warmth filling the spaces between them.

Liria's sunstone flared with her own magic, casting long shadows until she forced the brightness to recede.

"Why do I feel like that scepter should have been left in the Vault?" he muttered as they carefully made their way farther into the temple.

"Because you have no sense of adventure."

Cal scoffed. "My bondeds were accused of murder. I was hit with backlash while removing a slave collar. Humans are inciting civil war and murdering elders. And I was shot with an arrow. I don't need more adventure."

"Well, you're getting some anyway, because that's blood." Liria bounded into the smaller room with the air of an excited puppy, stepping around a crude circle etched into the floor with a star in the center.

The smell of smoke was stronger here, and he traced the source to a pile of ash in the center of the circle.

"What is this?" he asked, stopping beside Liria when she crouched, tapping a small bottle with the end of her scepter.

"Some kind of ritual," she said, carefully picking up the bottle. The insides were coated in dark red, and when she sniffed it, she grimaced.

"Blood. It's still fresh, but these feel like old preservation spells. Whosever it is, I can find them. Or at least whoever used the blood."

"Do it," Cal said. The sooner they found Justice or anyone else responsible, the sooner they could focus on restoring the city.

Liria set the bottle and scepter aside before pulling her small dagger free from her wrist sheath. She made a quick cut across her fingertip, squeezing a bit of blood into her palm. Then she picked up the bottle and spilled the last few drops of blood inside next to her own. She mixed them both with her thumb and smeared it across the scepter's sunstone.

With barely a word, the stone flared with brilliant white light, filling the room with heat and an almost inaudible ringing sound.

Cal squeezed his watering eyes shut and threw an arm over them, but it didn't help. The amount of magical power was suffocating, easily more than twice what Rashi had summoned, and he feared he'd find Liria dead when it finally faded.

The magic winked out with enough force he felt his teeth vibrate, and he staggered from the sudden change in pressure, crashing to the ground on a knee. He braced himself for the backlash, but there was nothing more. Only an echoing stillness, until his kingsguard rushed in, swords drawn, looking as disoriented as he felt.

"It's fine," he said, lifting a hand and pushing to his feet. He was relieved to find Liria still standing and unharmed. More relieved still when he saw the faint golden wave of magic emanating from the sunstone, stretching deeper into the temple. "You found him?"

Liria nodded, running her fingers through the wave in awe. "I think it's whoever used the blood."

"Justice, then," Cal growled, flexing his fingers.

Finally they could end this. He couldn't imagine Justice was capable of all of this on his own, but getting rid of even one snake was a start.

He looked over his men, recognizing three of them. Thallan, Rina, and Aire had served him for years. The other was new enough he didn't know the elf's name, so Cal pointed to him, unwilling to take him farther without knowing him better. "Let Faelan know what's happening, and bring a dozen of the guard to start searching the tunnels here."

Liria was already disappearing into a deeper alcove, and he hurried after her, the rest of his kingsguard close behind. He wrote a quick sigil in his mind and set it above the entrance to one of the many tunnels branching beneath the roots of the temple. The soft light would mark the path they'd taken, drawing on the ambient magic in the air to sustain itself for the next several hours.

Then he descended into the darkness, following the glow of the staff ahead of him.

Ages ago these tunnels would have served as safety through the nights and storage for food and weapons. Now they were all but forgotten, thick with dirt and clumps of foliage growing in the rare slash of dimmed sunlight.

The path was winding, dipping under large ylren roots as it went deeper underground. He trusted his guards to be marking their path as the air grew stale and heavy with the smell of damp earth, the tunnels narrowing enough that even one person struggled to get through at points. The light of the sunstone continued guiding them deeper, until the roots finally lifted up and away from them, revealing an area not unlike the Vault beneath the palace, shaped by magic and divided into smaller chambers.

And there, near the entrance, was light shining beneath a door.

The wave of magic brightened, stretching through the door before fading completely.

Cal started for it, but Liria and his kingsguard stopped him.

"You are King now," she hissed. "Bad enough you came here, but I'm not losing my head because I let something happen to you."

"And I'm not going to continue standing back and doing nothing while he destroys my city," Cal snarled, shoving past them. "Search the other chambers. If Justice is really here, the Black Sun should be close."

He stopped in front of the door with the light. If this was a trap, this would be the perfect place for an ambush, but he heard nothing aside from the others close behind him.

He summoned magic around his hand. He couldn't make a barrier like Haru or call on the trees around them like Rashi, but sun magic had its uses, and Liria was right. He couldn't be reckless. Certainly not after he'd asked Rashi not to be reckless again.

Closing his eyes, he focused his intentions on the light shining from his hand, manipulating it until it formed an image of himself in the air in front of him. It wasn't perfect. Anyone who looked close enough could see that it wasn't solid, but it would work well enough to give them the advantage if there was a trap.

He opened the door, and his image half walked, half glided through. The others shifted behind him, ready to defend and retaliate against any attack, but there was nothing.

Thallan slipped past him, and Cal followed close behind, the image of himself wavering as it moved to keep in front of them both.

The chamber was small, with bookcases lining two walls on either side of the door. A table covered in books, scrolls, and jars of amber liquid was shoved against the back, and slumped in a chair in the corner was Justice.

His eyes were closed and his skin was ashen, black veins creeping up his neck and around his eyes. His chest moved with wheezing breaths, and Cal didn't need a healer to tell him the human was dying.

He let his image fade as Thallan moved towards Justice, prodding him with his sword.

Justice stirred with a groan of protest. His rheumy eyes fluttered open, but it took a moment for him to focus on any of them. When his gaze landed on Cal, he jerked forward with a snarl.

"No," he rasped. "You should be dead."

"So sorry to disappoint," Cal replied. He stayed where he was, studying Justice and wondering just how the human had masked his hatred for them for so long. How any of the humans had lived beside them for centuries with this kind of hate festering in their core.

Despite humans attempting to annihilate every magical species that crossed their path, his father had offered them shelter after the war, after they'd created the Wound and lost their magic with whatever ritual or spell they'd tried to cast.

Cal had wondered sometimes if that had been a mistake. Even in the three decades he'd lived, there had been those few humans who tried to rally others to their cause. To leave the city and form their own. To protest that magic was unnatural, when their own lack of magic was the most unnatural thing in the realm besides the Wound.

Seeing Justice now, ravaged by whatever spell he'd cast that must have given him control over the Black Sun, Cal almost felt pity. A strange mix of disappointment and relief filled him as he realized he wouldn't need to publicly execute Justice. The man likely wouldn't even live long enough to get out of the temple.

"It's over," he said, hoping that were true, that with Justice gone, any of his supporters would fall silent. At least for long enough that Cal could hunt them down.

Thallan grabbed Justice's arm and hauled him to his feet.

"No," Justice snarled, stumbling and catching himself against the desk. His hand landed near a bottle of liquid, nearly tipping it over, and the way his expression twisted into deranged glee was their only warning, but it was enough that terror twisted in Cal's gut, remembering that bottles had started the fire in the library.

"Get out!" Cal shouted, as Justice picked up the bottle and smashed it on the floor.

Blue-white flames erupted as it shattered. Thallan screamed as he was caught in them, his attempts to put them out only spreading them farther and faster.

Cal doubled over as an echo of Thallan's pain ripped through him.

"Out!" Liria screamed.

Hands grabbed him and pulled him out of the chamber. "No!" he yelled, though he knew Thallan was already gone.

Justice stood still among the flames, his eyes glowing black as he stared at Cal, a cruel smile twisting his face, before the other bottles on the desk exploded and the entire chamber vanished beneath a surge of roiling flames.

"Run!" Liria shoved at Cal's back as Rina and Aire dragged him towards the exit by his arms, before he finally got his feet under him and his shock receded enough for him to think.

A quick glance back showed the flames weren't stopping. They were already eating their way through the other chambers and the roots forming the cavern, moving far faster than a natural fire.

They'd barely squeezed into the tunnels before the heat and smoke chased after them.

The path was marked with smaller sigils similar to the one he left at the entrance, but before they even reached the incline to start back to the surface, the smoke caught them. The heat was a breath behind, spreading unnaturally fast and pressing down on them.

Cal coughed, his heart thudding painfully as panic sliced through him. *Fuck.* He already couldn't see the next marker through the smoke. One wrong turn and they'd be lost for good, if the fire didn't catch them first.

He called on his magic as he stumbled forward, heating the air near their feet in an effort to circulate and push the smoke higher, but that only served to swirl it around them, the heat of the fire eating through the roots above them rushing closer.

*Fuck.*

He sank to the floor where the smoke was thinner and managed half a breath of damp air, closing his eyes and searching for the magic in the sigils. He sensed something else instead, a press of dark, cool magic reaching out for them.

Siren magic. There was water nearby.

"Get to the river," he called, choking on a lungful of smoke. His vision and concentration wavered, and he pulled his tunic over his face to help block the smoke. They had to move. The flames were getting close enough to throw light into the tunnel.

He crawled to the right, sure the water magic was emanating from that direction, but he couldn't see through the clouds of smoke.

Bright light flared around them, and for a moment he thought that was the end, the fire had reached them, but it was only Liria's scepter. The sunstone illuminated the area enough for him to see a gap in the roots, and he lurched towards it.

A few steps in and the dirt walls became more solid, like paved stone, broken by roots that had pushed through over the years. The heat and smoke diminished considerably, but they wouldn't be stopped for long.

He glanced back to see three coughing figures behind him before he continued on.

The path slanted down, winding around a large root, and immediately fell away. Terror jolted through him as his foot fell through empty air. He scrabbled for purchase on the root and held on long enough for the others to haul him back up.

"Fuck," he hissed.

Liria leaned forward, holding out her scepter and shining light over the edge. Water glimmered in the depths below. Very far below.

"We have to jump."

"Have you lost your mind?" Liria glared at him, and he remembered she couldn't swim. Despite all of Julius' efforts to teach her, she'd refused to enter any body of water bigger than a bath.

He coughed as the smoke caught up to them again. "We can't stay here. There's a siren nearby," he said, though by her grimace, she knew as well as he did that was no guarantee the siren would help.

They had a peace treaty, just like all creatures who had sought safe harbor in his kingdom after the war, but aside from the fishing vessels and riverside markets that traded with them, sirens didn't interact much with any land dwellers.

"Fuck, I'd rather be eaten than choke to death," Rina said.

Cal couldn't quite agree with that sentiment, but he wasn't going to die here when a path was still open to them.

Rina stepped over him and leaped off the edge. A long moment passed before there was a distant splash, and another moment, infinitely longer, before they heard a triumphant shout.

Aire clasped Cal's shoulder and followed.

Cal took a breath, gripping Liria's hand as the smoke and heat of the fire bore down on them.

"Fucking Julius is never going to let this go."

Cal smiled faintly. "Ready?"

"No," she snarled.

"Oh, good." He tightened his grip on her hand and tipped forward off the edge, pulling her with him, her ear-piercing screams certainly signaling their position to any sirens in the vicinity.

Then they hit the water and everything went quiet and muffled. He kicked back towards the surface and hoped it was the right direction, his lungs burning with the need for air even before the fall.

When he finally broke the surface, he sucked in a deep lungful of cool air, nearly going under again as Liria grabbed him around his neck. Rina and Aire latched on to her, supporting her between them.

"Now what?" Rina asked.

Cal opened his mouth to say he didn't know yet, when the light of the scepter caught quicksilver movement below them. His heart lurched into his throat as a siren surfaced, watching them with dark blue-gray eyes.

"King Callith," she said, her grin revealing a mouthful of sharp silver teeth.

Cal nearly flinched at the sight, turning it into a polite smile instead. "You have me at a disadvantage. I'm afraid I don't know your name."

Her grin grew even wider. "I am Rhaelopei, niece to Queen Adrene."

Suddenly, death by fire seemed a better alternative. "I'd very much like to speak with your queen. It's recently come to my attention that some of your people were being held in my prison."

"Yes," she said, "that is why I am here."

She ducked under the water and swam closer, surfacing less than an arm's length away. "Our people returned with alarming information. Your city is under siege. By humans." Her lips twisted in disgust. "I have a school of our best fighters. We will help you."

Cal couldn't hide his surprise completely. "And in return?"

Rhaelopei narrowed her eyes at him. "Humans are a threat to us as much as you. If you fall, we will certainly be next. Now come. It is a long way to the surface."

She swam up to him faster than seemed possible, grabbing his face with both hands and pressing her lips against his.

Magic washed over him as the Siren's Kiss granted him the ability to breathe underwater. She released him as quickly as she had grabbed him, before swimming to the others to bestow on them the same gift.

As she finished the last of them, the fire breached the paved walls above. They burst from the pressure of the heat, chunks of rock and root raining down on them.

"Down!" he shouted, then dove.

Fiery pieces of debris struck the water and continued to burn with the magic that caused the flames.

Rhaelopei swam to each of them, linking their arms together, before grabbing Cal's free hand and taking off, deeper into the water.

His lungs ached, refusing to trust in the magic he could feel wrapped around his body. It wasn't until the burning need for air overcame his fear of drowning that his lungs finally tried to draw breath. He nearly sobbed with relief when the magic worked and he didn't inhale water.

Only when the ache in his lungs eased did he notice Liria's fingers digging painfully into his arm, sure her nails had drawn blood. The sunstone still glowed on the scepter and lit the waters around them.

His stomach lurched when he caught the shadow of something huge moving in the depths, and he squeezed his eyes shut. If something decided to eat them, he'd rather not see it coming. It was terrifying enough to have the siren queen's niece pulling them through open waters.

He'd have to request an audience with the queen herself and ensure the treaty held despite humans imprisoning her subjects. If they made it back to the surface.

He wasn't sure how much time passed, his senses dulled by the pressure of water all around him. He just knew the longer they were in the water, more of the temple would burn, and more chance for the fire to spread to the rest of the city.

He trusted someone would see it before that happened, but the temple was the third ylren tree to be attacked, and they were all as important to the magical community as they were sacred.

None of the eight ylren trees had blossomed in over three Ages. Not since before the old creatures that haunted the nights began vanishing. Now there were only five left fully intact in the entire realm. Their destruction was as unforgivable as the slave collars.

If even now humans were determined to destroy the last inhabitable area on this side of the Wound, they couldn't be allowed to stay.

The pressure around them seemed to lessen, and he cracked his eyes open to see hints of light filtering from above. He let out a shaky breath of relief as the surface finally appeared. Then they broke through, and he was able to breathe actual air again.

Liria spluttered beside him as she came up, followed by Rina and Aire, who helped pull Liria to the edge of the canal they'd come up in.

He turned back to Rhaelopei, blinking in surprise to find her only a breath away.

"My queen will be here in two days," she said. "Until then, we will help."

She motioned farther down the canal where the river curved near the temple. Several sirens were there, guiding streams of water onto the flames. A dozen of his own men and city guards had formed a line to haul water in buckets, protecting the surrounding area against catching fire.

"Thank you," he said.

She smiled, silver teeth glittering in the light, before she sank back underwater and was gone.

Cal swam to the edge of the bank and grabbed Aire's hand. He'd barely gotten his feet back on dry land before a carriage raced down the street, narrowly missing knocking them back into the water.

As it jostled to a stop, the door flew open and Rashi tumbled out.

"What's wrong?" Cal demanded, meeting the fox as he rushed forward. The burst of relief that washed over him from the bond as Rashi crashed into his chest was staggering.

"You're all right," Rashi gasped.

His confusion only grew when Haru stepped out of the carriage. "What happened?"

"Apparently, you nearly died. At least three times," Haru replied, slipping his hands into his voluminous sleeves as he stood nearby, looking Cal over with a critical eye. "You seem fine to me."

"I wouldn't say I'm completely fine," he murmured, eyeing the thick smoke rising from the temple.

The flames were under control, at least, though he doubted much would be salvageable once they were put out.

The afternoon had barely started and he was already exhausted. And as much as he wanted to let Duaia and Julius rest, now that Justice was dead, they needed to figure out their next steps. He desperately hoped that with Justice dead and the vial of blood in their possession, no one else would be able to control the Black Sun.

"We need to get back to the palace." He turned and found Liria leaning heavily against her scepter. "You still have the rest of the blood?"

She reached into her pocket and pulled out the small vial, whatever spells were woven into it enough to have kept it from shattering.

Without letting go of Rashi, he turned to Rina and Aire. "Report to whoever has taken command here. Let them know I've gone to speak with Duaia."

He motioned for Liria to join him in the carriage, letting her get settled before sitting across from her, Rashi stuck to his side as if he'd never let go.

"I'm fine," he murmured, running his fingers through Rashi's hair and stroking along the base of his ears.

"You nearly died," Rashi snapped, his face buried against Cal's shoulder despite the water still dripping from his clothes.

He couldn't deny that. "Yeah," he said softly, pressing his fingers against his temple. "We'll explain everything when we're back at the palace if you want to hear." He was sure D would try to lock him in his rooms after this, but at least he had the excuse to leave in two days to meet the siren queen.

Haru sat next to Liria, watching Cal through narrowed eyes. It was the familiar predatory look, but he could almost see the concern lurking in the expression.

The carriage lurched forward, the slight rocking familiar enough that he relaxed, closing his eyes so he could catch his breath.

"Chances of them having more of those bottles of fire?" he asked quietly.

Liria made a sound somewhere between a grunt and a curse. "Probably very likely."

He was afraid of that.

As much as it hurt to lose another ylren tree, they needed to ensure the remaining ones were protected against fire. The spells would be easy enough to put in place, they would have already been woven into the thresholds Ages ago. But peace bred complacency, and that complacency ended today, even if he had to go through every building himself. Which, now that he thought about it, he likely would.

Thresholds on public spaces usually didn't hold long, but now that he'd taken the crown, the city belonged to him, and he had a clear intention of protecting his people from a specific threat. He just had to believe that would be enough if Justice's death didn't end this.

When the carriage finally rolled to a stop and they climbed out, he decided to put his theory to the test. The palace might be the largest ylren tree in existence, but its boundaries were his home. Not just the palace itself, but the courtyards and gardens and stables surrounding it had been his sanctuary until he was old enough to venture past them on his own.

The wall of living roots that served as the border between the palace and the city rose up on either side of him as he stopped inside the gate. He pressed his hands to one side, tipping his head forward to rest against the ancient wood. He pushed a slow breath out of his lungs, reaching for the threshold as he would reach for the ley lines.

A moment later, he felt them shiver and respond, as if the magic itself were waking from a long, deep slumber.

"There you are," he whispered, nearly dizzy with the possibilities if this worked.

He reached deeper, tapping into the ley lines and coaxing the magic through him to strengthen the threshold. There was a moment of resistance before the magic surged through him, answering his call to protect against fire, against intruders, against the shadows wreaking havoc in his city. Those intentions were already there, dormant like he'd thought, and they brightened to a near blinding glow even behind his closed eyes.

He heard Rashi's soft laugh of delight and Liria cursing at the influx of magic and Haru's soft hum that felt like approval.

The magic rushed through him into the roots forming the threshold, igniting the spells woven into the roots next to them, on and on around the entire grounds, then up into the ylren tree itself. The air hummed as the magic grew brighter, until color itself washed away beneath the brilliant golden-white light.

He was tempted to reach farther, into the still living roots of the previous ylren tree that had been sacrificed to form the walls of the city itself. It would be easy from here, to connect everything as it once had been Ages ago. Before the war. Before most of their elders and knowledge were lost. Before old enemies had proven to be patient enough to lurk in their midst, with hate and loathing festering for three hundred years.

As if sensing his intentions despite the lack of a completed Fate bond, Haru said, "That's enough."

Cal huffed and finally let the magic fade. The light diminished, though the roots continued to glow a soft amber not unlike Haru's eyes.

He straightened and turned, groaning as his entire body protested being used as a conduit, especially after the abuse he'd already put it through. His nerves tingled and burned with the residual magic, though he knew trying to expel it would only exacerbate the pain.

He breathed deep as he walked, smiling as Rashi's hand slipped into his own.

"That was both amazing and stupid," Liria said dryly.

"You can have an opinion on my stupidity when you learn how to swim," he replied, ignoring her glare as he headed into the palace.

Guards and courtiers alike were staring at the soft glow inside, and Cal stopped Zaos long enough to let him know what was happening, trusting him to spread the word before anyone could panic.

A servant moved to intercept them as they neared the stairs, and Cal slowed as he recognized Aster.

The young man dipped into a quick bow and approached. "Your Majesty," he greeted. "Princess Calaesynne wishes to see you."

Cal hid a wince. "Of course she does," he whispered to himself. She'd been stuck handling court for the past few days and likely wanted answers. "In the throne room?"

Aster nodded, glancing at the glow still emanating around them with wariness, even though he was trying hard not to. His gaze quickly focused on Cal again.

"It's nothing to worry about," Cal said firmly. "Just some protection wards."

"I see," he said, but he didn't seem convinced. Since he was human, Cal couldn't hold that against him.

He turned from the stairs, trying to release Rashi's hand to let them go back to his rooms ahead of him, but Rashi remained attached like a leech.

With a slight shake of his head, he led the way to the throne room. "Liria?"

"Food for an army to be brought to your rooms?" she guessed.

He glanced over with a brief smile. "Please."

She peeled away and headed for the kitchens.

When they reached the throne room, it was in the process of being emptied, word of his return likely having reached his sister the moment he stepped out of the carriage. The three of them moved to the dais where Synne sat on her throne on the left. Vesryn stood behind her, but he moved closer as the doors closed behind the last of the courtiers.

"There was another fire?" she demanded.

"That's not the only thing," Cal said. "Justice is dead."

# CHAPTER 21

WHEN THEY'D settled in his sitting room, Cal somehow found himself on one of the sofas the moment he'd returned from changing into dry clothes, with Rashi tucked into his side. In Cal's usual chair sat Haru. He'd expected some kind of comment or annoyed growl from the dragon by now, but he seemed unbothered by Rashi clinging to Cal, which he was grateful for. He wouldn't admit it aloud, but Rashi's warmth and presence beside him helped keep him grounded in the present.

He knew he'd be seeing flames and Justice's ravaged face and Thallan's death in his dreams, whenever he finally managed to sleep, but for now, he could focus on what needed done.

By the time he and Liria recounted everything that happened, the food was gone and silence filled the room as they considered their next steps. The vial couldn't be used to track who the blood belonged to, which suggested it was an ancient relic that had survived the war. Why Draekor would have stored his blood to begin with was a question with too many unpleasant answers.

What was more concerning was that when they tried to track who had given it to Justice, it resulted in the spell fizzling out before it could lead to anyone. Only shadow magic had ever been able to completely obscure spells in such a way. From the records he'd read when he was younger, Cal knew the humans' ingenuity to use magic to hide magic was what had made them so dangerous.

"So somewhere there's a human who's regained their magical capacity," Cal said quietly.

"Or they found an artifact that was made to hide its owner from scrying," Liria offered.

Cal could only hope that was the case. "The guard who released Justice to his quarters," he said, glancing at Duaia, "did he ever identify the page?"

She scoffed and shook her head. "Only that it was a human, which is more than half of the servants. Or was. I'm told several more have disappeared since the last fire."

He knew he should be concerned about that, for the labor issues it would cause if not their reasons for leaving. Either they'd all been aware of Justice's plan and knew he'd failed, or there was still a plan to take the city for themselves in an attack that required more bodies. Or they were all descendants of the Black Sun and there was someone else with another vial who could control them.

"They're scared," Synne said, and everyone turned their attention to her.

She huffed softly, as if that should have been obvious. "This morning alone I heard at least three comments of humans being responsible for the library and the recent deaths. How we should be doing something to punish them or kick them out of the city before they do more damage. The entire court was ready to join the rush to the temple, and most of them were ready to fight, not put out a fire."

She shook her head, running her fingers through her hair. "Even if we told everyone that Justice was responsible and is dead, his hand wasn't the one firing the arrows. His hand wasn't the one to burn our history to ashes. Our people are scared and angry, and the humans know they've been living here at our lenience. And with word of what was really happening in the prison spreading, they're afraid all the creatures here will retaliate."

"And they might just do that," Julius murmured. "Three trees. Even without the food and books inside them, the ylren trees are sacred, not just to us."

Cal sighed and pressed his fingers against his temple. Even if he'd prepared for the idea of civil war, he hadn't considered it starting from their side.

"We need to ensure their safety," he murmured. "The palace should be safe even if they attack here. Tomorrow I can try to do the same for the other buildings, starting with the granaries and the academy."

Securing the ylren trees would be easy enough; it was the rest of the city he was worried about.

"Start telling everyone to strengthen their own thresholds," Haru said. "I haven't seen a single one in the city that's been tended recently."

That would help, but he wasn't sure it would be enough. "Will that at least ease the fear and anger?" he asked, turning to Synne. She'd always been more attuned to the heart of the city.

Silent looks passed between them all before Synne offered a hesitant shrug. "It should at least appease them for a day or two. If we can ensure we won't lose the other granaries, we can stave off the fear of starvation for a few months."

Rashi's sigh was sleepy from where he'd slumped into Cal's lap after eating, his head resting on Cal's thigh and the rest of his body on the verge of sliding to the floor. "I'll start fixing the crops tomorrow."

Haru growled. "Two hours," he said. "One after breakfast, one after lunch."

Rashi tipped his head enough to shoot a glare Haru's way, but it was more petulant than angry.

Cal tugged at one of Rashi's ears before rubbing at its base to soothe him. "I'm going to go test one of the granaries and make sure I can secure it like the palace."

"Now?" Liria asked incredulously.

He glanced out the window. It was still early enough that he could at least get one done and have time to rest before tomorrow. His shoulder ached, and his entire body felt like he'd lost a fight against a girallon, but he couldn't ignore the restless need to *do* something, and the granaries were a fraction of the size of the palace. They shouldn't require him to channel nearly as much magic. He might even check the city's walls, just to see if he could secure them as well, even if it would take days before he could attempt that without burning himself out.

Rashi grumbled as he sat up. "You're not going to nearly die again, are you?"

Julius snorted quietly and stood. "I'll make sure he doesn't do anything reckless."

Rashi narrowed his eyes at Julius as if doubting him before he gave a resigned sigh.

"I promise not to run into any more tunnels," Cal said, squeezing Rashi's shoulder before following Julius out.

They took a carriage to the nearest granary in silence, and Cal took the chance to breathe and let his mind go blank for at least a few moments. That was a mistake. As soon as he closed his eyes, Thallan's shocked face as his body was engulfed in too-fast fire rose up to haunt him.

Thallan had served as a palace guard for a decade before Duaia suggested his move to Cal's princeguard several years ago. He had a younger brother who was on his own now. Cal would have to ensure he was taken care of.

"This isn't over yet," Julius said softly.

Cal gratefully focused on him as he tore himself free of fire and smoke. "What isn't?"

Julius narrowed his eyes and waved his hand as if to gesture at everything. "I'm still Seeing you stabbed and left for dead."

Cal groaned. He'd forgotten about that, with everything that had happened. Had it even been a week since he found Haru and Rashi in the prison?

"That's not going to change," he said, staring out the small window. Even Juls couldn't change his visions, though he seemed to have a bit more luck with manipulating them than Cal ever had.

"Just promise me you won't go to the prison alone," Julius said tightly.

Cal tilted his head and glanced over. "Is that where I get stabbed?" he asked. That would explain Julius being so uneasy every time the prison was mentioned. "I shouldn't have a reason to go there again." Not unless Aelin found something truly horrible. "But I promise I won't go alone."

Julius nodded, his jaw working like he wanted to say something, but there was a conflicted hesitance in his eyes. "There will be an eclipse soon," he finally said.

The thrum of soft magic in the words made his skin prickle and his heart race. He waited for Julius to say more, though he knew he wouldn't. Cal rarely had the privilege of knowing what Julius Saw anymore.

"And?" he eventually prodded.

Julius hesitated before shaking his head. "I just know it's important. It's the last thing I can See."

"What does that mean?"

"There's nothing past that point. After the eclipse, everything is empty. I can't See past it."

If humans had managed to wipe out all magical creatures, that was exactly how he imagined the future. Except that didn't tell them what they needed to do.

"Right, then," Cal muttered, rubbing his eyes. "I'll just wait for the eclipse to know we all die."

"Don't be an ass."

The carriage rolled to a stop, and Julius kicked him as he climbed out. "Let's get this over with."

"Don't sound so excited. I might think you actually enjoy being my personal guard," he said, snickering at Julius' bland stare. It was a small bit of normalcy in a sea of disaster, but he was grateful for it.

# CHAPTER 22

THE CROPS were dying.

Rashi sighed as he sat in the dirt between rows of leafy greens, leaning back against Haru's leg where he insisted on standing watch. This was worse than the blight that plagued his own village.

His family lived far enough from the Wound that only some of their crops were affected, the dark purple-and-black spots tiny enough that a communal spell healed them, but he could see the Wound from here, and the blight was so much worse.

He plucked a leaf from the nearest plant and stared. It was covered in the same shimmery purples and black as the one Julius showed them, with a few splotches of dark, wilting green.

"They said everything was fine a few days ago," Rashi murmured, rubbing his fingers over the leaf. The texture was a bit waxy, nothing at all like the soft and tender it should be.

"It's the rot," Haru said, sighing when Rashi elbowed his leg. "The *shadows*. I noticed after Kithiel was attacked that they're growing."

He'd hoped that had been his imagination. He might be getting used to the strange feel of the magic here, but sometimes he couldn't help but recoil when he reached for it, sure that something was reaching back. How the people here could stand to draw on their magic, he couldn't understand. Even if they'd never known magic without the shadows polluting it, how could it not offend their instincts?

"You can't heal all of this," Haru said.

"No…." He hadn't expected it to be this bad. Rows upon rows of crops, stretching all the way up the hill, and he couldn't sense a single fully healthy plant. Even the grass and weeds outside the plots were starting to turn.

Rashi studied the plants directly in front of him and shifted to his knees. He set the leaf aside and shoved both his hands into the soil, breathing in the rich scent of disturbed earth. He wiggled his fingers deeper as he called healing energy into them. Healing was as easy as asking nature to move for him.

The gentle magic eagerly wrapped around his hands and followed as he coaxed the energy into the roots of the plants and up their stems, into their leaves.

He opened his eyes as the glow and magic faded, only to find nothing had changed. He tugged his hands free of the soil and spread apart the leaves of the nearest plant, hoping to find a green leaf somewhere, but there were none. If anything, all hints of green had vanished completely, leaving only the strange purples and black.

"I don't understand…," he muttered, reaching for the next plant to find the same. "It worked at home."

He slumped against Haru's leg, staring out over the rows of crops again.

"They weren't as affected as this," Haru said, running his fingers through Rashi's hair.

That was true. The blight had barely touched their crops before the village healed the gardens, soil, and water with a day-long casting. Even though the spells had worked, the blight still returned every season.

"They can't *all* be this far gone," Rashi grumbled, pushing to his feet and trudging up the hill. There wasn't much difference in the plants as he moved higher and closer to the sea, not until he neared the top, where the blight was tiny spots of discoloration like in his village.

He stopped in a row of root vegetables and carefully dug one up. The entire plant was mostly healthy.

"Good," he breathed, burying it into the soil again. Then he pushed his fingers deep and focused on healing the few plants in front of him. This time, the foliage returned to its natural bright green, not a speck of blight to be seen, and he sat back with a giddy laugh of relief.

Less than half the crops were spread out in front of him. Not nearly as much as he'd hoped to save, but he hoped it would be enough to replace what was lost to the fires and theft.

"One hour," Haru reminded him.

Rashi tipped his head back with a soft growl. "I'm fine. I at least need to get this row and the next done. We don't know how fast it's spreading."

Haru sighed his displeasure, but he didn't argue, so Rashi moved down enough to deal with the next set of plants.

"Are you going to complete the bond soon?"

"Why?"

Rashi rolled his eyes at the suspicion. "I'm just wondering what else you expect from him. He accepted you being a dragon, and he even returned the remains of your relative as a sign of good faith."

He let the healing energy form and guided it into the plants to do its work, then moved down again. It would have been easier to do the entire row at once, but that would drain him quicker and wouldn't be as efficient. Small batches would take longer but required less magic.

And it prevented Haru from attempting to drag him off for overexerting himself. He may have still been recovering from the backlash, but it wasn't nearly as severe as everyone seemed to think.

"He likes you," Rashi added, brushing soil off his hands and watching Haru through his lashes, smirking when Haru looked away. That did nothing to hide the spark of pleased surprise along the bond.

"Every time he sees you, there's a twinge of awe and… yearning?" He grinned and continued down the path. "Don't you think he's attractive?"

"He's an elf."

"All elves are attractive, then?" he asked, laughing.

He didn't even have see Haru's glare to know it was there; he felt it along the bond.

"Yes, yes, elves are so evil. They can't be trusted. They're as deceitful as fae and twice as vicious," he mocked. "They're not nearly as bad as the humans here," he added under his breath.

Rashi fell silent and focused on healing what he could. He didn't quite manage to reach the end of the second row before he felt the first warning of burnout. Haru knew him well enough that he didn't try to hide the wave of dizziness and merely accepted the offered hand to get to his feet.

He leaned all his weight into Haru as they headed down the hill, thankful that Cal had assigned them a carriage, a driver, and two guards.

Rashi had protested that morning, sure the resources could have been put to better use, but he was glad for it now. "You think this is what we're supposed to be doing here?" he asked, fighting the tug of exhaustion once they were settled in the carriage.

"If not, then Fate should have given us better signs," Haru muttered.

"You mean better than Her bond you're refusing?" he asked innocently.

Haru scoffed. "If you want to sleep with him that badly, then do it."

"Maybe I will." He sighed and pressed his face into Haru's shoulder. "Why are we fighting about this?"

"I'm not fighting," Haru replied. "You have my permission."

Rashi pushed closer as he focused on their bond, surprised when he truly did only feel a calm acceptance regarding Cal, when before there'd been hurt, resignation, and fear. He wasn't sure how or when Haru's feelings had changed, but Cal had obviously gained Haru's trust, even if he was still hesitant to complete his own bond.

He wiggled his fingers in between Haru's and squeezed. "Thank you," he said softly.


THERE WAS food waiting when they returned, and after eating and showering, Rashi sprawled on the bed for a quick nap, only to wake as the sun was setting.

"Fuck," he groaned. He'd wanted to try to at least finish that row of crops before tomorrow, but even he wasn't willing to venture into the city at night. Considering they'd been attacked in daylight, who knew what might happen under the cover of darkness, even with the giant sunstones casting light over most of the city.

He rolled out of the bed and stumbled into the sitting room where he could hear others talking, giving a sleepy wave to Cal, Julius, and Faelan before sinking into Haru's lap with a yawn. He hated magical burnout. He hated recovering from it even more.

"Did you tell him about the crops?" he asked Haru.

"No."

Cal paused as he was reaching for a bowl on the table. "What about the crops?" he asked, opening a pot and ladling stew into the bowl before passing it to Rashi. "Can you fix them?"

Rashi took the bowl and inhaled the rich scent of thick broth and vegetables. "I can, but not nearly as many as I'd hoped."

"Whatever you can do is more than enough," Cal said, sitting back in his chair.

"Afamrail took a new inventory," Julius added. "We should have enough to last through winter until the first harvest. So long as there are no more extravagant feasts."

Cal muttered something about not wanting the first one.

"Does that mean no festival?" Rashi asked. He'd never been to a city festival. The closest his village had was the celebration of spring, when winter finally released its hold and the trees and flowers began blooming again.

Cal and Julius shared a silent look, and Rashi watched curiously as he ate his stew.

Finally, Cal sighed. "Most of the supplies have already been allocated for it. The bigger problem is that a large portion of the city's labor has gone missing."

"They're likely in the tunnels," Julius muttered. "D already sent scouts along the coast, all the way to Syll Taesi. No one has seen anyone new, much less a few thousand humans."

"Then they're in the tunnels," Cal said, sounding resigned. "That doesn't help us."

"Why not?" Rashi asked, his ears twitching back when Cal tilted his head in confusion.

"The tunnels are formed by the roots of the ylren trees. Not just the ones still standing. The first tree that was transformed into the walls was much larger than this one."

Rashi remembered the way the walls of the courtyard had lit up as Cal activated the dormant threshold. If those had been the roots of the palace, he could barely imagine how deep and far they must go. They'd have to stretch all the way into the Wound and the sea just to support the height of the tree. This was already the largest building and tree he'd ever seen. The thought of an even larger one….

"Oh," he said. "You'll never find them underground."

Julius laughed, though there was an edge to it. "That would be the problem."

Rashi slid off Haru's lap to refill his bowl.

"So not only are the crops a problem, but now you have a shortage of labor," Haru said. "Where, precisely?"

"Everywhere," Cal said, rubbing his forehead. "Most of the dock workers are gone. Half the market is closed." He stopped and glanced at Julius. "We need to gather any food supplies from there before they spoil."

"I'll take care of it," Faelan said. "The tavern is close enough that I'll send anything there."

Cal nodded and started to run his fingers through his hair, but the crown kept him from getting far, and he returned to rubbing his forehead instead. "The water supply is the biggest concern."

"Most of that is self-sustaining now," Julius said.

"Not if they sabotage it."

Julius flinched as if he hadn't considered that. Rashi hadn't either, but if the humans were willing to kill and burn sacred sites, they would certainly have no problem sabotaging the water. If their goal was to kill all magical creatures, why hadn't they done that already?

Faelan stood and slipped out of the room.

Rashi finished his stew in the silence that fell, devouring a third serving before finally setting the bowl on the table. Then he cleared his throat. "There was something else with the crops," he said quietly, wincing at Cal's resigned sigh.

He hated bringing even more terrible news to him, but he'd never seen anything like the plants he'd failed to restore. He was more interested in the fact that his magic had seemed to work, just not in the way he expected. The plants hadn't died. Despite the strange colors, and that their structure had completely changed from what they should have been, they were perfectly healthy plants.

"You think it's not an infection?" Cal asked after Rashi finished explaining.

"I don't know. We treated it like a blight because it appeared mostly as black veins in my village. But these are strange. I want to study them closer tomorrow."

"Even if it's not a blight, we don't know if the Wound is making them poisonous. Maybe we should burn them."

"No," Julius said, his voice sharp enough they all turned to stare at him. There was a flicker of magic, and Julius closed his eyes, gritting his teeth and breathing slowly as if through pain.

"Fuck," Cal hissed, leaning forward with an anxious expression. "What could the crops possibly have to do with anything?"

"You're a Seer," Rashi whispered, as shocked as he was delighted. He caught the faint glow of Haru's eyes as he examined Julius with his dragon sight, glad he hadn't been the only one who didn't know what Julius was.

The magic faded, leaving Julius pale and slumped against the sofa. "I don't know," he murmured. "I don't understand why, but the crops need to stay."

Rashi moved around the table and sat beside Julius, lightly touching his temple and pouring a gentle pulse of healing energy into him.

With a groan, Julius went limp, the tightness around his mouth easing. "Thank you," he said, cracking his eyes open. Already his color was returning.

"Of course." Rashi squeezed Julius' shoulder before returning to Haru's side. His ears twitched as he watched Julius and Cal have an entire conversation with only their expressions. It was thoroughly entertaining, until it truly sank in that Julius was a Seer.

"You know what's going to happen."

Julius stiffened, both his and Cal's faces twisting with guilt.

"You both know. How bad?"

They shared another silent conversation before Cal sighed. "You may as well tell them."

His lips twisted in dismay, obviously wanting to protest, but he didn't. "Yes, I'm a Seer. Most of my life, I've been Seeing parts of the events from the past few weeks. And nothing past them."

Rashi instinctively found Haru's hand when the dragon tensed, threading their fingers together. "What does that mean?"

"I assume it means either I die, or the humans succeed in whatever they're planning."

"That's not going to happen," Rashi snapped. They didn't come all this way to find Cal just to watch everyone die. "What do we do to stop them?"

Julius spread his hands in a helpless gesture. "Whatever they're planning is going to happen soon. My visions get shorter near the end, nothing but flashes of disconnected images." He tilted his head, staring into the distance. "There's a point when everything is empty, but the crops…. It feels like they're needed for after."

"We won't burn them, then," Cal said, but Rashi sensed the frustration and helplessness underlying his words.

He couldn't imagine the burden of knowing this was coming years in advance. It would have driven him mad.

Julius nodded and pushed to his feet. "You should get some rest. We'll get the academy's threshold done tomorrow," he said before taking his leave.

Rashi leaned back against Haru and pulled his feet onto the sofa as he faced Cal. "You were able to secure the granaries?"

"Yes," Cal said, a fleeting pulse of satisfaction echoing along the bond. "They should be protected well enough to withstand an attack. The academy should be easier despite being larger. There are already wards and protections against wayward spells in place," he added with a wry smile.

Rashi felt the familiar twinge of awe and yearning, there and gone again, when Cal studied them.

"Juls is right. We should get some sleep. You look like you're still recovering."

Rashi wrinkled his nose. "I'm fine," he said, smacking Haru's hand when it tried to pinch him. "I know my limits," he added with a soft huff.

Cal stood with a shake of his head. "Please do not overexert yourself. If you'd like to come, I'm meeting with the siren queen tomorrow. I'm hoping she'll be amenable to assisting us if we run short on food supplies."

Rashi leaned forward with an eager "Really?"

Cal laughed. "If you'd like. You're both welcome to come," he added with a quick glance at Haru. "Good night," he added before disappearing into his bedroom.

Rashi sighed and flopped across Haru's lap, reaching up to poke his cheek. "You are coming with us."

Haru gave him a pained look. "Of course."

With a hum, he trailed his fingers down Haru's neck and chest as he tried and failed to ignore the strange flutter of nerves in the pit of his stomach.

After a drawn-out silence, Haru sighed and grasped Rashi's fingers. "Why are you hesitating?"

Rashi swallowed hard and gripped Haru's hand in return. "What if he doesn't want me?"

"He does," Haru said dryly. "He's wanted you from the moment he found us in the prison."

"He wants you too," Rashi whispered.

"Maybe." Haru squeezed his hand before nudging him off his lap. "Go, before I change my mind." He pressed a kiss to Rashi's lips before going to their bedroom.

Rashi huffed softly and stayed on the sofa, flicking his ears towards Cal's room and waiting until he finished his shower. Then he took a deep breath and moved to knock lightly on the door.

"Come in."

He cracked the door open and poked his head inside. "Hi," he said, slipping into the room when Cal smiled at him.

"Something wrong?"

"No." He closed the door behind him and leaned against it. "I was hoping you'd like to have sex."

A flush crept up Cal's neck as he froze, staring at him with wide eyes.

Rashi bit his lip to hide a grin as Cal's flustered surprise squashed the nerves in his own gut. He pushed off the door and into Cal's space, grasping the bottom of his sleep shirt before tugging.

Cal leaned into him, settling his hands on Rashi's hips. "What about...?" He trailed off with a quick glance at the door.

"Haru knows I'm here. It's all right."

Cal relaxed, sliding his hands up Rashi's back with a hesitant smile. "You're sure?"

With a huff, Rashi nudged Cal towards the bed, pushing him until he sat. "More than sure," he said, straddling Cal's lap and leaning in to nuzzle his neck. He breathed deep, closing his eyes as he focused on Cal's scent, so different from Haru's. Where the dragon smelled like deep frost and fresh-cut mountain wood, beneath Cal's lemongrass soap, the elf was bright sunshine and crushed basil.

Rashi dragged his nose across Cal's cheek. "Can I take you?" he whispered, grinning when the immediate response was a deep groan.

Cal's hands flexed on Rashi's hips, pulling him closer. "Yes," he gasped, tilting his head to brush their lips together.

Rashi moaned and opened up to Cal's questing tongue, fisting both hands in silky golden hair and tugging. He lifted up enough to change the angle of the kiss, kissing Cal from above as he stroked his thumbs against the delicate points of Cal's ears. When that earned a full-body shudder, he grinned, the bond becoming a thrumming echo of pleasure between them.

He broke the kiss just enough to ask, "Do you want—"

"Yes," Cal gasped.

Rashi huffed a laugh and nipped Cal's lips. "You don't even know what I was going to say."

Cal opened his eyes, only a thin ring of blue visible in the low light. "I want anything you want to give me."

A soft whimper escaped him as he traced his thumb across Cal's lips. Something of his nerves must have made it through the bond, because Cal's expression shifted from lust-filled to concerned.

"What is it?"

Rashi swallowed and sank his weight across Cal's thighs. "Haru isn't… the only one with a glamour."

Cal tilted his head, sliding a hand up to cup Rashi's cheek, his gaze moving to Rashi's ears in confusion, but his eyes lit up a moment later. "You have a tail," he said, his other hand sliding to Rashi's lower back, where his tails were hidden.

"Three," Rashi whispered. He let out a slow breath before adding, "I was born with two," and braced himself for Cal's fear or disgust.

Tails were a direct reflection of a fox's age and magical power. Most of his kind were well into their first century before they ever manifested a second tail. He wasn't even in his third decade.

"Can I see?"

Rashi blinked at him, still expecting something other than the eager excitement in Cal's eyes. "Really?"

"Yes."

"You don't think it's unnatural?"

Cal leaned forward, resting their foreheads together. "No. I'm curious how you have three, though."

Rashi smiled and wrapped his arms around Cal's shoulders. "It appeared after Haru and I consummated our bond."

"Are you going to get a fourth after tonight?"

"Fuck, I hope not," he muttered. "It takes forever to regain my balance."

He ignored Cal's snickering and closed his eyes, releasing the glamour hiding his tails. Once they were free, they flicked and twitched wildly as if with minds of their own. One of them twined itself around Cal's arm, another his hip.

Cal grinned and sank both hands into the tails. "They're soft."

Rashi swallowed a whimper at the intense pleasure sparking like lightning through his body, which only intensified when Cal's fingers found the base of his tails and dug in. He buried his face against Cal's neck, grinding their hips together. His ear twitched from the puffs of hot breaths as Cal chuckled.

"Does it feel that good?" he teased.

With a growl, Rashi lifted his head and found the tip of Cal's ear with his teeth.

Cal's sharp hiss was satisfying, and he laughed as Cal toppled him to the bed in response.

"You are wearing far too many clothes," Cal grumbled, shoving Rashi's shirt up and off.

Once free of it, Rashi stretched out with his arms over his head, lowering his lashes as he wiggled his hips before lifting them.

Cal watched him with a mix of amusement and open desire that heated Rashi all the way to the tips of his tails. "Am I doing all the work tonight?" he asked, tugging Rashi's pants down his legs, pausing far too many times to caress newly exposed flesh.

Rashi bit his lower lip as he watched, relishing the slow exploration, his flesh prickling from the light touches.

Cal tossed the last of Rashi's clothes to the floor before settling between his legs, trailing his fingers up the inside of one thigh before closing around Rashi's erection.

The touch wasn't as intense as when his tails were tormented, but it was still enough that he pushed into Cal's hand with a shamelessly needy moan.

Cal leaned over him, keeping his hand in place and pressing the other into the bed next to Rashi's head.

"More," Rashi whispered, gripping Cal's hair with both hands and pulling him into another kiss. He hooked his legs around Cal's hips to keep him there, then eagerly lost himself to the warm pleasure of exploring Cal's lips and tongue. His fingers teased the delicate tips of Cal's ears, matching the rhythm of the hand expertly stroking him.

Even when Cal's arm eventually gave out and he pushed it under the pillow for leverage, neither of them was in any rush to move on. For a small eternity, their existence narrowed to the slow build of need and desire between them, the bond expanding and sinking deeper into their cores.

When Cal finally broke the kiss, it was to ask, "Shall I ride you?"

"*Please*," Rashi groaned. The only thing that would be better than being inside Cal, was being inside Cal while watching him take his pleasure.

Cal retrieved a bottle of oil from the bedside table and started to pour some into his hand, but Rashi regained enough of his senses to snag the bottle, rolling his hips to throw Cal off and switch their positions.

"Change your mind?" Cal asked, blinking up at him in surprise.

"No." He nudged Cal's legs up and apart. "But I want to do this for you."

Cal smiled and planted his feet on the mattress, keeping a knee up as the other fell to the side. One of Rashi's tails settled over Cal's thigh, and the elf immediately buried his fingers in its fur, his other hand wrapping around his own cock.

Rashi refused to let either of those things distract him as he poured oil into his hand, warming it between his fingers with a pulse of magical energy, then pressed a finger into the elf.

Cal exhaled at the intrusion, his muscles twitching before he forced them to relax.

Rashi took his time working his finger deeper, curling and flexing as he watched Cal's reactions, enjoying the play of pleasure on his face and along the bond. By the time he'd worked three fingers in, he'd learned how to push Cal to the edge and bring him back well enough that he was on the verge of frustration.

Cal's entire body was flushed with warmth, hair damp and sticking to his forehead, his stomach coated from his continuously leaking cock.

"Gorgeous," Rashi breathed, pressing his fingers in deeper to hit the spot that made Cal toss his head back with a sweet moan.

"Rashi," Cal gasped. "Please."

Rashi hummed and pulled his fingers away, stretching out next to Cal and tracing his fingers over the elf's chest, one of his tails brushing back and forth against Cal's hip.

"Sneaky little fox," Cal groaned, as another tail passed over his cock.

Rashi smirked and kissed Cal's shoulder. "Do you not want to ride me anymore?" he asked, blinking innocent eyes at him.

Cal let out a strangled laugh and crawled on top of Rashi, planting openmouthed kisses across his chest and up his neck. Once he was straddling Rashi's thighs, he found the oil and got his revenge by dripping it directly over Rashi's cock, then spreading it around with a single finger.

Rashi clutched the sheets as he squirmed, working a tail between them to rub against Cal in retaliation, only for the elf to capture it with his other hand, tugging sharply. He yelped, his vision going white at the edges from the intense pleasure.

"Fuck." Now who was the sneaky one? "Caaaal," he whined, pleased when Cal gave up tormenting him and shifted forward.

Holding Rashi's cock steady with one hand, Cal slowly sank down onto it.

Light burst inside him and he gasped, nearly ripping the sheets as he twisted his fingers in them, struggling to keep still.

"Cal," he chanted, "Cal, Cal, Cal." He squeezed his eyes shut, hardly daring to even breathe until Cal was fully seated.

After a few steadying breaths, Cal leaned down, covering Rashi's eyelids in feather-soft kisses. "You're not really going to make me do *all* the work, are you?" he teased, tracing his tongue across Rashi's lips.

Rashi groaned and gave up his last tentative shreds of control. He gripped Cal's hair with one hand, pulling him into a deep kiss, and dragged the nails of his other hand down Cal's back to grip his ass. His tails twitched wildly before wrapping around Cal's thighs, teasing against where they were joined.

Cal shuddered, whimpering against Rashi's lips before tearing his mouth away. He planted a hand against Rashi's chest as he sat up, bracing his other hand beside them as he began moving.

"Yes," Rashi gasped, releasing Cal's hair in favor of exploring his chest and stomach, the long, lithe expanse of sun-kissed, sweat-dampened flesh. "Gorgeous," he breathed, unable to stop touching every bit he could reach.

Cal's smile was blinding as he leaned back and began moving in earnest.

Rashi pulled his knees up and planted his feet on the bed to give them both leverage. When Cal gazed down at him through lowered lashes and wrapped a fist around his own cock, Rashi was sure he'd ignite into flames. Then he lost the capacity for thought as his existence narrowed to the sounds of Cal's ragged breaths and sharp cries of pleasure, the slick slide of Cal's hand and the slap of flesh meeting flesh, the thick scent of sweat and sex, the sharp tang of magic beneath.

Release slammed through him before he was ready for it, leaving him choking for breath as his muscles went taut. His grip on Cal's hips turned bruising as he held the elf in place, his cock pulsing and filling Cal with his spend.

When he could finally breathe again, he slumped into the bed, managing to tangle his fingers with Cal's and stroke him to completion before he lost even that strength.

Cal collapsed beside him, and they lay in silence for several long moments, until their breaths steadied and bodies cooled. "Stay the night?"

Rashi smiled and snuggled in closer, tucking himself against Cal's chest as he drifted to sleep.

He didn't rest long before he woke again.

Cal had shifted to his stomach in his sleep, the covers tangled around their legs.

It took some effort to free himself; then he settled between Cal's thighs, kissing his way up the smooth skin until he could spread Cal's cheeks and delve his tongue into the tight, hot depths of him.

Cal shifted with soft, sleepy gasps of pleasure, but it took until Rashi worked two fingers in alongside his tongue for him to truly wake.

He urged Cal to his knees before taking him from behind, Cal's shouts muffled by the pillow as Rashi stroked him to completion before finding his own.

The third time they came together was on their sides, too spent to do more than lazily grind against each other between wet kisses, until they coated each other's stomachs.

When morning came, they were stuck together by their dried spend and sweat.

Cal huffed softly against Rashi's throat as he carefully pulled away. "We should have cleaned up last night."

Rashi grumbled, trying to pull Cal back in. "Too early," he groaned, rolling over to shove his face into Cal's pillow when the elf proved too awake and coherent for his own good.

"Rashi," Cal called with a soft laugh, gently tugging on his tails. "Come shower with me."

That was enough to wake him, at least enough to roll out of bed and glue himself to Cal's back, wrapping his arms around Cal's waist to let him lead the way into the bathroom.

The hot water felt amazing, and he drifted back into a doze, grumbling when Cal laughed at him.

"You're not fond of mornings, are you?"

"Mornin're for sleep," he mumbled, humming in pleasure as Cal washed him from ears to toes, even taking time to wash the mess out of his tails. He tried to return the favor, but he didn't manage more than washing Cal's ass and groin.

He was even generous enough to use a bit of healing magic, though not enough to remove the ache entirely.

"Is Haru as insatiable as you?" Cal asked. "Should I be worried?"

Rashi grinned and kissed his way across Cal's chest. "He can be, but no. Now that I have two of you, I might finally be sated." He nipped at Cal's lips and shifted to rinse, watching Cal wash himself.

When they'd finished and dried, he dressed in one of Cal's shirts, enjoying the spark of desire along the bond, and the way the overlarge shirt hung nearly to his thighs.

Breakfast was already waiting for them on the balcony, along with Haru, who eyed him with exasperated amusement thrumming along their bond.

Rashi offered a cheeky grin and planted himself in Haru's lap before helping himself to a slice of toast. "When will the queen be here?" he asked as Cal sat beside them.

"Soon. She doesn't like being near the surface during high sun. And good morning," he added to Haru.

Haru inclined his head in greeting and discreetly breathed in Rashi's scent, settling an arm tightly around his waist.

Rashi tilted his head in invitation, taking a large bite of toast after adding a generous amount of butter and fruit jam. He watched Cal through his lashes as Haru pressed his face into Rashi's neck.

Cal returned the scrutiny with a curious expression and sipped his strong tea. "Does he smell different?"

Rashi choked on his toast, grabbing the table for balance as he coughed while laughing. "Oh," he gasped. "Oh, ow." He clutched at his side as he continued cackling, ignoring Haru's annoyed huff and Cal's bewildered surprise.

"Yes," Haru answered. "He smells like sex and impudence."

"Doesn't he always?"

"Hey!" Rashi wiped at his eyes and forced himself to breathe through the lingering giggles. "You two are not allowed to unite against me."

Cal raised an eyebrow and snagged Rashi's forgotten toast to take a bite. "I don't recall making that agreement."

Rashi widened his eyes with an exaggerated gasp. "Haru, are you going to let him do that to me?"

"You fucked him, now you get to deal with him."

Rashi gaped at him, simultaneously surprised and delighted, and also relieved that Haru accepted his new dynamic with Cal so easily.

"Well then," he huffed, trying for indignant as he got to his feet, but it only lasted a moment before he kissed them both on the cheek. His tails swished as he went to dress in his own clothes.

If he was going to meet a queen, he couldn't do it half-naked.

# CHAPTER 23

THE MEETING with Queen Adrene went better than he could have expected, thanks to his bondeds.

Adrene was utterly charmed by Rashi the moment he said that her algae-green hair, styled in its complicated crown of braids, was fabulous. And Haru impressed her simply by being the first dragon she'd ever laid eyes upon, though his ability to hide swords in his sleeves didn't hurt.

By the time she bid farewell, the sirens had agreed to help supply them with fish and edible seaweed should their rations run low before they could fix their crops. As well as help protect their water supply. The springs that fed their wells and the rivers were near the academy, close enough to the sea that the sirens would be able to sense any changes if their protections failed.

Since they were near the crops, Cal joined Rashi and Haru after they left the docks, Julius and a small guard following close behind. If he couldn't burn the strange plants, he at least wanted to see what they were dealing with.

The moment the fields came into view, it was obvious which ones Rashi had failed to heal, because they were more than twice the size of the surrounding plants. Instead of their crops, there were three giant, leafy bushes in brilliant purples and blues. One had a red flower with long, curved petals. He could smell the sweetness of it from several feet away and could already see ants and flies feasting on what looked like nectar pooled inside.

"What the fuck?" Rashi stopped in front of the bushes, his utter disbelief matching Cal's on the bond. "This is some trick. Right?"

Julius crouched in front of the flower and leaned in to sniff it. "I've never seen any plant like this," he said, reaching into the leaves of the next bush and pulling a smaller flower into view, this one with the petals peeled back and a small yellow bulb-like fruit forming at its center. "Amazing."

He stood and brushed his hands off, pausing when he turned and found Cal glaring at him. "What?"

Cal raised an eyebrow. "If I had done that, you'd be bitching at me for days." He glanced at Haru, whose silence felt different than usual. "What is it?"

Haru shook his head. "The magic in them feels strange."

"Strange like how the magic here feels strange to you?"

"No. Not quite." Haru sighed and tore his eyes away from the unfamiliar plants. He started to say something before a pained expression crossed his features. "I suppose there are no records to look through now."

Cal's breath hitched at the reminder of the library. "There might be some in the palace." He knew they had several historical records, but something like a reference book of plants would have certainly been in the library. "Maybe the elders would recognize them."

"Luckily they're all in the palace," Julius said, shrugging when Cal looked at him in confusion. "Our sisters decided it would be best to keep them within the protections you put up. We can ask them later. If you're wanting to do the threshold at the academy, we need to head there before lunch."

"Right, yes. Be careful," he said to Haru and Rashi, who was staring at the bushes as if they were the most interesting things he'd ever seen.

With a shake of his head, he turned for one of the carriages. Sitting wasn't entirely pleasant, but at least Rashi had healed the worst of the ache. Once they were on their way, he eyed Julius. "You're sure we can't just burn them? Would it really be worse if we did?"

Julius rubbed his eyes. "All I know is they're connected to whatever is happening."

"I don't like this."

"At least you've only had to live through all this once," Julius muttered.

Cal winced, but Julius waved a hand at him before he could say anything.

"I'm just glad we're getting to the end, one way or another."

Cal nodded and fell silent, using the rest of the ride to focus his magic.

The academy wasn't as large as the palace, but it was significantly larger than the other ylren trees. He hadn't been there in years, but he remembered the threshold being stronger. Without someone of royal blood in attendance, they likely would have gone lax.

"Did you See Haru and Rashi?" Cal asked, his thoughts drifting in a rare moment of stillness. "In your visions, did you See them before they came here?"

"Yes, but never close to you," Julius replied, answering what Cal had really been asking. "I wasn't sure they were bound to you, only that they would become important to us."

"Important to you?" Cal asked, his smile widening when Julius narrowed his eyes. "That should have been your first clue."

"Oh, do fuck off, Your Majesty," Julius muttered.

Cal laughed, still chuckling when the carriage arrived and he climbed out after Julius. It was late enough in the morning by now that most students were in classes, so they were undisturbed as he walked along the boundary. He stopped when he found a spot where the roots were exposed enough he could spread both hands out against them.

The threshold responded almost immediately, far less dormant here where various wards were routinely tapped into. He closed his eyes against the brilliant golden glow as the threshold lit up, pouring a steady flow of magic into them as he pulled all the protective spells into place.

There were various shouts from the academy, windows opening as students and professors noticed what was happening. He'd sent word of his intentions to the head custodian, but it seemed communication was as effective as ever.

When he'd finished, he turned towards the academy and waved, smiling innocently at Julius' aggrieved glare as they turned to leave amid excited screams.

"Must you start rumors or cause a commotion every time you go outside?"

"If it means keeping everyone from panicking, yes."

Cal stumbled a moment later as dizziness swept over him, catching himself against the carriage door. His breaths came sharp and fast as everything spun briefly, as if he was falling.

The strange feeling passed quickly, but he could feel Julius staring at him, waiting for an explanation that he didn't have.

"I didn't think I used that much magic," he said anyway, settling into his seat and ignoring Julius' dubious glare. "I'm fine."

He was still a bit dizzy, but it was fading, and he motioned Julius inside so they could get back to the palace. While he wanted to take one of the elders to try to identify the plants, he also didn't want to risk them being out in the open if there was another attack coming.

He didn't get the chance to decide if the risk was worth it; the moment they arrived, he knew something was wrong.

"Fuck," he hissed. He didn't have to reach for the threshold. As soon as they crossed it, the magic swelled against him with urgency, something disturbingly close to panic thudding against him.

"The elders," Julius breathed, running for the stairs.

Cal didn't hesitate to follow, up to one of the guest floors and into a small suite of rooms.

Inside was chaos, every healer in the palace crammed inside. The air was filled with the weight and sharp scent of dozens of healing spells, but he already knew they wouldn't be enough.

At least two of their elders lay unmoving, tea staining the carpet next to them. The cart with refreshments had been knocked over, spilling more tea and pastries across the floor. Aster was pressed into the corner behind it, knees drawn to his chest, staring with wide eyes.

"No...." This couldn't be happening. He'd put the threshold in place to keep this from happening.

"Rashi," he managed to get out, blindly grasping for Julius' arm until he could latch on to it. Their healers couldn't do much against poison, not the ones that killed quickly, but maybe Rashi could.

Julius cursed and rushed from the room. Even if it would take far too long to retrieve Rashi from halfway across the city, they had to try.

He took a steadying breath and found Duaia across the room, her hands hovering over Ardreth's chest. A green glow similar to Rashi's healing magic surrounded her fingers, but it kept flickering and sputtering out.

He sank to his knees across from her. "How can I help?"

She barely acknowledged his presence as she summoned the magic again. "Keep them alive."

"How?"

"Bonds," she said through gritted teeth, cursing as her magic flickered out again.

He wasn't sure how the bonds could possibly be the key, but he trusted Duaia enough not to question it. He closed his eyes and focused on the dizziness and breathless sensations inside him.

If he could feel them dying, maybe he could hold on to the connections to keep them here.

He braced a hand on Ardreth's shoulder, hoping touch would give him what he needed to find the connection between them.

"Please don't let them die," he whispered, magic building around his head as the crown activated.

He gasped as the presence of every elf in the city suddenly pressed against his senses, covering him with delicate white threads, shivering with fear and panic and anger and laughter and—

Too much. Far too much.

He tightened his grip on Ardreth and found the thread connected to him, pushing away the more distant ones as he narrowed his focus to the elves in this room. A moment later, his entire body was wracked with pain, his chest squeezed in a vise. He could barely breathe through it and instinctively pulled back, but the moment he did, one of the threads turned black and snapped.

There were shouts across the room, but he couldn't understand them over the pounding rush of blood in his ears.

He didn't need to hear them. He knew what it meant. Another elf dead. Another elder lost because of his incompetence.

He couldn't fail here. His father had been trapped by a slave ring, but he didn't have that excuse.

Cal pushed into the magic of the crown, his lungs wheezing as he struggled to breathe like every elder left alive. Even as he latched on to the white threads around him, another one flickered black and snapped, the loss hitting him like he was back underwater, darkness surrounding him, without a Siren's Kiss to keep him alive.

He wrapped the remaining threads around himself without bothering with a spell. He had no time to weave one even if he'd known what would work. He could only hang on and pour his intention into the magic and the threads themselves, willing them to live.

The crown pulsed with more energy, burning so bright that he could see it behind his closed eyes.

The desperate need for air diminished and he could focus on the heat of the magic, guiding it along the threads. Except it wasn't enough.

Another thread turned black, weakened, and then snapped.

"No!" he shouted, grasping for the frayed end as it fluttered just out of his reach. He couldn't lose another. He poured all the magic he could into filling the space of the broken thread, but it was no use.

Magic couldn't replace life.

But life could.

The crown hummed with a surge of power. The sharp scent of ozone thickened in the air, his lungs burning from the tangible weight of magic. When he grasped for the fading end of the thread again, he latched on and held, dragging it back together.

It was still black and thin, but it was connected, a single thread once again.

Only when the thread grayed did he realize the magic was drawing on his own life force to restore it.

There was more shouting around him, and what might have been his name, but everything faded to a dull roar of noise.

He focused on each breath searing his lungs, trying to count them. He gave up after five and tried thinking of something else instead. That was even harder. Even thoughts of Rashi and their wonderful night together were ripped to shreds beneath the pain and burning in his lungs.

When his hands went cold, he knew he was in trouble, but he couldn't let go. There were only seven threads left, and each one was flickering gray, kept intact only by his magic and life force. If he let go now, they were all dead. He was sure they were all dead anyway, himself included, when a hand clasped the back of his neck and magic flooded into him.

He gasped at the onslaught, finally managing to fill his lungs with air, the pain momentarily swamped beneath cool magic and the sense of a Fate bond settling into place.

As the torrent of Haru's emotions crashed through him, all he could hope was that he didn't die shortly after the dragon finally deemed him worthy enough to touch. He gladly sank into the cocoon of Haru's worry and furious determination to keep him alive, Rashi's fear a more distant current of torture.

Minutes could have been hours, or hours could have been minutes. Between the Fate bond vying for his attention, Haru's magic steadily coursing through him, and his grip on the threads, he lost track of time.

When the first thread returned to a solid, pure white without a speck of black, he knew Rashi had saved them. So long as Rashi's magic held out, they could all make it through this.

He tentatively released his hold on the restored thread, and the drain on his magic noticeably lessened. With each subsequent thread he let go of, relief and hope that they might finally save someone filled him.

And then the last one glowed bright and strong and faded from his grasp.

The magic in the crown vanished abruptly and he found himself on the floor, his head resting on Haru's knee, the dragon's hand still holding the back of his neck in a firm grip.

When he tried to sit up, that grip tightened, accompanied by an alarming draconic growl that made him freeze. "Right," he whispered, wincing at the raspy sound of his voice. He'd just stay there, then.

There was a flurry of motion nearby, and then Rashi collapsed next to him, his hands fluttering over Cal's face and chest as if searching for injuries.

"I'm all right," he rasped. When he swallowed, his throat felt raw.

"Fucking liar," Rashi snarled, grabbing one of Cal's hands with both of his own. "You're freezing. You could have *died*, you absolute *fuck*." He choked on a sob, scrubbing his face against his shoulder.

Cal's chest lurched with guilt, and he carefully pushed himself up enough to pull Rashi into his chest, slumping against Haru's himself. "I'm sorry."

"Good," Rashi muttered, "but I'm going to hate you for a few days."

"That's fair," Cal said, pressing his cheek against Rashi's ear before risking a look around the room.

All seven of the elders he'd held on to were recovering, but his gaze stuck on the two near the sofa with spilled tea around them.

He hadn't known either of them well, though he knew one of them used to be a diplomatic advisor, before the Wound.

"Hey," Rashi whispered, moving a hand into Cal's line of sight and forcing him to look away. "You did what you could."

"Yeah…." And it still hadn't been enough. They were only alive thanks to Rashi. "Thank you," he rasped. "Both of you."

Haru's arm around his stomach tightened and Cal blinked down at his wrist when a brilliantly white, scaled tail coiled around it.

When Duaia dropped to her knees next to them, Haru growled low in his throat. She paled, shooting him a wary look before focusing on Cal.

"I'm so sorry," she said. "I didn't mean for you to…." She trailed off, taking in the room and paling further, appearing more worn than Cal could ever remember seeing her. She closed her eyes and drew in a shaky breath before lightly touching Rashi's shoulder. "Thank you both. We can never repay you for how much you did today."

Rashi shook his head. "You don't have to," he said, clasping her hand, which earned a faint smile.

"Who did this?" Cal asked.

Duaia sobered immediately and shook her head. "Aster fetched refreshments while we settled the elders here. It was in the tea…."

Cal looked for Aster and found him still on the floor, a look of shock on his face. "Aster. Do you know who prepared the cart?"

Aster blinked and turned his head to look at Cal. "No. It was waiting outside the kitchen like usual."

"Whoever it was, they're not collared," said Duaia. "I've been using the seeking spell a few times a day to make sure."

"Justice is dead. Why would—" he started, but he fell silent as he realized what he'd been missing.

He'd assumed Justice had been using slave collars to further his own plans, but considering the depths of depravity within the prison alone, there were certainly those even without station who'd helped him of their own free will. Who were surely within the palace walls right now, still trying to destroy them.

He couldn't let this happen again. If they were still in the palace, they couldn't be allowed to escape.

The crown flared hot enough to burn.

He barely noticed the three of them flinching away from him as the palace itself trembled beneath them. He managed to get to his knees, planting both hands on the floor as everything lit up in a blinding gold light that faded as quickly as it had come.

"What the fuck was that?" Duaia snapped.

Cal panted for breath, his heart racing as he braced himself for a backlash that never came.

"I'm not sure," he finally said, instinctively reaching for the threshold of the palace. It practically vibrated against his senses with the amount of power in it. "But I think I just sealed everyone in."

"By the Wound," one of the healers across the room gasped, staring out the window.

He got to his feet with help from Rashi and Haru. When they made it to the nearest window, they were greeted by the sight of a shimmering golden bubble encompassing the entire palace.

"What the fuck did you do?" Duaia breathed. "How are you powering this?"

"I'm not," Cal replied faintly, staring at the ward.

As much as he hated the idea of whoever was responsible for this being trapped in here with them, at least no one was getting past that. So long as he got it up before they were outside the threshold, they could finally put an end to this.

"It's pulling from the ley lines," Haru said, sounding impressed.

"That's impossible," Duaia said, eyeing Cal as if she'd never seen him before. "That kind of magic was lost years ago."

"Apparently not," he replied, turning to survey the room. "Where's Julius?"

"He gave us his horse to get here and said he'd run back," Rashi said.

Which meant he was trapped outside the ward and would certainly make Cal's life a nightmare later if he couldn't get inside.

He reached for the threshold again, finding it surprisingly easy to alter it enough that Julius and no one else would be allowed passage.

With that taken care of, he pushed away the fatigue and weakness in his body, turning his attention back to the more important issue: Finding who was responsible for this and stopping them for good.

"Can you cast a spell to force everyone in the palace into the throne room?" he asked Duaia.

"No," she said, at the same time that Haru said, "Yes."

They eyed each other a moment before Duaia scoffed. "I might have been able to this morning, but I wasted too much energy failing to master Rashi's healing magic. And compulsions weaken when spread out that far."

"I can make a shield and slowly shrink it," Haru offered.

"Brilliant," Cal said, pretending not to notice the warm flush of pleased surprise along the new bond between them. "You can do it now?"

"It will take some time to get it in place, and an hour or so to shrink it."

"And that's if no one tries to break through it," Duaia muttered.

Haru nodded. "But we can assume anyone who fights is likely responsible for the attacks."

Cal leaned against the windowsill as he considered that. With the ward drawing power from the ley lines, there was little chance of anyone getting through without some major spellwork, and anyone trying that hard to get out was who they were after. "What do you need for this?"

"A layout of the palace and the grounds would help."

"I can get that for you," Duaia said.

"While you do that, spread the word that everyone needs to start moving to the throne room on their own. I'll meet you there to start speaking with everyone."

"No," Rashi said sharply, glaring at Cal when he raised his eyebrows in surprise. "You nearly died. You need to rest. Both of you do," he added to Duaia.

Cal shook his head. "We can rest after this is taken care of."

Rashi narrowed his eyes. "And when your enemy is trapped in a room full of your people, you expect them to give up without a fight?" he demanded. "Or to best them when you can barely even stand on your own?"

Cal opened his mouth to protest, but Rashi jabbed a finger into his chest.

"You are going to rest while Haru forces everyone to the throne room, and by then we'll have a plan of how to proceed."

"I can rest while sitting on my throne," Cal muttered, but the way Rashi's eyes sparked and he stepped closer with a sharp smile let him know he was in trouble.

Rashi pushed up on his toes so his lips brushed Cal's ear as he whispered, "If you want anything like last night to happen again, you will not be difficult."

Cal glared even as heat crept up his neck. "I am not being difficult," he hissed.

"Good," Rashi replied, taking Cal's hand and twining their fingers together. "Then we'll rest until Haru's shields have done their work. And you can rest after you spread the word," he added to Duaia.

She nodded, not bothering to hide her delight, the traitor.

When even Haru refused to take his side, Cal resigned himself to being pulled out of the room, leaving the elders to the healers and guards.

Rashi kept hold of his hand all the way to his bedroom, where he promptly pushed Cal down, crawling over him to lie on the other side.

Cal remained sitting, eyeing the door and considering his chances of getting out before either of them could stop him. Considering Haru lingered near the door and eyed both of them with exasperation, he didn't give himself good odds.

"What did I do to deserve being bound to two of the most reckless creatures alive?" Haru muttered, barely loud enough for Cal to hear.

Rashi scoffed. "You'd be bored without us."

"I like boring," Haru replied, sitting on the floor with his legs crossed. "Now be quiet and rest," he added, gathering magic around himself.

Cal sighed and finally stretched out next to Rashi. "I should be doing something."

"You can't do everything," Rashi said. "You saved seven elves, and if this works you might have to do something like that again soon."

Cal winced and truly hoped it wouldn't come to that. His entire body ached from the strain of the first time, though he hadn't noticed until he stopped moving.

"Maybe we shouldn't put everyone in the same place," he said, staring at the ceiling. He didn't expect a human to be able to poison everyone at once. He doubted many would trust any food at all if they'd heard what had happened, but if their enemy had more of those vials of fire….

Could he trust the threshold to snuff out the flames before someone died?

"It will take longer, but I can guide humans to another location," Haru offered.

"Yes," Cal said, relaxing slightly.

At least that would offer some protection. He couldn't fathom how an elf or other magical creature could be responsible for any of this. Not without a slave collar forcing them. He had to wonder whether the humans who had fled the city were part of some bigger plan, or if they knew what was happening and refused to be part of it. Surely not all of the ones who'd vanished had simply feared for their lives. Maybe the only humans left inside the palace walls were enemies.

That was a terrifying possibility. More than half of the palace staff was human.

Rashi sighed beside him and shifted closer, resting a hand on Cal's chest. "You should be resting."

"I'm lying down," Cal said. What more could he possibly want? After a moment, he pushed up onto an elbow to look at Haru. "Can your shields extend underground?"

"Yes."

"Can you make them an enclosed sphere like the ward? Most of the tunnels are sealed off, but there are servant and secret passages that lead out of the palace."

Haru nodded and closed his eyes.

A long moment later, Cal felt the thrum as the first of Haru's shields lit up, forming along the inside of the ward, close enough the magics echoed against each other.

He dropped back to the bed and stared at the ceiling again, each new section of shield a soothing vibration along his senses. He curled his fingers around Rashi's hand on his chest and tried to truly rest. He knew he needed it. He'd been more than exhausted for weeks before he ever found them in the prison, and the last several days were anything but relaxing.

"When this is over, I'd like to spend at least a full day, just the three of us," he said quietly.

"That sounds like a good plan," Rashi said, pressing closer.

"Are you implying my other plans aren't good?" he asked.

"Wellll, I think I'm starting to understand why Faelan refers to Julius as the sage."

"And what does he call me?"

Rashi grinned against his shoulder. "Impulsive seems to be a common theme."

Cal grunted softly, though he couldn't exactly deny it. "Everyone's a traitor," he grumbled, rolling to his side and sprawling over top of Rashi.

"There, there," Rashi said, laughter in his voice as he pet Cal's hair. "Now sleep so I can try to heal the damage you've done."

"Save your magic," he said, closing his eyes, though he doubted he'd fall asleep. "We might need it later."

Rashi hummed and ignored him completely. He brushed his fingertips against Cal's temple, a gentle pulse of healing magic spreading through him and guiding him into sleep.

# Chapter 24

P_UTTING THE_ shields into place was easy. Haru had been perfecting his shields for nearly four hundred years. Even making one the size of the ward to encompass the entire palace didn't take too much effort, though it took a considerable amount of energy. Thankfully, he could follow what Cal had done with the ward and anchored the shield to draw its power from the ley lines as well.

The hard part was when it came time to reduce its size while keeping it intact, and without letting anyone escape or trapping them somewhere.

A guard brought him a map detailing every floor of the palace, and he spread it out on the floor in front of him, using it as a guide as his shield shrank from the size of the ward, to the ylren tree itself. Everyone on the palace grounds must have already been ordered inside, because there was no resistance.

"Need any help?" Rashi whispered from the bed. The faint, soothing pulse of his magic faded as he was finally satisfied that Cal was no longer on the brink of death.

"No," he murmured. "You need rest as much as he does."

Considering the state of nearly everyone in Cal's circle of trust, he hoped the results of the poisoning hadn't been part of some brilliant plan. They'd exhausted themselves over and over again, suffering loss after loss, expending all of their energy just to keep on even footing and bracing for the next crisis.

None of them were in a position where they could give up, but he knew they couldn't keep going much longer.

He turned the map a bit to better orient himself, then closed his eyes. As the shield shrank past the outer walls, he focused on each area alone, flexing and stretching the shield to clear a room, then resting it in a doorway to keep anyone from entering before moving to the next.

Time passed in silence as he worked from the bottom up, clearing the empty tunnels first and then up each level, leaving the top floors for later.

At some point, he sensed Julius pressing against part of the shield and allowed him through, expecting he would make his way up to them.

Haru continued shrinking the shield, surprised by how little resistance he encountered, but then he reached a floor closer to the center of the palace.

A human stood in the center of a small room and didn't move. When the shield shrank further and pressed against them, they stumbled forward, towards the door, but then stopped again.

He hesitated, cracking an eye open to study the map, fairly certain that the human was in one of the offices on the floor dedicated to officials.

He shrank the shield further, guiding the human out of the room and leaving them standing outside the door as he moved on, only to find another in the next room. He swore softly and considered simply forcing them out like the first, but this was obviously part of something. He didn't sense a slave collar at work, and he didn't sense the shadows like he had when Kithiel was attacked either, but he suspected either the rot in the magic was still growing stronger, or he was becoming accustomed to it to the point he couldn't sense it any longer.

Much like everyone who lived here.

Even when the Black Sun attacked them, he hadn't sensed much other than active magic.

He anchored the shield where it was and hastily added another, smaller barrier that he hoped blocked most of the doorways on that floor. Then he sought out Duaia's magic, finding her on the same floor.

He got to his feet and glanced at the bed when Rashi stirred from his doze.

"Wh's wrong?"

"Something strange," Haru said. "Stay here. Let him sleep some more."

Rashi glared at him, but the effect was ruined by his sleep-mussed hair and the lines on his cheek from the wrinkles in Cal's shirt.

"I'll let you know when we're done," he added, leaning over for a quick kiss.

Then he quietly left and made his way down the spiraling staircase.

The air was heavy with fear, which only grew more oppressive as he neared the center of the palace. The halls were eerily empty, no guards or servants or wandering courtiers. Other than the unmoving humans, he sensed most everyone else had already gathered in the throne room.

The sorceress was still where he'd sensed her, and when he slipped into the office, he found her slumped against a large desk covered in books, scrolls, and items emanating magic.

He cleared his throat and pushed away the flicker of guilt when she startled awake.

The dark smudges under her eyes were worse than ever, and she'd lost weight. "Are you done already?" she asked, swaying to her feet and brushing back her hair.

"Not quite," he said. Rather than trying to explain when he wasn't sure himself, he motioned her to follow.

A few doors away there was a human, standing completely still and silent in the center of the room, their eyes vacant as if they weren't aware of anything. His second shield cut through part of the room, and he adjusted it to cover the doorway as they stepped inside.

"What the hell?" Duaia muttered. "Who are you?"

There was no response. They didn't even blink. If not for the fact that Haru could see their chest moving, he would have assumed they were dead.

He stepped farther into the room, slowly walking around them, but he still couldn't feel any slave collar at work. He let his sight slip as Duaia continued asking questions in vain. A single black tendril of magic wrapped around the human's neck, hidden under the high collar of their shirt, writhing with shadows and stretching nowhere.

This was no Fate string or Death thread. He'd never heard of anything like this. He didn't dare try to touch it after what happened with Kithiel.

"There's a collar," he said, moving to stand next to Duaia.

She frowned at him before stalking forward, tugging open the top of the human's shirt.

That was enough to make them move. They lunged at her with a high-pitched shriek, fingers curled as they slashed at her like claws.

Duaia cursed and threw her arms up, light flaring around them in a defensive spell at the same time that Haru grabbed the back of her shirt and pulled.

He spun and pushed her to the door and through the shield, following her through, but not before sharp nails caught the back of his neck and gouged his flesh.

He hissed and turned to make sure his shield held.

The human slammed their fists into it twice before going still, except now their eyes were full of the same writhing black shadows that wrapped around their neck.

"Release us," they said, their voice echoed by a dozen others all along the hallway.

"Fuck," Duaia breathed. "Those are shadow collars."

"The original slave collar?" Haru asked with disgust. "Someone else has a vial of blood?"

She shook her head, more in disbelief than denial. "What are the chances there was more than one?"

"More likely than there being a descendant."

Duaia scoffed at him before motioning to the human, then down the hall, where others were trapped in rooms, all under the control of someone who couldn't exist.

The Shadow King died. His son died. He had no other children.

The thrones were bound to bloodlines, but the Shadow Throne had also been destroyed. No other human should have been able to inherit the power.

"Release us."

Haru couldn't stop the grimace at the disturbing chorus of voices speaking as one.

"Why should we release you?" Duaia demanded, stepping closer to the shield.

The human turned their head and focused on her, an eerie smile pulling at their lips. "Release us or we die." They pulled a small dagger from their sleeve and pressed it to their throat.

Duaia cursed and rushed down the hall, Haru close behind, but they found what he expected in the next room, and the room after that.

Humans with shadows for eyes and daggers at their throats, some of them younger than the first.

"Let them go," Duaia said.

Haru hesitated, unwilling to release potential threats when they were finally getting closer to the one controlling them.

She whirled on him, her eyes full of desperation and panic. "Some of them are children. I won't have their blood on my hands," she snapped. "Let them go!"

With a growl, Haru let the secondary shield drop.

The humans all stepped out of their rooms, most of them turning and moving down the hall, but one of the smaller ones gave them a mocking bow. "Now bring us the stone."

"What stone?"

"The one the prince-king locked in his desk. We'll be waiting in the interior garden." With that, they turned and followed the rest of the human puppets.

Haru tucked his hands into his sleeves. "We should go there now and end this, before they have time to gather."

"They're already ready for us," Duaia muttered. "They realized they couldn't break the protection spells to get what they wanted. All of this was just to get our attention."

She stalked down the hall to an office across from her own.

The door was open, and inside was a mess, books and papers tossed across the floor, the chairs overturned. The desk was swept clean, everything shoved off to a pile on the side.

Duaia picked her way across the room and crouched beside the desk.

Even from the doorway, Haru could see that someone had taken something sharp to the wood, trying to break into one of the drawers. Broken glass had shattered everywhere, scorch marks on the floor and side of the desk, like someone had tried to start a fire, only for it to be snuffed out.

With a few twists of magic, a drawer popped open and Duaia groaned. "Fucking idiot," she hissed, pulling out a small piece of stone that glowed with dark shadows.

The unnatural feel of rotting magic made Haru's teeth ache. "You're going to hand that over to them?"

She gave him a scathing glare and shoved the stone into a pouch at her hip. "For now, I'm going to go kick your bonded's ass."

# CHAPTER 25

CAL WOKE gasping for air, thrashing against an unseen attacker as he suffocated. His lungs seized, and for a moment, he was sure someone else had been poisoned, but this felt different. Pressure on his neck and chest, like someone was choking him.

Not him. Someone else.

The crown flared with magic as he reached for the threads, seeking the one flickering and fading. He expected it to lead somewhere in the palace, but it stretched farther, across the city, directly to the prison.

"No," he gasped, flinching as hands landed on his shoulders. He shoved away so violently that he tipped off the bed, crashing to the floor.

"Cal!" Rashi shouted, landing beside him.

Cal ignored him, reaching for the thread and pouring magic into it, but Aelin was too far away to make any difference.

The thread darkened and snapped, and the pressure on his chest vanished, letting him breathe again, only for him to choke on a sob.

"Cal," Rashi whispered, grasping his arm.

From a room close by, Liria started screaming, no doubt feeling Aelin's death through their twin bond.

Rashi startled halfway to his feet, grabbing Cal and pulling him up.

His legs were unsteady, but he forced them to work, stumbling in the dim light as Rashi pulled him to the door. "Why is it dark?"

They should have woken him after a few hours. What the fuck happened?

"Haru said not to wake you," Rashi said. "He had a problem with the shields."

Cal knew he should focus on that, but the only thing he could think was that Aelin was dead and it was his fault. He should have made sure Aelin had proper protection rather than a single guard. Aelin wasn't much of a fighter; he'd never needed to be. As Truth Seekers, the twins were living symbols of integrity, and their word was as good as law.

When they reached the main door of his rooms and threw it open, Liria's screams became louder, but a moment later they cut off.

Cal froze in shock as the snapped thread reformed. There was only one way that was possible, and resurrection spells were as forbidden as slave collars. Pulling away from Rashi, he hurried down the hall to Liria's room, shoving the door open without knocking to find her collapsed against a sofa.

She was pale, strands of hair sticking to her tear-stained face. "I didn't know," she gasped. "I swear I di—I told him not to."

Cal gripped the doorjamb for balance and stared at her, unbelieving. "You knew," he said tightly.

"He said he wouldn't! He promised." Liria swayed to her feet, a pleading expression on her face, but they both gasped as their bonds with Aelin activated again.

Cal doubled over, pain exploding in his chest like he'd been stabbed. He lurched forward as his legs gave out completely, hitting the floor as he struggled to breathe through Aelin's second death.

Rashi shouted at him, but Cal barely heard him.

The thread snapping again was just as painful as the first time. If Aelin had cast the resurrection spell on himself as thoroughly as Cal suspected, it wouldn't be the last. He would keep coming back until the magic powering it ran dry.

Cal panted for breath and pushed to his knees, latching on to Rashi when the fox appeared by his side. "I need to get to the prison."

"You're not going anywhere like this," Rashi hissed, his worry nearly overwhelming as it crashed through their bond.

"Aelin is dying," he said through gritted teeth.

"Then we send someone, but not you!"

Cal sneered and shoved to his feet, stumbling as he turned for the door.

"I'll go," Liria said.

Cal turned sharply, and she jerked back several steps, staring at him with wide eyes. "You are not going anywhere," he snarled. "You are forbidden from leaving this room until this is over."

The crown flared with magic, the threshold of the room shifting to enforce his words.

"Cal," Liria pleaded. "Callith, please, I swear, he promised he wouldn't use it."

He ignored her. He couldn't afford to be swayed. She knew that kind of blood magic was forbidden. She should have come to him or his father the moment Aelin even mentioned it.

"Bring me the scepter."

"Cal—"

"Now!"

Liria flinched and retreated to her bedroom, returning a moment later with the scepter and handing it over.

They both nearly dropped it as the resurrection magic activated and Aelin returned to life once again.

"Fuck," Cal hissed.

He wasn't sure how many times Aelin could come back, but forbidden or not, no one deserved to come back just to die again. He had to get to the prison to stop the cycle.

He stalked out of the room and turned, running straight into Haru's chest. Hands on his shoulders steadied him, and for a moment he was distracted by the fact the dragon was touching him, the bond between them bright and as full of concern as Rashi's.

"What the fuck is going on?" Duaia demanded from beside them.

"Aelin is dying. In the prison."

"Wonderful, another distraction," she muttered.

Cal snarled, pulling himself upright, sunlight sparking around his hands and the crown. "What the fuck did you just say?"

Duaia lifted her chin, refusing to back down. "It's obviously a trap."

"I don't care."

"I do! And until you relieve me of duty, your safety is my responsibility."

"I'm going," he snapped, shoving past them.

He took a few steps before he stumbled into the wall, his vision spinning as pain cracked along the back of his head. He reached out blindly, catching himself against the floor, choking as his stomach heaved and emptied itself.

"Fuck," he gasped, his body shaking with the force of the connection even as it cut out again.

Rashi gripped his shoulder, soothing the aftereffects with his healing magic. "It's getting worse," he murmured.

"And further apart," Cal gasped, his stomach still twisting with nausea. "I don't know how much time he has left."

"You won't even make it to the prison like this," Duaia said.

That didn't matter. "I have to go."

"I'll go," Haru said, and they all turned towards him with varying degrees of surprise, Rashi's shock rivaling Cal's own, considering Haru never went far from him.

"Thank you, but I still have to go with you."

"Why?" Rashi demanded.

Cal swallowed, grimacing at the sour taste in his mouth. He glanced at Duaia before quickly looking away. "Because that's how Juls Saw it," he said, ignoring her vicious swearing. "He Saw me in the prison, being stabbed."

As much as he didn't want to be stabbed, he didn't want to see how much worse everything would be if he didn't go.

"Then we change it and Haru goes instead."

"No! I won't risk making it worse by cheating Fate."

"You won't," Haru said. "I'm a dragon."

When they stared at him in confused silence, he sighed. "I can cast more than just a glamour." Then he closed his eyes, magic swirling around him with a brief impression of snowflakes filling the air.

When they faded, Cal was suddenly staring at himself. "That might work," he said faintly.

Haru nodded, speaking with Cal's voice as he said "I'll get Aelin. You can deal with the humans." He turned into Cal's rooms, walking right for the balcony.

Cal lurched to his feet with a strangled sound of shock as Haru leapt onto the railing.

The burst of freezing air as magic swirled around Haru again punched the breath from his lungs. He watched in astonishment as Haru's body melted away entirely, shifting into something far bigger. He caught only a brief glimpse of brilliant white scales and a long serpentine form before the dragon disappeared below the balcony.

Cal had just enough sense to adjust the new ward to allow Haru through before he crashed into it, though he suspected even the ward couldn't hold back a dragon for long.

Rashi sighed, and Cal slowly turned towards him, raising an eyebrow at the sappy smile on his face.

"Can you turn into a fox?" He knew most beastkin could shift into their animals, but he'd never seen one do so before.

Rashi's smile turned into a cheeky grin. "Yes. And if you manage to go a day without trying to die, I might even show you."

Duaia snapped her fingers at them with an irritated sigh. "Focus." She opened her pouch and pulled out a stone teeming with shadows.

Cal recoiled, instinctively calling light around his fingers and pushing Rashi behind him. "Where the fuck did that come from?"

She raised an unimpressed eyebrow. "From your desk."

"I've never—" he started, shaking his head, before remembering the strange stone he'd found in the Vault. "I found something in the Vault, but it didn't look like that. I was going to give it to you to study."

"Whatever it is, this is what they want."

Rashi stepped around him, leaning in for a better look. "That feels old."

Duaia frowned as she studied the stone, turning it over in her fingers. "Older than most artifacts," she said after a long moment.

Which meant several Ages old. Even if it had been in the Vault, that shouldn't have been possible. Most of their artifacts had been lost in the war or when the Wound exploded into existence, and creating them took a tremendous amount of magic and knowledge they no longer had. The only things he knew of that were that old were the ylren trees and—

"You don't think…," he said softly.

She swore as she shoved the stone back into the pouch. "Part of the Shadow Throne? What else could it be?"

"You're not going to hand it over, are you?" Rashi asked.

"I don't think we have much of a choice," Duaia said, taking a breath. "Whoever it is has inherited the bloodline. They've put shadow collars on most of the humans left in the palace, if not all of them."

"No," Cal said, refusing to believe a new Shadow King was in his city. In his palace. "That's not possible."

"There's no other explanation! I might have believed his blood survived in an artifact and allowed Justice to control the Black Sun, but old blood wouldn't give anyone this much power. They're threatening to kill the humans they've taken if we don't hand the stone over."

"So let them," he snarled.

"Cal!" Rashi stepped away from him, eyes wide with shock. "You can't mean that."

"After what the humans have done? To you? To this city?" he demanded. "They tortured you and Haru! Burned a granary and our food, the library, the temple, killed and poisoned our elders. Everything they have done has been to destroy us!"

Cal clutched his chest with a gasp as Aelin's connection returned. Weaker than before, but it was there. If Haru didn't get to him before he died again, Cal wasn't sure he'd come back.

"Cal," Duaia whispered, "some of them are barely older than children. You cannot possibly hold them responsible."

"Maybe I should," he hissed.

Rashi grabbed Cal's face with both hands. "You are better than that. And if you don't think so, or you don't want to be, too bad. I'm not going to let you be responsible for children dying." He turned to Duaia without waiting for a response. "Where are they?"

Duaia glanced between them, expression torn about taking orders from Rashi, but in the end, her desire to prevent humans from dying apparently took precedence over her loyalty.

Cal sneered and followed. He would have to remember the limits of her allegiance in the future.

He gripped the banister on the way downstairs, using the scepter like a walking stick. He feared he'd feel Aelin's next death at any moment, but either Haru had found him in time, or he'd managed to escape. He refused to think of the alternative.

"Where's Juls?" Surely he'd returned by now.

"In the throne room, keeping the peace."

Duaia moved quicker when they reached the throne room floor, moving to the internal garden on the east side.

Two young girls in page uniforms stood at the entrance, their eyes nearly black with the shadows swirling in them, each holding a dagger to their own throat. "Have you brought it?" they asked in unison.

Cal gritted his teeth. If he ever saw another enslavement spell when they were done with this, he'd execute everyone involved himself.

"Yes," Duaia answered.

The girls turned and entered the garden, leaving them to follow.

The sunstones that should have lit the path were dim, only the thin slices of pale moonlight through the high windows offering any illumination. The shadows seemed deeper than they should have been, thicker, shifting despite there being no breeze to stir the plants.

"Why are we willingly walking into the trap?" Cal muttered.

"Do you have a better plan?" Duaia hissed.

"Yes," he snarled back, "but you didn't like it."

When they reached the fountain in the center, more than a dozen human servants surrounded it, all with shadows in their eyes and daggers to their throats. The only one without a blade sat on the edge of the fountain, his leg drawn up with an arm resting over his knee.

It took Cal a moment to recognize him in the twilight, and another to believe it. "Aster?"

"Draekor, actually," Aster replied, sounding bored. "Not that it matters. Where's the fragment?"

"Somewhere safe," Cal answered before Duaia could hand it over. "Why are you calling yourself Draekor?"

Aster sighed and motioned to one of the humans. A young man stepped forward and went to his knees beside the fountain. "Hand it over or he dies."

Cal grabbed Duaia's wrist when she reached for the pouch. "You intend to kill your own people?" he asked incredulously.

"I'll kill anyone I have to. Now give me the fragment."

"So you can kill us instead?" He eyed the gathered servants and pages, but they were all motionless. There was no way to save them all. The moment he tried, they'd all slit their own throats, and even Rashi wouldn't be able to heal each one.

"Eventually," Aster said. "Maybe I'll let you live tonight if you hand it over. Now."

"Let them go," Cal said. "Release them. Let them leave and we'll hand it over."

Aster laughed. "This isn't a negotiation."

Moonlight flashed against the blade as it moved, cutting deep and quickly enough that the base of the fountain turned dark with a spray of blood.

Duaia screamed and lunged forward, but Cal hauled her back, both of them going to their knees when she fought him. "I'll kill you," she snarled, still fighting Cal's hold, and he wasn't sure which of them she was threatening.

Cal looked back at Rashi for help, only to find him gone. His heart skipped at the thought of Aster somehow taking him, but he felt nothing along the bond aside from a calm determination. He didn't know what Rashi was planning, but he'd need time.

"That's enough!" he shouted, not daring to relax his grip even when Duaia sagged against him. He tensed when he felt her pull on the scepter, but he released his hold and let her take it, trusting her to have a plan. He hoped it was a better one than walking into the gardens.

Aster leaned forward. "Hand it over, or your sister is next."

Cal's breath stuck in his lungs. No. The throne room was safe. Julius was there. So was Vesryn. Neither of them would let anything happen to Synne. She'd kill the attacker herself if she had to.

Aster smiled, baring his teeth in delight. "You think any of them are willing to kill sweet, tortured little Kithiel?" he asked. "Shall we test them? It took so long to bring him under control, it would be a shame not to let him play. He has a blade to your sister's heart right now."

"You're lying."

"Am I? Go see for yourself. Or rather, send your pet fox." Aster sat up and looked around. "Where are you, Rashi?" he called, a sneer twisting his features. The shadows around them seemed to thicken, choking out what little light there was.

In response, the crown pulsed with magic, offering enough illumination for Cal to see a few paces around him. "I'll go," he said, pushing to his feet.

Aster focused on him, his bored facade cracking. "No, you'll stay. We can't have the plant fucker interfering."

"Too late," Rashi called, as the plants around them moved.

Sharp, whip-like cracks resounded as roots and vines lashed out, wrapping around the humans and forcing the blades away from their throats. Several more sprung out of the darkness, aiming for Aster's limbs, but he threw himself to the ground and rolled, snatching a fallen blade in each hand on his way to his feet.

He couldn't have been older than fifteen, but he moved with the skill of someone twice that age, slicing through the vines with ease. He didn't notice the one from above until it wrapped around his throat.

Cal snarled and snatched a fallen dagger, heating it with a burst of magic as he rushed forward. Aster freed himself from the vine strangling him, blood smeared on his neck where he'd cut himself, and whirled on Cal with a frustrated shout.

Duaia's fireball lit up the gardens as it struck Aster's face, burning hot enough that it singed Cal's skin as it passed.

Aster screamed, thrashing wildly as he tried to put it out, drops of liquid fire raining down from his face. He tripped over the edge of the fountain, going under in a burst of hissing steam.

The shadows thinned around them, moonlight slicing through the gloom, before the shadows converged with force. They thickened and darkened, roiling like fog and spiraling higher.

Cal flinched as the wisps of tangible black nothingness covered his hands and arms, the crown's brilliance sputtering out as the darkness rose over their heads and blocked out the light again.

He stepped back with a curse, hearing the water churn before Aster let out a breathless laugh. "Fucking… Vile…," he panted. Wet squelches followed as he climbed out of the fountain.

Cal slashed in the direction of the sound, the glow of his dagger hardly cutting through the shadows, but the tip struck flesh and Aster hissed.

The shadows twisted around Cal as a blade sliced in front of his face.

"D!" he called, ducking and slashing low. A blade whistled through the air just above his head and he lunged forward, catching Aster's legs and knocking him to the ground. A fist slammed into the back of his head and he grunted, working his dagger around and jabbing it into Aster's thigh.

Aster snarled, the shadows shuddering around them, slices of moonlight lancing through the dark.

Cal nearly gagged on the thick stench of charred cloth and flesh.

Plants rustled nearby, and vines cracked through the air again, wrapping around Aster's neck and wrists.

Then pain exploded in Cal's back and Rashi screamed, the vines holding Aster twitching before going lax.

Cal's lungs seized, though he knew it wasn't his pain. He reached through the bond for Rashi, but it wasn't his either. It was radiating from Haru. Even knowing that, his body refused to draw breath without a fight.

He fumbled for the dagger in Aster's thigh, but Aster got his good leg free and kicked Cal in the face.

Bright, intense pain turned his vision white as his nose crunched and he tasted blood. "Anytime, D," he choked out, scrambling back. There was a flash of silver as Aster pulled the dagger from his leg.

Shadows swirled as Aster stumbled to his feet, limping towards him.

Cal wrapped light around his hand, the crown flaring with magic and dissipating the shadows around them, and he got a decent look at Aster. More than half his face was bloody, blistered, and blackened, one eye swollen shut. Cal formed the light in his hand into a ball and threw it at Aster's face, kicking out when Aster flinched. His foot caught the bastard's knee, but Aster snarled and shoved himself forward as he fell, driving the dagger towards Cal's chest.

He twisted to the side, but it wasn't far enough. The blade sank deep into his shoulder and struck the floor beneath him.

"Cal!" Rashi yelled.

Cal's teeth fused together with pain. Fine. He was fine. This was nothing compared to Taegen or Yrasne or the others Aster had murdered. Nothing vital was hit, and his lungs might have shuddered when he tried to breathe, but they still worked.

So long as they won this fight, any injury was worth it.

Light sparked around his fingers but sputtered out with his scream when Aster ripped the dagger from his shoulder.

"Death to the Sun," Aster sneered, lifting the blade for another strike.

"Stop!" Duaia shouted, the force of the spell knocking the air from Cal's lungs. For an excruciating moment, he was suffocating, before the spell's intentions released him.

Aster froze, his dagger suspended above Cal's heart.

Then the second wave of magic hit and the stone base of the fountain cracked, water cascading over them. It spiraled up and around Aster, encasing him in a sphere. Bright light sliced through the remaining shadows as the scepter's sunstone lit up, burning away the gloom like fog at dawn.

Cal crawled backward with his feet and an elbow before rolling to his side, spitting blood as he struggled to his knees.

"Can't hold this long," Duaia said through gritted teeth.

He was about to suggest she drown the bastard when the humans moved, no longer bound by Rashi's vines. "No!" he yelled, as several puppets rushed towards Aster to drag him from the water. The rest converged on Duaia.

The sunstone's light flickered out and water flooded the floor as she lost her hold on the spells. Blue lightning crackled in a wide dome around her, striking a few of the humans, but that spell was for dissuading and paralyzing, not causing injury.

Cal staggered to his feet, calling light around his fingers. He threw it at the nearest human when they raised a dagger, blasting it from their hand.

An explosive force threw the humans around Duaia back a few feet, but they'd gotten what they wanted.

One of the young girls clutched the pouch with the fragment, and she scrambled towards Aster. She took three steps before vines wrapped around her torso. Without hesitating, she threw the pouch. More vines lanced through the air, snagging the pouch strap, but another human puppet was already reaching for it, ripping it free.

Then it was sailing through the air again, into Aster's hands.

He pulled the stone out with a deformed grin, and the shadows exploded.

When they cleared, Aster and his slaves were gone.

# Chapter 26

Cal twisted away from Rashi for the second time as he staggered out of the garden.

"Hold still," Rashi hissed, frustration sparking along their bond as he reached his hand to Cal's shoulder again.

"We need to get to Synne."

He could heal later. His shoulder didn't hurt much, despite the blood trickling down his arm and fingers, his shirt failing to absorb any more. Not like the sharp, throbbing agony in his face. He couldn't breathe through his nose, his eyes were swelling shut, and he kept tasting blood at the back of his tongue.

Duaia wasn't faring much better, with the gashes on her arms from daggers and cuts on her face like someone had gotten their nails into her, but none of that mattered.

Aster had the stone, and who knew what his next move was going to be. Whatever it was, Cal wouldn't let it involve his family.

The screaming started before they reached the stairs. Nobles and courtiers rushed out of the throne room, shadows wafting around their feet like smoke.

"Fuck," he hissed, shoving past them to get inside.

"Cal! Wait!" Rashi yelled, but his protests were lost beneath the sudden rushing of blood in Cal's ears.

Fear slammed into him when he pushed clear of the mob to find Synne on her throne.

Kithiel stood beside her, shadows wrapped around his throat and filling his eyes, with the tip of a dagger pressed to Synne's chest.

Vesryn stood a few paces behind the throne, sword clutched in his hand and his expression twisted with distress.

Julius was sprawled against the steps of the dais, dazedly struggling to get to his knees.

"Away from the throne, Princess," Aster snarled from a few feet from Julius, his human puppets wrapped around him like a protective barrier.

"Fuck you," Synne sneered, her knuckles white where she gripped the arms of her throne. Her eyes flicked towards Cal, wide with restrained fear, before she looked back at Aster, but he was already turning, a mocking smile twisting his severely burned face.

Cal couldn't find any satisfaction in the damage; it wasn't nearly enough. He wanted Aster to burn to ash like Yrasne. To choke on his own blood like Taegen. To suffocate on his last breaths like the elders he'd poisoned.

Light burst around his fingers, his drying blood hissing from the intense heat, but before he could release it, Aster lifted the stone fragment in his hand.

The sunstones lighting the room went dark and the shadows thickened, more of them spewing from the stone in a never-ending wave of purple-tinged black. They filled the room between one breath and the next, rising over their heads and snuffing out the light.

Cal expected another fight, for Aster to come at him like he had in the gardens, but instead of an attack, the palace shook. He stumbled forward as the floor bucked beneath him, tripping to his knees. There was a deafening crack, like part of the ylren tree splitting apart, and the floor lurched again.

Rashi and Duaia crashed into him, latching on to his arms and dragging him to his feet.

He swayed into Rashi, the solid blackness around them lighting up with spots of sliding white dots. He knew they were a result of his own vision and not some new attack.

"Get Synne," he ordered, gritting his teeth against nausea and the deep, dull pain radiating from his shoulder.

Duaia's hand found his, pressing the scepter into it. "Maybe it'll like you better," she said, before she pulled away and vanished into the shadows.

As soon as the scepter was in his grip, it lit up with a soft glow of light. Enough he could see Rashi and nothing else.

"Cal, *please*," Rashi hissed, holding his arm with a bruising grip. "Your shoulder needs healing."

Cal started to protest and pull away, but Rashi's terror along their bond finally cut through his own fear for Synne and whatever Aster was planning. He swung the scepter in a low, wide arc, confirming there was no one in their immediate vicinity. "All right," he relented, before slowly sinking to his knees again.

Rashi followed him down with a sharp growl, muttering curses under his breath. "Fucking idiot," he said, anger lashing Cal through the bond, even as gentle warmth wrapped around his shoulder. "You keep *trying* to die. I fucking hate you."

What could he say to that? He wasn't trying to die, not really. But if living meant watching others die, when nearly dying himself could save them, what choice did he have? "I'm sorry."

"No, you're not. Don't fucking lie to me, you bastard."

Cal snapped his mouth shut, tightening his grip on the scepter and staring into the shadows.

The palace continued to tremble under them, the shouting and bursts of magic across the throne room muffled, as if coming from the other side of the city.

For a moment, with the shadows blinding them to anything but each other, knowing D and Juls would protect Synne with their lives, he could breathe and think again. Only then did he realize he still felt Haru's bond, strong and vibrating with annoyance and frustration.

Thank the Sun for that particular vision not ending in tragedy.

"We need to get the humans away from Aster," he murmured, grunting as something shifted in his shoulder with a sharp snap. Numb relief flooded down his arm, and his breaths shuddered with the sensation.

The green glow vanished despite the fact he could still feel a wound in his shoulder. But it was no longer bleeding and the nausea was fading, so further healing could wait.

Rashi pulled away with a glare, before swallowing hard and blinking quickly as he caught himself on Cal's arm. "I can handle the humans," he said, his breaths coming short before he drew in a slow, deep breath to steady himself.

Cal recognized the signs of burnout easily enough, but they both knew there was nothing to be done about it. Not until Aster was stopped. He'd have to trust that Rashi would hold out until then.

He squeezed Rashi's hand as they got to their feet. "I promise I'll try to live."

With a fierce growl, Rashi pulled him in for a kiss that was more teeth than lips, before tearing himself away and following after Duaia.

Cal took a breath and called on his magic to seal the throne room and to protect everyone outside it.

Power hummed through the crown as it warmed, the threshold around him sealing as tight as the one surrounding the palace. The scepter pulsed in his hand like it was asking to be used, so he raised it, needing to see what was happening around him. The ancient artifact sang a high-pitched tone as it unleashed blinding white light, fracturing the shadows filling the room.

Near the dais, small orbs of concentrated light wavered in the air above the others. Vesryn stood between Synne and Kithiel, blocking Kithiel's quick, short thrusts and slashes with his sword. Vesryn's blade was angled in an effort to disarm rather than injure, but Kithiel's movements were as skilled as Aster's as he retained his weapon.

Synne's back pressed against the wall as she threw orbs of light at the four humans trying to join Kithiel. Her attacks aimed for their eyes, forcing them back as they stumbled, momentarily blinded.

Duaia was surrounded by the rest of the human puppets, fending off their attacks with her sword while striking them with paralyzing spells that barely slowed them down.

Near the throne, Julius stood off against Aster, his hands glowing bright red with concentrated light.

Aster struck at Julius with two blades, shadows dripping from them like poison. Every time he opened a path, he lunged for the throne, and every time he neared it, the palace trembled before could Julius forced him back again.

Around them, the shadows twisted, but Cal caught movement within them.

The purple tinge within them had solidified, flashing like violet lightning, twisting and zipping through the shadows as if trying to break free of them.

He turned the scepter to the thick black surrounding the violet and more light sliced into the shadows, burning them away and leaving a misshapen, shimmery violet mass behind.

It hovered in the air for a breath, before it split apart with something eerily close to a shriek of torment, vanishing beneath a fresh surge of shadows.

As disturbing as that was, he couldn't pay any mind to it. Familiar blue magic crackled through the air, striking the human puppets and knocking one to the ground, but the rest continued lashing out at Duaia.

Cal rushed for Aster as the sound of creaking wood echoed through the room.

Branches of the ylren tree reached inside itself, sweeping several puppets off their feet, pinning them to the floor.

Cal spun the scepter in his hand, swinging it like a club as he lunged at Aster's back. It whistled through the air when Aster ducked and spun, kicking Cal's legs out from under him.

He fell with a grunt and rolled, bringing the scepter up in time to block a dagger going for his throat.

Aster twisted away as Julius swung at him from behind. He spun, slicing in return, leaving a shallow red gash across Julius' chest.

Then Aster turned and rushed for the throne again.

"Fuck!" Julius raced after him, leaving Cal to get back to his feet on his own.

Before he could take a step, more branches swept wildly across the area. He ducked as one nearly took off his head. Another struck Aster in the chest, but not before he touched the shadow stone to the throne.

The palace shook again as the throne sundered open. The power stored within exploded in a visible ripple of raw magic that threw everyone off their feet.

Cal hit the floor yet again and groaned, his shoulder stinging as the force of his impact tore it open anew. He rolled to his stomach and considered crawling to the throne. At least then he'd already be on the floor for the next attack.

Aster's laughter echoed with sinister delight.

When Cal pushed up enough to see what had happened, the throne had gone dark, the once-bright sunstone crumbling into black sand.

"No," Cal breathed, the crown weakening in the wake of the throne's destruction. He gathered all the magic it could give him as he braced against the scepter, dragging himself to his feet. He threw a hand forward and unleashed the magic as a wave of burning sunlight.

Aster laughed again, spreading his arms and taking the hit to his chest. The magic fizzled out, swamped beneath the endless dark of countless shadows.

He smirked. "My turn." He held his hand up, and a thick pitch-black stream erupted from his palm. It flew through the air towards Cal.

He threw his arms up to brace, light flaring around his wrists. The air filled with the sharp snaps and pops of opposing magics clashing. His light kept the shadows from sinking into him, but he slid backward from the strength of Aster's attack.

The shadows were so much stronger than they had been, as if destroying the throne had given Aster power.

The assault ended and Aster tsked, as if he'd expected Cal to be dead. Undeterred, he unleashed another wave, shadows converging around the humans and sinking into their bodies.

The branches restraining them burned away, crumbling to black sand.

As the human puppets got to their feet, shadows pulsed around them and formed around their hands.

"Fuck," Duaia hissed, no longer worried about causing harm as bright red flames replaced the crackling blue around her. "Stop them however you can," she shouted, flames meeting shadows in a dark, swirling inferno as the humans rushed her.

Vesryn was pushed back under the renewed onslaught of Kithiel and his own group of puppets, Synne's light barely making it through their shrouds of darkness.

"Now then," Aster said, turning back to Cal. "Who wants to be the host? The fox? Rashi!" he called, raising his voice. "Where are you?"

"Don't you fucking touch him," Cal snarled. The scepter flared with light, burning hot enough to rival Duaia's flames as it raced towards Aster.

Aster laughed, his image flickering as he stepped to the side, out of the path. At the same time, he lifted a dagger and launched it at Cal's chest. Shadows wrapped around it in midair and it vanished, reappearing in front of Julius before sinking into his gut.

Duaia's scream of denial rivaled Cal's own, his chest twisting with panic as Julius stumbled back.

Dull pain flared in his stomach, and his heart skipped, instinctively reaching for the thread connecting him to Julius. The crown sputtered to life, just enough for him to grasp the thread and hang on.

Aster flipped his other dagger between his fingers. "He'll die," he said, "but if you come out, little fox, I'll let you heal him a bit."

"Don't!" Cal shouted, but he knew Rashi wouldn't listen.

Aster snickered. "I promise to keep my word. Unlike your kind."

The long, thick drapes hanging on the side of the balcony twitched as Rashi stepped out of hiding.

"There you are," Aster said, his voice sweetly pleased, sounding even more sinister with his burns still oozing blood.

Rashi swallowed, flicking an apologetic look at Cal before rushing around the thrones and falling to his knees beside Julius.

"Don't," Julius gasped.

Rashi shushed him, a flare of green lighting up the dagger as he slowly pulled it free.

The twinges of pain in Cal's own stomach let him know it was a rough job, done quick and messy, the only concern to keep Julius from dying rather than restoring his torn flesh.

The dagger had barely slipped free before Aster snapped his fingers. "Enough," he ordered.

Cal hesitantly released his hold on Julius' thread, sure he would survive, at least long enough for him to finish the fight. But when he rushed towards Rashi, Aster unleashed another torrent of shadows at him.

The scepter flared to life again, pushing them back, but his skin stung when wisps of darkness slipped through the shield of light. Tiny strips of his flesh turned black where the shadows touched him. He couldn't move under the force of the attack. Could barely see through the dark engulfing him. But he could see enough.

A dark circle erupted around Rashi and Julius, sinking into the floor and turning it black. Five points of shadows raced through the inside, creating a star in the center, its points touching the circle. Five humans pulled away from the fight, taking up spots at the points of the star. The palace shook as they lifted their hands, dark light bursting from inside of them.

Rashi jerked upright as shadows wrapped around him.

Cal stumbled forward in a desperate attempt to reach him, flinching as his entire cheek burned, the flesh crumbling away. There was no way through. He'd be torn to decay before he ever reached them.

He stared at the sunstone, willing it to burn brighter, but the scepter pulsed in his hands, as if to say no. "Fuck you!" he snarled, slamming the tip of the scepter onto the floor.

Rashi screamed, and Cal gave up any hope of getting through the shadows in time. But if he couldn't get through, he'd call the shadows to him, away from Rashi.

He lifted the scepter, and it vibrated with power as he focused. Instead of pushing the darkness back, he let it come. Let it feast on the sunstone even as the light drank in the shadows. The hum of power in the scepter grew louder until his ears rang. Loud enough he barely heard Aster shouting at him as the scepter reached for more, pulling the darkness away from Rashi, away from the human puppets, sucking the shadows out of the room until they vanished inside the sunstone.

Darkness swirled inside the light, and a moment later, the sunstone cracked.

With a curse, Cal threw it aside, turning and covering his face. The sunstone exploded into sharp fragments of burning glass that cut through his skin.

When the air cleared, the shadows were gone, most of the puppets collapsed on the floor.

Kithiel remained standing, shadows thick around his neck and in his eyes.

Aster spun on Cal with murder in his own.

Cal snatched up the two broken pieces of ivory and wood left of the scepter, heat flaring around them as he waited for Aster to come to him.

Before Aster took a second step, something large passed by the window, the natural shadow of a dragon sweeping across the floor.

Cal startled with a breathless laugh of relief and awe, before Haru crashed through the balcony doors with a thunderous roar. White scales gleamed in pale moonlight, and Cal froze as he saw the sky, where the moon had turned red from the eclipse.

The shock of Haru's arrival momentarily froze everyone in place.

Aelin and Elwin slid off Haru's back as the dragon took in the scene with a single glance.

He immediately focused on Aster with a growl. He opened his mouth, spitting a stream of solid frost at him.

Aster jumped away with a shout, but his left foot and calf turned white and he stumbled. One of the human puppets moved closer, and he immediately latched on for balance.

"Kill her!" Aster shouted at Kithiel.

"No!" Cal turned as Kithiel lunged forward, pressing an already exhausted Vesryn in a furious effort to get to Synne.

The fragments of shattered sunstone pulsed red around him, still holding power. He drew it into himself and desperately called on what was left in the crown to find the thread attached to Kithiel.

The thread was thin and wrapped with shadows, but Kithiel was still part elf. Kithiel belonged to them, not Aster.

Cal slammed sunlight into the thread, ripping the enslavement spell away.

Kithiel immediately stopped, gasping for air as he stumbled back, his eyes and throat finally clear of shadows. With a sneer, he spun, hardly sparing Haru a second glance as the dragon hunted Aster like prey, backing him away from Rashi and towards the dais.

Kithiel stalked forward on silent feet, reaching the bottom step as Haru snapped at Aster with a loud growl. When Aster jerked away, Kithiel slammed his dagger into Aster's back.

Aster lurched to a stop with shock widening his eyes, staring down at the tip of the blade protruding from his chest. "Fucking… Vile," he wheezed, pitching forward as the puppet supporting him turned, driving her own dagger into Kithiel's throat.

"No!" Synne screamed.

Kithiel stumbled back, choking as he clutched his neck, blood spilling fast and red over his fingers.

Duaia stumbled forward to catch him as he fell, green healing magic already flickering around her fingers.

Rashi crashed to his knees on one side, Synne joining him with a choked sob on the other, adding their own magic to the mix.

Aster hit the floor with a heavy thud.

The stone fragment tumbled from his grip and bounced on the floor, landing near Cal.

With a snarl, he gathered the last flickering remnants of power in the scepter and shattered the stone to dust.

His moment of satisfaction was short-lived.

He jerked with a gasp as a deafening crack tore through the tree, only from far deeper. He felt it in his core, a white-hot lance of burning agony, like the ley line itself was ripped apart.

The floor split open where the circle had been drawn, and Julius barely lunged out of the way before shadows spewed violently from the fissures.

Violet flashed in the depths of darkness with a sound like thunder, growing brighter and larger, until an endless minute later, the shadows vanished.

Everything went silent as a mass of twisting violet hung in the air in their place. A moment later, it descended on Aster's body like a scavenger finding its first meal in weeks. It wrapped around Aster in a glowing, pulsing cocoon that seeped into his flesh, black veins spreading into his neck and face.

Finally, the suffocating weight of magic eased from the air and the ley lines calmed.

Cal took a hesitant step forward as he looked at Synne and Rashi and Haru, stumbling towards them with a shaky breath. Duaia and Julius, Vesryn, Aelin, Elwin. They were all alive, if not unharmed, though Kithiel was on the verge of dying. But even as he watched, Kithiel's bleeding stopped, and Synne slowly removed the dagger as Duaia and Rashi healed behind it.

A quick glance at Julius confirmed he was on his feet, an arm wrapped tenderly around his stomach, but well enough, considering.

Convinced no one else would die today, he collapsed against one of Haru's massive legs, his knees going weak with physical and magical exhaustion. "Think I'm starting to see why Rashi likes this form so much," he murmured, running his palm against warm scales.

Haru turned his head, focusing one eye on him with an unamused stare that made Cal laugh.

Aster's body shuddered, twisting on the ground as the sword slowly dislodged itself and slid free of his chest, clattering to the floor.

Cal and Haru both were already turning towards it, heat and frost mixing in the air between them, when the body went still, faintly breathing.

He lifted his hand with every intention of reducing Aster to ashes.

"Stop!" Julius shouted, shuffling forward. He eyed the body with his sour-lemon expression as Aster's flesh turned a shimmery purple, not unlike the crops. "Don't kill him. We'll need him."

As if in response to his words, lightning flashed in the sky, dark clouds gathering as thunder shook free what glass still clung to the balcony doors.

With a groan, Julius clutched at his head, wiping blood from his nose, but when he turned to Cal, it was with relief in his eyes.

"It's over. I can See again."

# CHAPTER 27

THE STORM lasted a week.

The heavy rainfall threatened to flood the city, but the sirens erected barriers over the canals and the beach. As the rains continued, the waters rose, pressing against the barriers to rise over the nearest buildings in towering walls of restrained destruction.

Julius was the only one who seemed unbothered. Every day he would assure them the storm would pass soon, with magic blanketing his words.

The gloom was fitting, as far as Cal was concerned.

Not long after the battle was won, he noticed his red Fate strings were gone. Not just his. According to Haru, all the red and silver strings that had connected them were gone.

Vesryn had appeared mildly guilty at that, though Cal assumed he was blaming himself for letting Kithiel get close to Synne with a blade.

He found himself staring at his finger, where the strings he'd taken comfort and placed hope in for the last thirty years were missing. The loss of his connection to Rashi and Haru was an empty void in his chest, like losing a piece of himself that he'd assumed would be there for the rest of his life.

It took a few days for their wounds to heal, and then, despite the constant rains, there was work to be done. The black sand of the destroyed throne and what dust was found of the shadow stone were locked in the Vault, safe under the powerful wards and suppression spells. Rashi and their best mages worked to restore the damage done to the palace and ylren tree. Duaia and Haru started the arduous task of emptying the prison of anything valuable so they could tear it down, moving the handful of true criminals to the remains of the library.

It was mostly a burned-out husk inside, but beyond the first three floors, the fires had hit a second threshold protecting the more precious and ancient books, where they were summarily snuffed out. A large portion of their knowledge and culture was still lost, though the upper seventeen floors were largely intact and unharmed aside from smoke damage.

Cal set a ward around the first floor and anchored it into the ley lines, locking the criminals in with tools and supplies. They were instructed to clean the mess, with a few guards to keep watch, and then ignored for the time being.

Synne kept Kithiel close as she handled the court, Vesryn watching over them both, and Julius remained at Cal's side as he dealt with everything else.

Cal threw himself into the work, starting with his cousins.

Aelin had been on the verge of dying again when Haru tore through the prison, finding him trapped in a room with three members of the Black Sun. They'd been no match for a dragon, until a fourth found him, stabbing him with one of the claws missing from the Vault's dragon remains.

If Aelin hadn't been there to stitch him back together with blood magic, Haru may have died. In light of that, and because the entire city knew by then what had happened with Aster, Aelin was spared the serious consequences for using forbidden blood magic.

Cal still revoked his Truth Seeker status for a year, and Liria's for six months, and they both swore never to use it again.

Only after his ruling did Julius admit to Cal, "I let him overhear me about a vision of Seeing him die."

Cal frowned at him. "Why?"

Julius looked away, staring at the still-falling rain. "The visions after his death were worse than the consequences of changing his fate."

Cal didn't ask, and he pushed away any doubts of just how much Julius manipulated his visions, and how dangerous that might be. He refused to think that the consequences of his mother dying had been better than another possible future. He'd trusted Julius his entire life, and they had survived the return of the Shadow King together.

Aster's body had been moved to an empty suite and sealed behind another ward tapped into the ley lines, with one of Haru's shields inside it. Whatever changes the magic inhabiting the body was making, it showed no sign of being done.

Replacing the throne was easy enough, as the second throne was untouched, and a new one was being carved from one of the blocks of sunstone in the Vault. But with the continuous storm, there was no sun visible for him to complete the ritual. Until the second throne was connected to both sun and ley line, the crown had limited power to draw from.

He rose early and retired late, hardly seeing Haru or Rashi except in passing. He knew he was being a coward, but with the connections between them broken, no longer bound together by Fate, he was sure they would be leaving soon. As soon as the storm lifted, they'd resume their original search for a way to restore the Wound.

Then, a week after it started, the rain finally stopped, the constant rumble of thunder fading away in the middle of the night. In the morning, the sun broke over the horizon, blinding in the clear skies and glittering on the raindrops still clinging to the city.

Not daring to risk another delay, Cal went to the throne room.

Most of the damage had been restored, but the circle and star etched into the floor would take longer to remove, as it had burned through the entire floor and would need to be cut out and patched. The new doors opened soundlessly as he stepped onto the balcony, and he tipped his face into the warm light.

As he breathed deep and reached for the Sun and the ley lines, the crown flared with power. He thought it would be difficult, connecting the three to the throne—the last time it had been done was when Ysildea claimed the power of the Sun herself—but it was remarkably easy. The throne linked to the ley line as if made for it, and the crown hummed, restored to its full power.

When he called tiny sparks of sunlight to his fingers, the magic felt different, like what he'd sensed in the oldest sunstones in the Vault, and he finally understood what Haru had meant by the feel of rot in the city. Until it was gone, he'd never noticed how muddled it had felt. Now it was purer, clearer, and he hadn't sensed anything like sentience in it since the violet mass took over Aster's body.

With the throne and crown fully restored, he breathed a bit easier, staring out at the slowly receding waters towering above the canals. Beyond them, he could just make out the crops on the hill, and even from the palace he could tell that more than half of them were the strange plants that had taken over.

Rashi had asked to study the crops as soon as the storm passed. He was likely already making his way there.

Cal turned to get back to work, but he stopped as a sweet scent caught his attention, like fresh honey with the sharp undertone of ozone. He turned again, searching for the source, and his breath stuck in his throat when he spotted the bright pink and violet flowers bursting from the higher branches of the ylren tree. When he looked out to the academy and granaries, he saw more of the same.

For the first time in over three Ages, the ylren trees were blooming.

# Chapter 28

With the end of the storm, Aster finally woke. Except it was certainly no longer Aster.

Where a human had been a week ago, there was now a tall, lithe creature with sable skin. Their bone structure was similar enough to an elf to be eerie, with pointed ears half as long again as Cal's own. But the strangest things were the jet black feathered wings, long enough to brush the floor, and the wide, deep-set eyes of solid, rich violet.

The creature stood in the middle of the room, staring at each of them without blinking.

Rashi nearly vibrated out of his skin beside Cal, having refused to be left out of this meeting.

Cal desperately wished he could have sensed Rashi's excitement along the bond.

"You're really a fae," the fox squeaked, shifting forward half a step, before freezing as that unblinking gaze landed on him.

When there was no response forthcoming, Cal silently cursed.

Fae had vanished from the realm long before the creatures that once ruled the night. The old customs were barely even remembered as myth, but everyone knew never to give their name to a fae, and he'd always remembered the tale of the elf who bought her freedom from a fae by giving them honey.

When there was a knock at the door, he cleared his throat, waiting for the servant to have ample time to leave, before opening it and pulling the cart inside.

"Would you like something to eat?" he offered, lifting the covers on plates filled with the fruit produced by the strange plants taking over their crops. "I'm unsure if these are poisonous or not. They appeared in place of our own crops some days ago, using the same magic you used to take Aster's body," he said, tensing as the fae's strange eyes stared at him, before focusing on the plates.

He let out a slow breath and reached for the lid on a small jar. "But this is honey, which I am certain is not poison," he said, relief filling him when he saw a flicker of response in the fae's expression.

He slid the jar across the cart, closer to the fae. "You're welcome to all of this."

The black wings shifted, feathers rustling against the floor as the fae stared at each of them in turn. Several tense moments of silence passed before they looked at the honey again.

Finally, they stepped forward. They picked up the jar and a spoon, then dipped it into the honey. They looked up again, almost hesitantly, before sticking the spoon in their mouth. Their violet eyes slipped closed with a soft moan. Then they stepped back, all the way to the far wall, where they sat on the edge of the window seat, eating spoonful after spoonful of honey.

Cal waited until most of the jar was gone before daring to speak again. "We have no intention of trying to keep you here," he said, intent on making it clear they wouldn't hold the fae against their will.

When the fae eyed him with clear distrust, he spread his hands, showing he had no weapons.

"We would like to know what happened before you leave, but you are free to go. If you require a trade for the information, we can bring more honey."

The fae sat up a bit straighter, pressing the jar into their chest. With another glance at the four of them, the fae finally spoke in a deep, dulcet voice. "My essence was trapped in the ley lines."

Cal listened with growing dismay and horror as the fae explained how, Ages ago, their family controlled the Shadow Throne. Until they'd made the mistake of trusting a human with their name. Between bites of honey, the fae told how the human had used their name to bind them, forcing them to kill their own family, until they were the only one left to inherit the throne. And then surrender it to the humans.

Before that happened, the fae had managed to seal the veil between this realm and that of the fae, cutting off the flow of fae magic into their realm. For Ages, they had served the human line, their name passed from ruler to heir in a never-ending cycle.

Until the time came when human thirst for power demanded more, and they began the war with other creatures in an attempt to take their thrones.

Sorren, the heir at the time, had demanded to know of a way to steal the magic by force, so the fae told him that if he sacrificed a fae to the ley lines, all magic could be stolen.

A smirk twisted the fae's lips as they took another bite of honey. "I didn't tell him that it could also be stolen by the one who was sacrificed."

So when the time came, Sorren betrayed Draekor, sacrificing the fae on the Shadow Throne. The result was the throne's destruction and the fae's essence being sucked into the ley line, where they proceeded to wrest control of the shadows, binding the magic with their own essence.

But the foreign presence in the magic tilted it out of balance, and before the fae could find a way to harmonize with the ley lines, the Wound formed.

Since then, they had been waiting inside the ley line for a chance to escape.

Rashi crept forward with an expression of utter awe. "It was your power," he said, "that changed the crops."

The fae nodded, scooping up the last drops of honey and licking them from the spoon with an expression of disappointment.

"And the Wound?" Rashi asked. "It can be restored now?"

The fae looked between each of them again, twirling the spoon over their fingers before tilting their head. "It needs magic."

Cal ignored the pang of loss and jealousy as Rashi and Haru shared a significant look.

"Do you plan to stay?" Cal asked.

The fae looked out the window, where the branches of the ylren tree swayed in the light breeze, the flowers sharing their sweet scent. For the first time, the fae smiled, and Cal could easily see how the stories always seemed to end with someone falling tragically in love with them, despite all the warnings.

"You have cared for one of our most sacred trees," the fae said softly. "I will stay. For now."

They retreated from the room, and Cal made a point of ensuring another small jar of honey would be sent up to the fae with dinner.

He and Julius ended up following Haru and Rashi out of the palace as they made their way to the edge of the Wound, Duaia and the others joining them along the way. Somehow, by the time they'd reached the gates, half the city had fallen in behind them.

Haru and Rashi stepped out into the wasteland.

Rashi turned back after several steps, when he realized Cal wasn't following, and grabbed his hand.

Together, the three of them walked out several paces, before Rashi turned to them both, sucking in a deep breath.

"You both combine your magic. I'll do the rest."

Cal raised an eyebrow and looked at Haru, who shrugged and flexed his fingers.

Frost chilled them, snowflakes and ice crystals swirling around and above their heads as the moisture was sucked from the air.

When Rashi turned an expectant look on him, Cal summoned his own magic, warming the air until a soft, cool rain fell around them, soaking into the barren earth.

Rashi closed his eyes, tipping his head back with a brilliant smile. He opened his mouth, sticking out his tongue to catch the raindrops. Then the earth shivered beneath them, fissuring apart with the rich, thick scent of damp earth and petrichor.

From the cracks, tiny sprouts of green grass emerged.

Cal's heart skipped, his chest constricting as he watched the grass grow higher and thicker, flowers following in their wake a long moment later. They bloomed unnaturally quickly in vibrant bursts of colors, their light, sweet scents blending with the grass and rain.

The return of foliage didn't extend beyond the large patch around them, but the land that had stood desolate and empty for three hundred years was finally green again.

He stared as he waited, counting the beats of his heart, sure everything would wilt and die as it always did when they tried to restore the land. But several long moments passed, and then several more, and everything remained fresh and healthy.

"It worked," he breathed, still not daring to believe. He would have sunk to his knees with the weightlessness of relief, if Rashi hadn't crushed himself into Cal's chest.

"It worked." Rashi laughed, pulling away from Cal to throw his arms around Haru's shoulders, then spun to shout to the others all hovering by the gates. "It worked!"

As shouts of disbelief echoed behind him, Cal stared out at the expanse of the Wound.

For the first time in years, he finally felt hope for their future.

# Chapter 29

"Of course you're going," Synne said, narrowing her eyes at him.

Cal returned the glare with his own. "Restoring the Wound can't be done in a few days, or even a few weeks."

"So?"

So? He was the king. The city was still recovering from the worst disaster they'd suffered since the end of the war, and she expected him to disappear into the Wound for months? Not to mention the lingering tensions between humans and the magical community, which several humans had already proven to now be a part of.

The humans who had disappeared were slowly returning as word of Aster's death spread. And with the fae's essence no longer bound to the shadow magic, the humans' access to it was restored.

Whether he had truly been Draekor, bound to a new body, or reincarnated, or anything else, was something Cal would likely never find an answer to, but that little detail had been kept tight between himself, Duaia, and Rashi.

Synne rolled her eyes. "You want to go. And they will need your magic to heal the land. I can rule just fine in your place."

Cal eyed her suspiciously. "Is that so."

She crossed her arms with a sullen glare, before quickly uncrossing them and lifting her chin. "Kithiel and I handle court well together."

With a groan, he pinched the bridge of his nose. "You are *not* taking him as a consort."

"In five years, I certainly will. In the meantime, dear brother, you are going to fulfill your duty to the kingdom and heal the fucking Wound."


And so, a week later, Cal found himself flying on the back of a dragon.

It was the most terrifying and thrilling experience of his entire life, especially with Rashi curled on his lap, snuggled safe in his arms as a large black fox with three tails.

The scenery could have been vastly improved, but that was exactly what they were here to do.

Haru set them down in what likely used to be a lush valley, directly above a small nexus in the ley lines.

Already, the fae's essence that had been draining the Wound of magic had released its hold. Instead of dead gray land, there were tiny shoots of fresh grass coming up in small patches. It was a far cry from healthy farmland, but it was a start.

It might take years, or decades, but if they could set up waymarkers with supply outposts, they could at least reestablish trade routes. They didn't need to restore the entire wasteland at once. Small areas that could be developed as settlements would be enough to start.

He slid off Haru's back after Rashi hopped down, grabbed the bags with their supplies, and set them aside. "Lunch first?" he offered, hating the nervous flutter in his gut as both Haru's giant dragon form and Rashi's much smaller fox form receded into more familiar shapes.

Without the Fate bonds, he had no guide on how to respond to either of them. No idea on what they might be thinking or expecting of him.

"We can eat later." Rashi hummed as he opened a bag for a blanket, shaking it out before spreading it over the ground. He added another on top for extra cushioning.

Then he toed his boots and socks off and stepped onto the blankets, turning to Cal with a grin and holding both hands out, wiggling his fingers in invitation. "This is more important."

"What is?" Cal asked, his heart skipping a beat at the implication, even as he knew that couldn't be what Rashi intended. He'd only shared that one night with Rashi, and none with Haru.

Rashi narrowed his eyes at him. "You've been pushing us both away, like an idiot. We let you because you had to take care of the kingdom first, but now you're ours."

"The bonds—"

"I don't give a fuck about the bonds," Rashi hissed. "You're ours. I've belonged to both of you from the day I was born. If Fate wants to be a bitch, fine. But I'm not giving you up. Either of you."

Cal swallowed hard, desperately wanting to believe that but not daring to hope it was true. Not yet. He took a slow breath and looked at Haru.

"I'm not willing to let Fate decide this either," Haru said quietly, coming up to stand beside Cal. He lifted a hand and brushed his fingers against Cal's cheek, before leaning in to press their lips together. "And I have no desire to listen to Rashi complain about losing you for the rest of my life."

"I heard that," Rashi muttered.

Cal's laugh was a release of nervous excitement. He looked from Haru to Rashi and back again. "You're sure?"

Haru nodded and slipped his own shoes off before stepping onto the blanket.

Cal took a deep breath and joined them, and immediately found himself with Rashi pressed against his front, with Haru a warm, solid presence against his back.

Rashi grinned and nipped at Cal's lower lip. "Too many clothes," he murmured, licking his way into Cal's mouth.

He closed his eyes with a moan, burying both hands in unruly black hair as Rashi and Haru made quick work of both his clothes and their own. He shivered as he was left naked between them.

"How do you want me?" he asked, breathless and embarrassed by how overwhelmed he felt. Vesryn had been his sole source of experience before Rashi, and occasional sex with another elf was vastly different from being with two men who he'd hoped to spend the rest of his life with.

Rashi leaned up and kissed a smile against Cal's lips. "For now, just like this," he said, before gracefully sinking to his knees. His hands slid down Cal's chest and hips before resting against his thighs.

Cal's breath hitched twice as he watched Rashi lean in and nuzzle against his hip, before dragging his tongue along the underside of Cal's cock.

Haru's quiet growl was a gentle rumble against his back, followed by warm lips against his neck. He tipped his head to the side, shuddering as teeth scraped against the sensitive flesh. Then his knees threatened to give out as Rashi took him completely into his mouth.

Cal's hands twitched as he sought something to hold on to, reaching for Rashi's head, but Haru caught his wrists in a firm grip and held them against his shoulders. Something long and cool wrapped around his waist, and he blinked down, finding Haru's tail there, pinning him against the dragon with far more strength than he would have expected.

When Rashi's hands gripped his hips, he was effectively trapped in place, powerless to escape even if he'd wanted to.

Escaping was the absolute last thing he wanted. This…. Being held by two people who wanted him, despite the loss of their bonds, was more than he'd ever dared dream of having. If they were truly offering this, he intended to hold on and never let go.

Haru shifted behind him.

Cal gasped as Haru's hot, thick length pressed against him, followed by a hot, wet tongue sliding up the side of his neck. The sound that escaped him was closer to a whimper than a moan, but neither of them seemed to care.

If anything, they both seemed intent on overwhelming him with sensations.

The end of Haru's tail flexed, curling over his right hip and under his thigh.

Cal yelped as his leg was lifted into the air. Heat spread through his entire body as Haru's cock settled in the cleft of his ass with the movement.

A deeper growl rumbled against his back as Haru rocked his hips, the head of his cock catching on Cal's entrance.

"Fuck," Cal gasped, his hips bucking with pleasure. He didn't get far thanks to Haru's tail, but Rashi hummed around him and swallowed him deeper, and Cal stopped trying to retain any control. He let Haru take his weight and gave himself over to both of them, losing himself in the pleasure.

Haru's breath against his ear sent shivers down his spine, and the tongue and teeth that followed drew a long moan out of him.

When Haru pulled him around far enough to guide Cal's arms around his neck, he didn't resist, eagerly parting his lips with a hum of pleasure as Haru kissed him.

He curled his fingers in silky silver hair and relished having Haru's hands on him, one exploring his chest while the other gripped his hair, holding him in place. The dragon's questing tongue was distracting enough that he hardly noticed the loss of Rashi's mouth on him, until warm hands gripped his ass.

Haru swallowed his desperate moan when Rashi's tongue pushed into him.

Cal's legs threatened to cramp as he sought enough leverage to move, to find friction for his now neglected cock, but they both had firm grips on him.

Haru's tail kept his leg held up at an angle, so all he could thrust against was empty air. Fingers kept a tight hold on his hair, forcing his head back so Haru could claim the entirety of his mouth.

Rashi's tails pressed soft, teasing touches against his legs, his hands nearly bruising Cal's ass, keeping him spread and open for Rashi's tongue.

His moans grew louder and sharper until he was nearly mindless with pleasure, needing more than they were giving him. He shuddered as one of Rashi's tails rubbed against his aching cock, tearing his lips away from Haru's with a gasped "Please."

Rashi's heat vanished, and Cal choked on a sob at the loss, but the fox returned quickly. An oil-slick finger pressed into Cal from behind as Rashi's mouth wrapped around him once again.

He cried out in pleasure, squeezing his eyes shut with a gasp as his release hit him with an intensity that left him breathless.

Rashi moaned around him, swallowing Cal's spend before pulling away.

Cal's strength failed entirely, and he sagged between them, offering no help at all as they gently lowered him to the blankets.

When he cracked his eyes open, Rashi was grinning at him, brushing Cal's hair back from his face.

"I hope you're not done yet," Rashi said, leaning in for a quick kiss, before Haru tugged the fox back.

Rashi yelped, laughing as Haru pulled him into a kiss as deep as the one he'd given Cal.

He watched in fascination at the way Rashi arched his lithe body into Haru's. At the way Haru gripped Rashi's thighs and guided them over his own.

The bottle of oil was within reach, so Cal grabbed it, spilling more than was needed over his shaking fingers, his body still recovering from his intense release. He set the oil aside and rolled closer, pressing his lips against Rashi's back. He fondled the base of Rashi's tails with one hand and pressed a slick finger into him with the other.

Rashi tore his mouth from Haru's as he keened. His nails left red lines on Haru's arms as he bucked and twisted between them.

Cal dragged his tongue up Rashi's spine, getting to his knees so he could kiss his way across Rashi's shoulders and neck. He caught Haru's eye and smiled, warmth spreading through him when Haru's eyes darkened and the end of his white tail wrapped around Cal's ankle.

It didn't take long for Rashi to become a squirming, pleading mess between them, especially after Haru's fingers joined Cal's in working Rashi open.

Cal could have gladly spent all afternoon driving Rashi into a frenzy, but Haru stopped him with a quiet "Enough."

When Cal pulled his hand away, Rashi slumped against Haru's chest, gasping for breath between soft sounds of frustration, but he recovered quickly enough. When Haru lifted the oil and handed it to him, Rashi took it and turned on Cal with a grin. He glanced down, grin widening at the sight of Cal's returning arousal.

"Good," he purred, sliding off Haru's lap, pushing Cal onto his back in the same motion. He settled on his knees between Cal's legs and nudged them farther apart, wasting no time in pouring oil into his hand. Then he resumed his earlier task, this time with his fingers.

Cal groaned, gripping the blankets with both hands as he pushed into Rashi's fingers. "Fuck," he hissed. "I'm ready, just do it."

Rashi snorted and nipped the inside of Cal's thigh. "I'm not the one you need to be ready for."

Cal blinked in confusion before focusing on Haru, his eyes traveling down the pale flesh of his chest and stomach to his cock. He swallowed as he got a good look at it for the first time.

The same white scales edged in pale blue that were scattered across Haru's body also covered his thighs and hips, reaching all the way to the middle of his very thick cock. There, the scales faded into a series of tiny ridges, wrapped all the way around, nearly to the tip.

He must have stared too long, because Rashi chuckled and kissed his stomach. "Don't worry, it feels good," he said, twisting his fingers and pushing them in deeper.

Cal let out a strangled sound that was a mix of need and apprehension, which wasn't eased at all when Haru looked at him like he had those first days, with the distinctive air of a predator.

Haru slowly crawled closer and leaned over Cal. His long hair was a feathery touch against Cal's chest as he pressed their lips together. He grasped Cal's wrist and guided his hand between Haru's legs.

Cal's breath stuttered as he carefully wrapped his fingers around Haru, sliding his thumb against the soft texture of thin scales, so different from how they felt in his full dragon form. The ridges were more surprising. They were firm but flexible, and gave slightly beneath the pressure of his fingers when he squeezed them.

Haru's breaths came hot and quick against Cal's shoulder, his body shivering as he held himself still.

That was enough to erase any lingering uneasiness Cal might have had. They may have lost the advantage of the Fate bonds, but Haru had no intention of harming him.

He tilted his head enough to nuzzle into Haru's neck, lightly biting as he gave a firm stroke from the base of Haru's cock to the tip.

Haru shuddered and twitched away with a strangled growl that made Rashi cackle.

"You already found one of his weak spots."

Cal grinned. "His neck or his cock?"

"Mmm, both." Rashi snickered and pulled his fingers away, sprawling against Cal's side as Haru took his place between Cal's legs.

His breathing quickened as Haru poured oil over himself, then grasped Cal's hips, lifting him up before slowly pushing into him. "Oh," Cal gasped, his hands twisting in the blankets as his body arched from the sensations. It was like nothing he'd ever felt before. The ridges pressing against his insides sparked tiny flames of pleasure in places he never knew existed.

Rashi hummed and climbed on top of Cal, pinning his wrists next to his head before kissing him, his tongue delving past Cal's lips and gradually exploring deeper, as if matching Haru's pace.

By the time Haru was fully seated, Cal's lips were kiss-swollen and stinging from the numerous nips of Rashi's teeth, his chest heaving as he fought for air.

Rashi sat back with a smug grin, licking his lips before glancing over his shoulder. Then he planted his hands on Cal's chest and lifted up.

One of Haru's hands settled on Rashi's hip as the other wrapped around Cal's aching cock, holding it steady as Rashi sank down onto it.

"Fuck," Cal hissed, his eyes rolling back in pleasure as Rashi's tight heat enveloped him. His hands landed on Rashi's hips as he fought the instinctive urge to bury himself deeper. But he quickly realized he didn't have much leverage to do anything. Like earlier, they had him exactly how they wanted him, unable to take more than they were ready to give.

"Please," he gasped, prying his eyes open to gaze at them.

Rashi took him in completely, rolling his hips in a lazy circle that made them both groan.

The fox bit his lower lip and did it again, meeting Cal's eye with a grin as he leaned back against Haru's chest. He lifted his hands to hook around the back of Haru's neck and turned his head to plant a kiss on his cheek. "Doesn't he look good like this?"

Haru hummed softly in agreement, his hands sliding over Rashi's chest and stomach. "You both do," he murmured, before wrapping a hand around Rashi's arousal and stroking.

Rashi arched with a sharp cry, pushing into Haru's hand and grinding onto Cal in the same movement.

Cal groaned and bucked his hips, jostling Rashi enough that he lifted up and slammed back down.

Haru grunted and finally moved, gripping Cal's thighs as he leaned forward and began thrusting in earnest, settling into a deep, steady rhythm.

"Yes!" Cal shouted, his toes curling as his entire body lit up with pleasure.

He wouldn't last long, certainly not with both of them intent on destroying his ability to think. He slid his hands into the fur of Rashi's tails and tugged, relishing the sharp, desperate groan and the way Rashi shuddered between them.

Haru snapped his hips forward, driving in deep, and Cal's vision went white at the edges, his body going taut as he neared release.

"Magic," Rashi gasped, his hips bucking wildly into Haru's grip. "Call on your magic. Both of you."

Cal couldn't comprehend what he was saying until he felt the air around them go cold, his breath frosting above him. The air crackled as tiny shards of ice appeared, glittering in the sunlight.

"Cal," Rashi said, breathless. "Your magic."

Cal reached for the Sun and it answered, the ice crystals glowing brighter as light filled the space around them. Heat followed, warming the air again, turning the ice to a cool rain that soaked them and the ground around them.

Rashi's magic followed, first in a faint tremble beneath them, and then in an explosion of damp earth and green growing things.

Rashi grinned in delight and leaned down to catch Cal's lips with his own. "Now we can finish," he murmured, biting Cal's lip hard before sitting up again, tipping his head back as he moved in earnest.

The momentary distraction of their magic combining faded, and Cal was left holding on to Rashi as pleasure crashed through him.

Rashi shuddered above him, his body tightening around Cal as he spilled over Haru's fingers.

Cal gasped as he followed after, tingles of pleasure chasing each other all the way to his toes as he came.

Haru gave a few more deep thrusts before he joined them, filling Cal with his spend.

Rashi was the first to move, toppling off Cal and collapsing next to him with a breathless laugh. "Amazing," he moaned, nuzzling into Cal's neck.

Haru carefully shifted to lie on Cal's other side, his hand resting on Cal's stomach as he curled into him.

Exhaustion settled into Cal's limbs, and he yawned, glad the ground had turned even softer under the blanket. The mostly barren land around them had turned green as far as he could see, and he hoped that meant they could restore it faster than he'd thought.

"Rest," Haru murmured into his hair, tightening his arm around Cal.

Cal hummed softly and closed his eyes to do just that.

They didn't rest long. The sun was still bright when he woke to Rashi's mouth on him, already hard and so desperate for release that he didn't resist at all as they put him on his knees.

Rashi took him from behind as Haru settled in front of him and took his mouth. The scales and ridges were a new and interesting sensation on his tongue, and Cal thoroughly explored each and every one of them before Haru gripped his hair, holding him still and spilling down his throat.

He fell into another doze the moment Rashi finished with him, waking only long enough to eat sometime later.

When he woke again near sunset, it was to find Haru on his knees, Rashi spread open beneath him, their lips locked in leisurely kisses as Haru slowly moved inside him.

Cal felt like he was intruding on an intensely private moment, but he couldn't tear his eyes away, his body already heating.

When they paused for breath, Rashi glanced over with a smile, reaching for Cal's hand and pulling it to his lips. He kissed across Cal's knuckles before suckling the tip of a finger into his mouth, which was all the invitation his cock needed to fully harden.

Cal groaned and tugged his hand away, not wanting to intrude.

Haru lifted his head from leaving a mark on Rashi's neck and turned to him. "Join us."

Cal swallowed and looked at Rashi, who snatched his hand again and pulled. "Get over here."

Haru found the oil and pressed it into Cal's hand, then shifted himself and Rashi onto their sides, Rashi's back to Cal.

He poured oil onto his hand and quickly coated himself before hesitating. "You're sure?"

"Go slow," Rashi said, his tails lifting up as if in invitation.

Cal rested a hand on the fox's ass, staring at where Haru was already buried inside, groaning quietly when Haru pulled out. He shifted closer and pressed against Rashi's back before taking Haru's place with a slow, deep roll of his hips. He buried his face into Rashi's neck as he held there a moment before pulling out. He shuddered as Haru's cock slid against his when the dragon pushed inside again.

He tipped his head back and found Haru's lips as they traded places again, moaning around the slick slide of their tongues. The next time he pushed into Rashi, Haru joined him, and he broke the kiss with a gasp as they all went still, Rashi trembling and panting between them as they slowly pressed in together.

Haru's tail coiled around Rashi's leg, lifting it higher and giving them more room.

Rashi keened and arched between them, his nails leaving red marks on Haru's chest, his head nearly smashing into Cal's nose.

Haru wrapped an arm around Cal and gripped Rashi's hair over his shoulder, forcing the fox's head back and keeping him still.

Rashi whimpered and tightened almost painfully around them. "Please," he whispered.

Cal slipped a hand between them, finding Rashi's leaking cock and slowly stroking him.

Rashi keened again and shuddered, but he kept still, and Haru carefully rolled his hips to press in deeper.

Cal hissed as the ridges of Haru's cock pressed into him, sliding along his length. He tightened his grip on Rashi in an effort to keep still himself. He buried his face in Rashi's neck again and breathed deep, waiting for Haru to pull out, then pushed in completely.

They settled into a matching rhythm, one pushing in as the other pulled out, keeping Rashi filled the entire time. The pace wasn't as slow as when Cal had woken to watch them, but only Rashi seemed bothered by the fact neither Haru nor Cal were in any hurry to finish.

The heat and pleasure built slow, consuming him from the inside out, but Cal refused to give in. He wanted this to last forever, the three of them intimately connected. Haru's hard cock against his own, both of them gripped by the tight heat of Rashi's ass. Rashi's tails shifting wildly over every bit of bare skin they could reach, his cock covering Cal's hand in a steady stream of hot, thick fluid.

Cal groaned into Rashi's neck, breathing in the thick scent of the three of them and sex, the occasional hint of fresh grass on the breeze.

He opened his eyes at the sound of kissing, a deep moan escaping him at the sight of them sharing breath, tongues twining together in wet kisses. He pulled his hand away from Rashi's cock and buried it in Haru's hair instead, dragging him closer for his own kiss.

Not to be left out, Rashi turned his head to press his tongue into the kiss too.

It was messy and could hardly be considered kissing, but it was perfect.

Still perfect when Haru shifted to pin them both down, his face buried against Rashi's ears with soft grunts of pleasure, his thrusts quickening then slowing into shallow, sharp jerks of his hips.

Cal and Rashi both gasped as Haru came, the heat of his spend nearly overwhelming.

Rashi whimpered when Haru slid free a moment later, only mollified when Haru grasped his chin and gave him a deep kiss.

Then Haru stretched out beside them, completely focused on them with half-lidded eyes.

Cal flushed as Haru's gaze lazily skimmed over them, but he refused to be intimidated. Not when Rashi was squirming with need against him.

He pushed Rashi forward and onto his knees, nudging them as far apart as they would comfortably go. Then he pressed a hand to the back of Rashi's neck until his cheek was resting on the blankets.

"Cal, please," Rashi gasped.

"Right here," he breathed, pushing into Rashi with a single thrust. He didn't bother with a slow pace this time. The moment he sank in completely, he pulled out, quickly plunging back inside, the slick slide of his thrusts obscenely loud from Haru's spend. He moved his hand from Rashi's neck, bracing his weight on the ground as he gripped Rashi's cock with his other.

He held his hand steady as the fox gasped and immediately began fucking into his fist, Rashi's hands twisting in the blankets as he chanted, "Yes, yes, yes."

Cal tipped his head back with a groan as he chased his own pleasure.

They came together after several more thrusts, collapsing to the blankets in an exhausted, panting heap of boneless flesh.

For the first time in years, Cal fell asleep easily and slept deep, confident he was exactly where he belonged.

He slept through the night, the nightmares from the past weeks thankfully held at bay, and woke to the sunrise, without the thick scent of sex in the air for once. His entire body ached in a delicious way he could gladly become accustomed to.

He stretched carefully and pushed up on an elbow, smiling as he found Rashi curled between him and Haru, still sleeping soundly.

Haru cracked one eye open, a tiny slice of amber watching Cal for a moment, before he went back to dozing. His tail twitched where it was draped over Cal's hip.

Cal resisted the urge to press a kiss to Rashi's shoulder, not wanting to wake him. He carefully got to his feet instead before walking several paces away to relieve himself.

It wasn't until he turned back that he noticed his hand, and the golden threads stretching out from his finger.

He stopped completely as he lifted his hand, turning it over and back again, sure it was some trick of the light. But no, the threads were there, linking him to Rashi and Haru as surely as the red Fate strings had.

He stumbled back to the blankets and dropped to his knees. "Wake up," he said, gently shaking Rashi's shoulder.

The fox grumbled in protest and burrowed into Haru's chest. "Fuck later," he mumbled.

Cal snorted and tweaked one of the too-many fluffy black tails, stifling a laugh when the fox yelped and rolled over, blindly kicking in retaliation. "Look," he said, grasping Rashi's hand where his thread ended and lifting it between them.

Haru yawned and propped his chin on Rashi's shoulder, blinking at Rashi's hand a few times before quickly pushing up on an elbow.

Rashi stared at his hand with wide eyes, a grin slowly breaking out on his face. He reached for both Cal and Haru's hands, laughing with delight when he found the ends of his strings. "This is real?" he breathed.

"True mate bonds," Haru whispered, staring at their hands, awe shivering across the renewed connection between them.

Cal laughed, leaning down and finally giving in to his need to kiss Rashi. He reached for their bonds and pushed his own delight and elation into them, grinning when the same sentiment echoed back from them both. He leaned in further to kiss Haru before stretching out on his side, content to watch Rashi admiring the threads between them.

With the bonds restored, he doubted he'd ever have reason not to be content again.

"Oh," Rashi said, as if suddenly realizing something. "This means I can do this again." The utterly devious tone should have been warning enough, but Cal still wasn't prepared for the intense lust that filled their bond, or the image of Rashi stretched out naked between them, much like he was now, the only difference being a bed instead of blankets.

Cal rolled into Rashi, stifling a laugh that was mostly a groan into unruly black hair. "You're insatiable."

"Mmmhmm," Rashi replied brightly, wiggling between them until he found the oil and pushed it into Haru's hand.

Cal shook his head with a soft laugh. He certainly doubted he'd ever want for sex again either.

As Haru shifted behind Rashi, he tilted his head, staring at the fox's ass. "You have four tails now."

"What?" Rashi growled, twisting around to see for himself.

Sure enough, four tails wildly twitched and flicked between them, rubbing and curling against all the flesh they could reach.

Cal couldn't help his laughter as Rashi lurched to his feet, only to tip to the side as if drunk with a shouted, "Fuck!"

# Epilogue



*Three weeks later*

DEEP INTO the slowly recovering Wound, Rashi shook Cal awake after yet another intense round of sex.

"Cal," Rashi hissed. "Cal, wake up."

With a groan, he cracked his eyes open. "What?" he grumbled, seeing the moon was still high. They'd barely even slept an hour.

"Is that a unicorn?"

Cal stared at Rashi for a long moment before tipping his head back to follow his gaze. There, near a large tree they'd grown that morning, stood a pure white unicorn, staring at them like they were the strangest creatures it had ever seen.

"Fuck," he said, and then, "No. Go back to sleep."

"Do you think I could touch it?" Rashi asked, awe in his voice.

Cal groaned and reached over Rashi to shove Haru awake, too tired to restrain the fox from certainly being impaled.

He was here to help restore the Wound.

Creatures reappearing from myth were someone else's problem.

Keep reading for an exclusive excerpt from
*Mage's Marines*
by Saria Bryant!

# Chapter 1

MAX CRASHED to the floor, his vision swimming from the pistol cracking against his temple. The boot to his ribs was completely unnecessary; he was already caught. As he choked on air and the taste of blood, he forced himself upright. It wouldn't keep more punishment from raining down on him, but he'd be damned if he gave his father the satisfaction of seeing him writhe on the floor.

He swayed to the side, swallowing against the twisting of his stomach as the room spun out and away from him. He was intimately familiar with the signs of a potential concussion, but that was the least of his problems right now.

When he could finally focus, he recognized the dining room. Not the small one the family used. This was the big one, meant to impress and intimidate, which meant when he'd been dragged in here, he'd interrupted a business meeting.

A borderline hysterical laugh bubbled up in his chest and he pressed his hand to his mouth to keep it silent, focusing on the pain of his broken fingers to steady himself.

Blood trickled into his eye as he blinked at his father, who was staring at Max with familiar disappointment and loathing from the head of the table. He knew better than to look away, but he couldn't help it as his gaze slipped sideways, black and bright spots fighting for territory in his vision.

When he focused again, he was staring at a strange man sitting near his father, his bodyguard standing behind him. Handsome enough that even through the fog and muffled panic filling his mind, Max noticed the storm-cloud-gray eyes, strong, scruff-covered jaw, and black, silver-touched hair just long enough to run his fingers through.

That was all the confirmation he needed. He was delirious.

The laughter tried to escape again, but when Jake stalked into the room from behind him and bowed to his father, Max's blood went cold.

"Your son, as promised," Jake said, his lips twisting into a sneer as he glanced at Max.

"No," Max whispered, refusing to believe it. But how else had they caught him so quickly? He'd planned for *months* to ensure he got away clean. He'd learned plenty of lessons from his previous attempts. Everything had been perfect. He just had to get to the airport and he could disappear into Asia, where his father had no power and no contacts.

Jake was the one person he trusted enough to tell his plans to, who had promised to drive Max's car as a decoy while Max took his bike for the extra speed and maneuverability.

Max had even paid him a few thousand dollars for the trouble.

His father gestured to one of his men and Jake turned expectantly, obviously expecting some reward. "Your services are appreciated. Your betrayal to my blood is not."

Jake realized too late his mistake. "Wait," he said, but that was all he got out. He wasn't nearly fast enough to dodge the bullet.

Max flinched from the sharp, muffled sound of the silenced gun, unable to look away as Jake's body slumped towards the floor, before it was dragged away by his father's men. He should have felt remorse or revulsion, but that was hardly the first corpse he'd seen, and even the sting of betrayal barely registered against the dozen stabbing and pulsing pains in his body.

His father sighed, an exaggerated sound Max knew was meant for him. "I warned you last time I would not tolerate this nonsense again, Max."

Nonsense. Like him wanting his own life, away from the violence and blood his father traded in, away from the suffocating control that took away his choices of when and what to eat, when to sleep, when to piss, was nonsense.

"I'm sorry, Father," he said, the words slipping out before he could stop them, much less control the thick sarcasm that came with them. "I really thought this would be the last time."

Fury and disgust twisted the man's face before he straightened. "You are no longer my son. I should have disowned you the moment I learned you were a *twink*."

Max couldn't help it. The hysterical laughter escaped. Never in his life did he ever think he would hear that word from the homophobic asshole's mouth. The man had made no secret of despising Max's *proclivities*. Not since the day Max made the mistake of telling his mother that he found a boy cute when he was ten.

His life had been a waking nightmare ever since.

The punch to the back of his head to shut him up wasn't at all surprising. He nearly went to the floor again, but somehow stayed on his knees. "Dis'n me then," he slurred, spitting blood and hoping it stained the flawless wooden floor. "Or fuc'n kill me. I don't… care anymore." Death would be preferable to one more day in this hellhole.

He listed to the side as his vision wavered and went black.

# CHAPTER 2

CAIUS WATCHED the young man slump to the floor with a mix of shock and dismay. Instincts shouted at him to get a medic as the scent of blood filled his nose, but common sense stayed his hand. He was no longer an acting colonel. Technically, he was a civilian now, and sitting in a mafia boss' home wasn't exactly the best place to reveal that he had connections to the armed forces.

He didn't even want to be here, but as he intended to permanently move to Denver, and under shifter law he was technically alpha of a pack of three, he was required to make his presence known to any powers in play, including the underworld.

The last thing he'd expected walking into this meeting was to see Savino order his own son beaten and then murder someone.

He could smell Quinn's anxiety and rage behind him, but he trusted Quinn not to interfere. As much as they both might loathe the situation, they didn't have any power here, much less authority.

Still, when Savino motioned for one of his men, who pulled out a gun and aimed it at the unconscious man, Caius couldn't stop himself from clearing his throat.

"If I may," he drawled, sipping the tea he'd been given as Savino eyed him. "If you intend to kill him, perhaps you'll let me take him off your hands." He felt Quinn's eyes boring into the back of his head, but he knew he didn't need to explain. They'd both seen far too many innocents die at the hands of those in power, and if he could finally save one, he'd do it. Not that he could prove the young man was innocent, but he'd put money on him being more innocent than his father.

Savino made no effort to hide his distaste when he eyed Caius. "You ask me for my own son?"

Caius smiled faintly and set his tea down. "As you've just disowned him, I believe he belongs to no one, yes?"

He considered pressing further, but the sudden Spark of magic in the room made his breath catch. There was a mage here? Not just any mage, one who'd just come into their power, but he hadn't caught sight or scent of any children on the premises. No, when he followed the faint pull of magic, his gaze was drawn to the unconscious man on the floor.

Fuck. Savino's own son was a mage, and by the looks of it, not a single other person in this room besides him and Quinn realized it. As they were all human, that wasn't surprising. Shifters were far more sensitive to magic.

All the more reason to get his hands on Max. He may not have any sway in this city, but binding a mage to his pack before the Order found him would certainly change that.

He forced his heartbeat to calm and his face to show only mild interest. He couldn't risk revealing just how much he wanted Max. If Caius couldn't get the mage out of here, Max would be better off dead than with the Order.

Savino grunted softly. "A trade then. You are looking to start a business in my city, yes? You take Max. You give me fifty percent of your earnings for five years."

Caius bristled. No way in the seven hells would he let the mob have a finger in his businesses. He pulled out his wallet with a hum, tossing a few grand on the table beside his cup. "I'm willing to buy him outright, but a half-dead man who's obviously suicidal isn't worth more than this."

Max was worth everything Caius had in the bank and then some, but only if he got hold of the mage first. Once everyone else realized what Max was, Caius wasn't sticking around for the war unless he had a binding in place.

He pushed his chair back and stood, buttoning his suit jacket. "I've made you aware of my pack's presence here. That's all I came to do." He tapped his fingers lightly against the cash. "Shall I leave this?"

Savino stared at him through narrowed eyes, too old and shrewd to know there was a reason Caius wanted his son, but Caius hoped the old bastard assumed he was just a perverted shifter and nothing more. Finally, Savino waved his hand with a scoff. "Take him. He is not worth the trouble anymore."

Caius nodded, restraining his fierce smirk of relief, and motioned for Quinn to retrieve Max.

As soon as they were out the door, he pulled his phone out, searching for the nearest independent mage healer. Thankfully, there was one in the city, though over half an hour away from them.

While Quinn got Max settled in the back seat, Caius slid into the passenger seat and put the address into the GPS. Once Quinn was behind the wheel, they were off.

"I can't believe you managed that," Quinn hissed as they sped out of the neighborhood and onto the main streets.

"Neither can I," he admitted, glancing back at Max, who was still unconscious. Not a good sign, but at least he wasn't leaking too much blood. "He's a bit old for his magic to Spark for the first time," he added quietly, turning back to watch the road.

"Maybe it was just waiting for someone who could keep him safe to show up," Quinn said with a cheeky grin that Caius ignored. Quinn had made it clear he was a romantic from the first day they'd met, but Caius put no faith in higher powers.

He'd seen enough depravity to know that if gods did exist, they didn't give a fuck about the people they toyed with. Which was why he had to do everything in his power to ensure the safety of his pack. If that meant binding a new, untrained mage to them, he would.

By the time they reached the clinic, Max was starting to come around, but at Caius' request, the healer was kind enough to give him a potion that knocked him out again.

Caius stood at the end of the bed with his hands clasped behind his back, watching the healer work. At any moment, he expected the Order to show up, but even he knew they couldn't show up that quickly. And any independent mage would have ample shielding and protections in place. At least he hoped.

His eyes tracked the healer's familiar, a small white snake, as it slowly coiled around Max's body, guiding the healer to the most severe injuries. He held his tongue until she finally sat back with a soft sigh and turned her attention to Max's fingers.

"Can you put a block on him?" he asked, meeting the healer's suspicious look with a calm gaze.

"Why? If he's on the run—"

"His magic just Sparked today."

Her eyes widened and she turned back to Max.

"I'd like to ensure the Order doesn't force his hand."

With a soft swear and a wince, the healer shook her head. "He wouldn't survive them," she murmured. "But it'll cost extra."

"That's fine. Just get him back on his feet."

Convinced Max would make a full recovery, he left her to it and stepped out of the room, finding Quinn slouched in a chair with his phone. Caius stretched his senses past the doors, confirming no other mages were in the vicinity, before sinking into a chair next to Quinn. Since they'd rushed from Savino's place, he hadn't had the chance to confirm if Quinn had managed his part of the job.

He might have been required to make his pack's presence known, but he wouldn't pass up an opportunity to keep an eye on a criminal. "Did you get in?"

Quinn tipped his head back with a grin. "Of course," he said. "Their security was a joke. Obviously, they don't expect anyone to be able to hack them from inside. Whatever plans they make, we'll be able to see."

Caius nodded, some of his tension easing. He may have gone in with the vague intention of keeping an eye on Savino's operation for when and if Caius built a pack strong enough to challenge him, but for now, he was only interested in making sure Savino didn't have regrets about selling his son. Or at least not acting on them if he did.

"What are you going to tell Lukas?"

Caius let his head fall back with a groan, tempted to bash it into the wall. Lukas had served with him almost as long as Quinn, but he doubted the sniper would be happy to hear he'd swindled a mafia boss' son from him. Though he hoped the fact that the son was also a mage would be enough to appease him. He doubted it, but he could hope. "The truth, obviously," he said on a sigh.

Quinn laughed. "Good luck. Put him on speaker when you do. I wanna hear."

That wasn't going to happen. Considering Lukas was still dark from whatever mission he'd been sent on, Caius likely wouldn't get a chance to speak with him until he returned home. For now, he was more concerned with getting Max healed and settled so they could bind him before anyone else realized what he was.

## SCAN THE QR CODE
## BELOW TO PREORDER!

Saria Bryant has been an avid reader since childhood and a fan fiction writer since middle school. They enjoy traveling and exploring, and learning about other cultures and languages.

They are constantly dreaming up new ways to torment their characters, playing servant to their cat, or feeding a caffeine addiction.

Their favorite stories are M/M/+ relationships with a healthy dose of angst and drama with an HEA. When not reading or writing, they can usually be found watching anime or playing video games.

Saria can be found on Twitter / Instagram / Tumblr @sariabryant.

Follow me on BookBub

A SERIES OF FATES: BOOK FOUR
FATES' HERITAGE
C.C. DADO

After their parents' murder, Kron and Kimber Ainsworth took refuge within the Easter Valley pack. Now Callum, the Ainsworth pack's new alpha, is looking for them. When timid Kron learns Callum is his fated mate, he panics and disguises his scent using an old family recipe—a plan that quickly demonstrates what happens when you try to fool with fate.

Callum never wanted to be a pack alpha, but a late-night bar fight rewrote his future. Leaving behind a nomad life, he heads to Easter Valley to solidify his position by mating an Ainsworth, only to find himself inexplicably conflicted. If Kimber is his true mate, why can't he stop his mouth from watering every time he sees her brother?

# Scan the QR Code
# Below to Order!

# August Li

# Granny Buchanan's Other Helper

Tyler has the mountains in his bones, and he can't leave sleepy Starling Hollow even if everyone else has. He has no prospects other than helping out Granny Buchanan, the local conjure woman, and trying to keep the old Greenbrier Inn from falling down. He knows neither one's long for the world, and he dreads the idea of being alone.

Granny Buchanan's as stubborn as the mountain, with a memory almost as long. She has no plans to leave Tyler alone—there's somebody right in her backyard who'd be perfect for him, and she's learned some tricks in her life.

But things more mysterious than Granny haunt the old mountain, and they have tricks of their own.

## SCAN THE QR CODE
## BELOW TO ORDER!

# THE
# GUARDIAN
## OF
# MACHU LLAQTA

# ARIEL TACHNA

Professor Victor Itoua has two passions: the legend of Philli-philli… and PhD candidate Jordan Harris. But while ethics rules and his own doubts keep him from admitting, much less acting on, his feelings for Jordan, nothing can stop him from researching the Philli-philli.

Even if it means the torture of spending six months in the Peruvian rainforest, searching for an elusive, possibly mythical guardian with the man he loves and can't have.

For Jordan, with his history of abuse and abandonment, Victor is the one good, constant thing in his life. When Victor asks him to come to Peru, Jordan packs his bag, prepared to follow Victor anywhere the legends take them.

Then, in a remote village, Jordan and Victor meet T'ukri.

T'ukri is shaken when he realizes who the outsiders are and what they are looking for. Though he agrees to guide them on their quest, he is drawn by a deeper calling. But the more he shares with Victor and Jordan, the more questions they have—questions whose answers require him to reveal secrets that could mean his death should the men he is falling in love with betray his trust….

# SCAN THE QR CODE
# BELOW TO ORDER!

# A GROWL, A ROAR, AND A PURR

K.C. WELLS

Lions & Tigers & Bears: Book One

In the human world, shifters are a myth.

In the shifter world, mates are a myth too. So how can tiger shifter Dellan Carson have two of them?

Dellan has been trapped in his shifted form for so long, he's almost forgotten how it feels to walk on two legs. Then photojournalist Rael Parton comes to interview the big-pharma CEO who holds Dellan captive in a glass-fronted cage in his office, and Dellan's world is rocked to its core.

When lion shifter Rael finds his newfound mate locked in shifted form, he's shocked but determined to free him from his prison… and that means he needs help.

Enter ex-military consultant and bear shifter Horvan Kojik. Horvan is the perfect guy to rescue Dellan. But mates? He's never imagined settling down with one guy, let alone two.

Rescuing Dellan and helping him to regain his humanity is only the start. The three lovers have dark secrets to uncover and even darker forces to overcome….

# Scan the QR Code
# Below to Order!

A PARANORMAL ROMANCE ANTHOLOGY BY
BRU BAKER, JENN MOFFATT,
TA MOORE & RHYS FORD

BAD,
DAD,
AND
DANGEROUS

WHEN THE KIDS ARE AWAY,
THE MONSTERS WILL PLAY....

When the kids are away, the monsters will play.

School's out for summer, and these dads are ready to ship their kids off to camp. Not just because their kids are monsters—whose aren't?—but because they're ready for some alone time to let their hair down and their fangs out. You see, not only are the kids monsters—their dads are too.

Even the most dangerous of creatures has a soft spot. These bad, dangerous dads love their kids to death, but they need romance.

Every year, for a few short weeks, these hot men with a little extra in their blood get to be who they truly are. And this year, life has a surprise for them. Whether they be mage, shifter, vampire, or changeling, these heartbreakingly handsome dads might be looking to tear up the town… but they'll end up falling in love. All it takes is the right man to bring them to their knees.

# SCAN THE QR CODE
# BELOW TO ORDER!

FOR **MORE** OF THE **BEST** **GAY** ROMANCE

www.ingramcontent.com/pod-product-compliance
Lightning Source LLC
Chambersburg PA
CBHW070522100726
47907CB00004B/946